SECRETS OF THE DEEP

THE MERMAID CHRONICLES
BOOK ONE

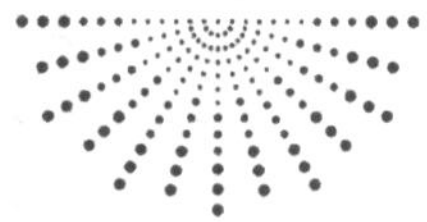

MARISA NOELLE

"Secrets of the Deep plunges readers into a world of mermaid royalty and forbidden love. A captivating fantasy romance!" – Kindle Reader

"Marisa Noelle creates a world filled with intrigue, danger, and a love that defies the odds. A stunning start to *The Mermaid Chronicles* series." – Amazon reader

"From the depths of the ocean to the heights of forbidden passion, *Secrets of the Deep* is a rollercoaster ride of emotions." – Book blogger

The Shadow Keepers

The Unraveling of Luna Forester

Plastic

The Unadjusteds Trilogy

The Unadjusteds

The Rise of The Altereds

The Reckoning

The Mermaid Chronicles Series

Secrets of the Deep

Quest for Atlantis

Fight for Freedom

Ghost Pirates

Vendetta

Denizens of Darkness

Vorago Returns

The Mermaid Chronicles Companion Guide

SECRETS OF THE DEEP PLAYLIST

Mermaid - Train
Thick as Thieves - Jack and Carly
All About You - McFly
What Lovers Do - Maroon 5
To Be With You - Mr. Big
I'm Yours - Jason Mraz
Leave a Light On - Tom Walker
I Won't Give Up - Jason Mraz
Tattoos Together - Lauv
What A Man Gotta Do - Jonas Brothers
Together – Sia
Beggin' – Maneskin
Memories - Maroon 5
Nothing Between Us – Westover
Flames - Donzell Taggart
Low Down - Venbee & Dan Fable

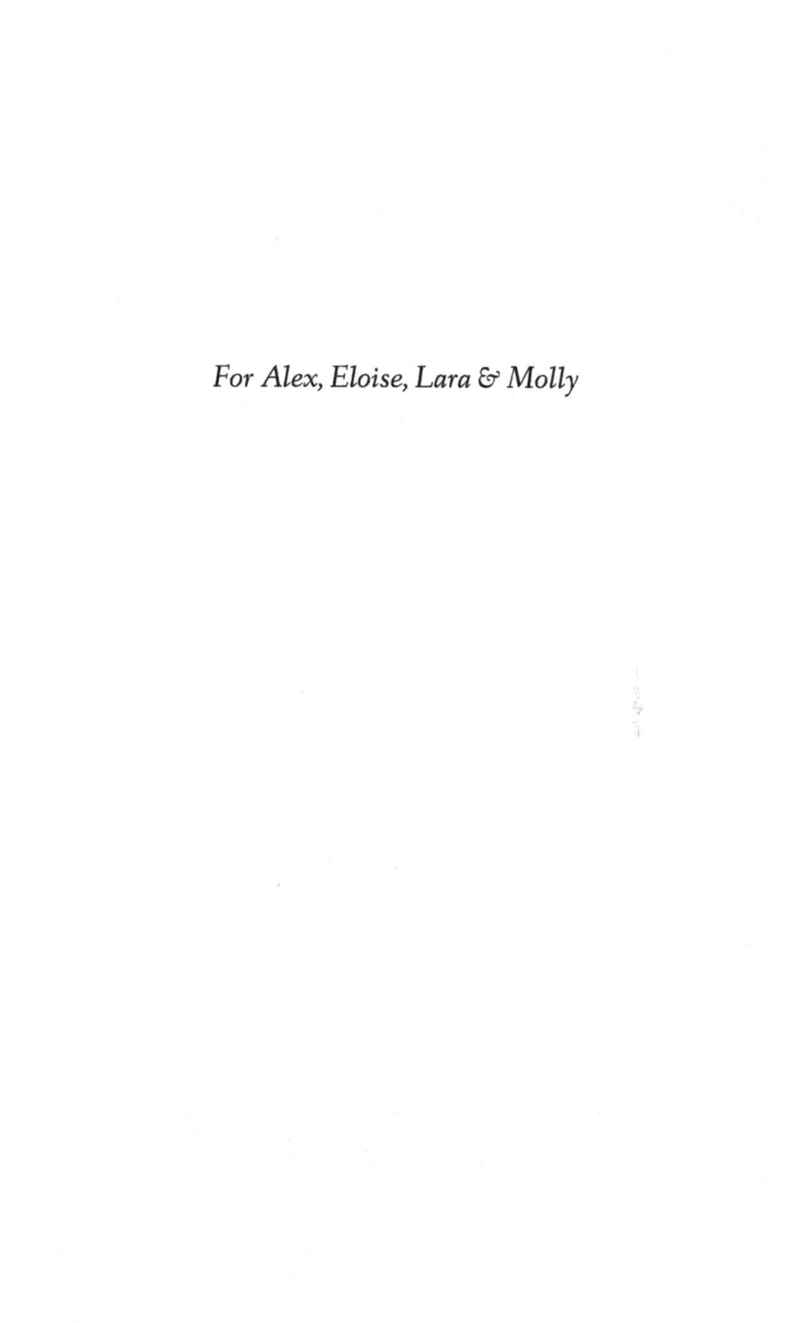

For Alex, Eloise, Lara & Molly

CHAPTER ONE

Shark Attack in San Francisco, 2 killed.

*A*nother one?

My scalp prickled as an overwhelming feeling of dread churned in my stomach.

"Cordelia..." Dad spotted me hovering in the hall. The remote rested in his hand, teetering on two fingers. It overbalanced and crashed to the wood floor, the batteries rolling under a chair.

I returned my gaze to the TV, which portrayed a sunny Californian beach oddly devoid of families and surfers. Instead, emergency vehicles and police dotted the length of the coastline, and thick, yellow tape prevented people from entering the water. Officials held hands to their foreheads to shield their vision from the sun and conferred in huddled groups. The tickertape scrolled by endlessly at the bottom of the screen:

Shark Attack in San Francisco, 2 killed.

A memory stabbed deep, leaving me winded and dry mouthed. Signs of a building panic attack. *Please, not today*.

The news report ticked on, and my heart thumped along with it. All the memories from five years ago slammed into me like a cartoon anvil. That made ten fatalities from shark attacks along the US Pacific coast this year alone.

What the hell was going on?

I'd made it my mission to understand shark behavior, and although they were territorial and often defended their patches of ocean, this behavior was unprecedented.

The warm flush of anxiety coated my skin, made my fingertips tingle. Dad stooped to retrieve the remote and batteries, then thumbed the power button. The screen went blank. We stared at each other, a myriad of unsaid things hovering between us.

"Breakfast is ready." He ushered me to the table. After sitting, he busied his hands with moving the jug of maple syrup and the plate of bacon and a thousand other unnecessary things.

"Here." He placed a mountain of waffles in front of me and proceeded to drown the whole thing in a gallon of maple syrup.

I pointed to the blank TV screen. "Are you going to ignore what we both saw?"

His shoulders sagged. "I didn't want you to see that."

"Too late," I said, putting the cap back on the maple syrup.

"You know shark attacks are rare, right?" He held a

forkful of waffle poised before his lips. "What happened to your mother, to Dylan—it's extremely rare."

"You've told me before, Dad. It was Sod's law. Wrong place, wrong time. A crappy, unfortunate accident." I couldn't meet his eyes. If I looked into those compassionate blues, tears might fall. "But the shark that took Mom and Dylan wasn't an ordinary shark. You must know that."

He frowned and somehow managed to pull his whole face into the gesture, stubble and all. "What else could it be?"

"You're the shark expert. You tell me." I chucked my knife and fork onto my plate. The clatter startled both of us. I took a breath, attempting to calm the building anxiety. "The fact that there have been ten fatalities this year alone tells me something else is going on."

Dad chewed on his waffle and swallowed carefully, then rammed in another bite. I wasn't about to let him off the hook.

"Tell me what you think. Go on." I picked up my knife and pointed it at the TV. "I want to hear your explanation."

"It is unusual," he said, running fingers glistening with syrup through his short beard. "I think illegal feeding, combined with the rise in pollutants and a decrease in prey, has made sharks bolder. That's what the chatter in the lab is, anyway. But—"

"But?" I questioned. Was he finally going to admit something was wrong? Not that I thought there was a mad scientist injecting sharks with illegal concoctions and turning them into murderous beasts...but something, something wasn't right.

"I don't know," Dad said.

"You guys work for the Navy. You're a marine biologist.

Surely you must have some ideas?" I jabbed my knife in little stabbing motions to emphasize my point.

He shoved his plate aside to lean over the table. "The chatter has turned...nervous. We have a meeting later." He held my gaze. "We're looking into it, Cordy. I don't share everything with you. You still won't get into a bath. And don't think I don't know you had a nightmare last night. I don't want to add to that."

I slammed my fist on the table. "We need to figure out what's going on."

"We?"

"You."

"I just said I was looking into it."

"That's not good enough." I rubbed the red spot on my fist where I'd slammed it into the table. "People are getting hurt. Like Mom. Like Dylan. Do you want more people to get hurt, like them?"

Color leached from his face. "Of course not."

"Then you need to do something."

"Like what? You want me to catch every great white in the ocean and stick it in a tank—"

"For fuck's sake!" I lurched to my feet. I remembered the jaws. I remembered the murderous black eyes. I remembered the blood. And the screams. The screams would always haunt me.

"Cordy..." Dad stood to face me.

"Do you think it was the same shark that attacked Mom and Dylan?"

Dad coughed and spluttered. He slapped his chest a couple times to ease the food down. "Cordy—"

"It could be." I pressed my palms against the table to stop them from shaking. "Who knows what your experiments are doing to them."

"Not *that*."

"Then we have two killer sharks swimming up and down the coast of California. Don't you think that's a little odd?"

"What I think," he said, after clearing his throat, "is that we should change the subject. This isn't getting us anywhere."

"You're avoiding."

"I'm not avoiding."

I swallowed around the emotion clogging my throat. "I don't want anyone else to die."

He put a hand over his heart. "I'll find out what's going on. Okay? Trust me."

I gave him a quick nod, easing back onto my stool. He had kept me alive after all. "I don't know how you can walk into a lab every day, look at those sadistic smiles, and not think about...what happened. How do you do that?"

He splayed his hands on the table. "You know why. For your mother."

I blanched. "Mom hated the water."

"She had anxiety."

"I know that."

Dad's voice lowered as he said, "A hormone in sharks' brains is showing promising signs of regulating anxiety. How can I not?"

A renegade tear slipped down my cheek. Dad picked up his half-eaten plate and chucked it into the sink, leaned over it to collect himself. I'd pushed him too far. Losing half our family hadn't happened to just me. Dad had lost his wife, his son. And sometimes I was so focused on and so terrified of my own grief, I forgot that.

"I'm sorry," I said.

Behind my head, the kitchen clock ticked a full sixty seconds. The hum of the refrigerator purred and clicked. A calendar hung next to it. The picture for September depicted an ocean scene with a boat uncomfortably similar to *The Big Blue*—our old boat.

"It's okay. You feel what you need to feel." Dad turned to face me, swiveled his baseball cap around a full three-sixty degrees and fiddled with the peak, pulling it lower on his brow. "I wanted to talk to you about your birthday."

"You're changing the subject."

"Not entirely."

I blotted my sticky lips with a paper towel. "I don't do birthdays. You know that."

He gave me one of his thin sympathy smiles. "I think it's about time you did."

I glanced at the clock. "I don't want to be late for school."

"You don't have to be there for a while yet."

I focused on the suddenly interesting condensation pattern my juice glass had made on the wood table.

"You're going to be eighteen."

Not looking at Dad, I ran my fingers up and down the side of the glass. "I'm aware."

"Cordelia."

I remained fixated on the tabletop.

"Cordy." His voice softened. "It's been almost five years."

"I'm aware of that too." I met his eyes, surprised to find them watery. "I think about them every freaking day."

He took the glass out of my hand. "So, what do we do now?"

I lifted a shoulder. "I guess we keep on keeping on."

Dad reached for my hand. "I don't think that's enough. I want you to be happy."

I blinked away the forming heat behind my eyes. "I want to be happy too. But I can't. Not without them. Not while other people are being killed by a serial killer shark."

Dad brought his coffee cup to his lips, must have realized it was empty, and put it back down. He blew out an extended breath, which ruffled the sparse hairs of his mustache. "What do you think Dylan would want you to do?"

I recalled the worst day of my life. The day he and my mother died. The day he tried to steal a bottle of beer from the cooler. At thirteen. "Something outrageous."

Dad raised his eyebrows. "You got that right. He'd probably try and kick Mom and I out and have a house party."

"Or buy drugs in Tijuana."

"Or set up a quad biking stunt in the desert."

"Or get a girl pregnant."

"He'd be more of a threesome person."

We smiled at each other.

"Will you at least think about it?" Dad asked. "It doesn't have to be a big deal. You could do something small with Trent and Maya."

"Maybe." Above my head, the kitchen clock continued to tick, and the refrigerator clanked and whirred. The calendar picture stared at me, mockingly.

Dad hovered. "You deserve it. We...I...you...need to move on—"

"I don't know how to move on when there's still a shark in the water killing people." My hands fisted.

Dad raised his hands. "I'm sorry. I pushed you too far."

Or maybe he hadn't pushed me far enough. Maybe I've given in to my fear. Maybe avoidance had become my middle name. But I didn't know what else to do.

"Just think about it, okay?" Gathering the rest of the dishes, he carried them to the kitchen sink. He rinsed them and loaded the dishwasher, the clang of the plates fraying my already unraveling nerves.

I made my escape. Rising from the table, I glanced briefly at the blank TV, picturing the widening jaws of the great white shark from my past. I shook my head, trying to dispel the image as I walked to my room.

"See you for dinner," Dad called. "I'll bring back some fish from the market."

"See you for dinner," I yelled back, just before the front door slammed closed.

Continuing down the hall, I didn't dare glance at the spare room or think whose room it used to be, and ignored the framed family prints dotting the hallway. I refused to take in the wide smiles and arms around shoulders of a life long ago and stepped into my room. Today was the first day of my last year of high school. A milestone, if I cared enough to think that way. Maya would be all over it.

I hovered in my doorway, my hand grasping the cool of the brass door handle. Inside, the scrunched pillows, askew lampshade, and twisted sheets spilling onto the floor revealed the extent of last night's nightmare. I wished, for the millionth time, that everything was different.

Tasting salt at the back of my throat, I struggled against a wave of exhaustion as I straightened the lampshade. Beneath it, I left the framed photograph of my family face down. I didn't have the strength to face that image today.

Sitting on my bed, I plucked my iPad from the twisted sheets and loaded a search engine. I gritted my teeth as I typed in my question. It was time to stop hiding. I couldn't rely on Dad to find the answers. I needed to know for myself.

Why do sharks kill?

CHAPTER TWO

$\mathcal{S}$harks killed because they were nasty fuckers.

With horrific images and thoughts of everything I'd read during the past hour assaulting my mind, I stared out my bedroom window at the sliver of ocean. It called to me, like it always did. The water wanted me. And I wanted it. But I couldn't give it what it wanted.

I hadn't been anywhere near water in five years.

I hadn't swum in the ocean. Not once. Nor a swimming pool, despite the disappointment of my coach. Missing out on the title of Allstar Junior Swim Champ was a bitter disappointment. For him. I didn't care.

I hadn't been able to take a bath either. Every time I tried to enter a pool of water, whether it be the vastness of the ocean or the once comforting enclosure of a bubble bath, I would feel the freezing ocean again. I would hear my family's screams. The dead, uncaring eyes of the beast that changed my life plagued me.

Showers I tolerated. Full sinks were a painful tantalization. I craved the water. But I feared it too.

I poked a finger into the middle of the filled sink, creating concentric ripples which disturbed my reflection. Even in my distorted image the dark circles under my eyes were obvious. Not a good look for a redhead. I was anemically pale at the best of times.

Turning on the shower, I waited for the water to warm, telling myself the icy needles weren't the frozen spray of the ocean. The shower door slammed closed, bringing back more of the past. I jumped, slipped, and banged my elbow on the wall. The memories were relentless this morning.

It's just a shark.

The one on the news. The one which had killed two people. But that's what Dylan had said too. *It's just a shark.* But sharks didn't attack forty-foot sailboats. They didn't capsize them. They didn't kill the people on board. Not in real life. And yet it had happened.

It's just a shark.

It was not just a fucking shark.

I slapped my cheek, trying to exorcise the intrusive images assaulting my mind. I'd never be on time for school if this kept up. I stood there, willing my accelerated heart to slow. It took a few minutes. And while drying myself, the rotting smell of decayed seaweed crawled up my nose.

"Stop it!" I admonished myself.

My phone bleeped.

First day of school!

A message from Maya. At least someone was excited. I smiled. She and Trent made the days more bearable.

I threw on a pair of denim shorts and a faded 'Guns 'n' Roses' T-shirt. Then I slipped my feet into my flip-flops and checked my appearance in the mirror. The dark circles were worse than I feared. I would have to opt for make-up. And sunglasses.

Although my hair hadn't needed to be washed, it wasn't exactly looking like I had just stepped out of a salon either. I pulled it into a ponytail and threaded it through the loop of my father's Navy cap.

When I had finished dressing, I toured the house looking for my keys, backpack, and cellphone, and opened the back door. Outside, I jumped into my Jeep Wrangler. Trent insisted it matched the exact shade of my hair. I wasn't entirely sure if he meant that as a compliment or an insult.

I shook off the remnants of the nightmare as I started the engine. But the news of this latest shark attack stayed with me. Ten people were dead. If Dad didn't think that was weird, then his head was buried in the sand.

A few minutes later I parked in front of the vast mission-style Point Loma High School and found Maya and Trent already bickering in front of our lockers.

"I can't believe you haven't grown out of Disney movies." Trent flicked Maya on her shoulder. He tapped a finger on a picture of *The Little Mermaid*'s Ariel taped to the inside of her locker door. "Hey, Cordy."

"Hey," I replied, opening my locker.

"It's not about a Disney movie," Maya carried on with the conversation, but touched my arm, letting me know she was there. "It's about Ariel. She's bold and beautiful and represents all that is female power. And besides, Disney is just the kiddie version. What happened to Ariel is a lot more tragic."

"She looks exactly like Cordy here," Trent said.

"Don't involve me in this."

"Exactly." Maya grinned. "If Cordy was a mermaid she'd look like Ariel."

Trent rolled his eyes and gained himself a poke in the ribs. "Hey!"

"Mermaids will rule the world once again," she said, her smile smug.

"News flash." Trent made an elongating rectangle with his hands symbolizing a tickertape. "Mermaids can't rule the world again. They never existed, so they can't exactly come back."

"Just you wait." She turned to face him, no longer wearing a smile, shaking her finger. "According to the lore—"

"Lore? Are you serious?" His laugh only increased the size of Maya's frown. "There's actually lore about mermaids?"

I stifled a giggle and checked my favorite blue pen was present in my pencil case. This was better. Being around Maya and Trent's constant banter often distracted me from my darker thoughts.

Maya crossed her arms and tapped her foot on the floor. "Yes, absolutely. Tons of it. Prophecies say the mermaids will replenish—"

"Maya!" He grinned, his honey eyes dancing with amusement. "Mermaids aren't real. Trust me, I would know. I'm the one who spends time in the water."

"Just because you surf doesn't mean you know everything

that exists in the ocean. In fact, you spend more time on top of the water than you do exploring the mysteries beneath the surface." She tossed her blonde hair over her shoulder as if she'd won the argument.

I shoved a few random items into my locker, trying to hide my laughter.

"And thank God for that," he exclaimed. "I wouldn't be a very good surfer if I spent most of my time under the water." He slammed his locker closed, having selected an army of books for the next three periods.

"Besides, I've seen one," she said, staring hard through a pair of thick, black glasses.

He rolled his eyes as he ran a hand through his messy, blond hair. "Not that again. You were ten. Full of make-believe. And your eyesight is shit." He wiggled the frame of her glasses.

She pouted and flicked his forehead with a thumb and forefinger. "I know what I saw."

"Hey..." I shouldered my backpack. "You guys want to do something for my birthday?"

"Ooohhh! Like a party?" Maya asked, clapping her hands. Trent winked at me, thanking me for distracting her.

"Well, maybe not a party per se," I said, "but something... something to mark the occasion."

"Good for you." Trent bumped his shoulder against mine. "Count us both in. Anything you want."

"Thanks." *Thanks*. I said it again with my eyes. He understood. Dylan was his best friend. He knew it was a big step for me. For him too.

"Maybe we could go away for a weekend," Maya said. "Or see a show, or go quad biking or..."

Her suggestions swirled around me, but I wasn't really paying attention. Someone across the hall caught my eye. A new kid. A guy. He had his back to me, but with the way he was struggling with his locker, it was clear he was a transfer.

My heart rate ratcheted up a notch and I had no idea why. Maybe it was just going to be one of those days; intrusive thoughts, intense anxiety, all culminating in a very public and very embarrassing panic attack.

I took a breath, watching the guy opposite struggle with his locker, and mercifully, the anxiety ebbed away. But something else took its place. The feeling that I knew this guy. I couldn't see his face, only the hard line of his jaw and the hint of a dimple in his cheek, a profile that was both rugged and undeniably handsome. As my eyes trailed down, I couldn't help but admire the way his toned muscles rippled beneath his shirt. There was something inexplicably magnetic about him, a pull that stirred a something hidden within me. Every detail of his presence captivated me, drawing me in with a blend of fascination and a growing, undeniable attraction.

"Close your mouth, Cordy, you're drooling." Maya pushed my chin up so my jaw snapped shut. "Who are you staring at?"

We all turned to look across the hall, but the guy was gone, him and his dimples and his deliciously oversized muscles.

"Um, no one," I said, as heat flashed across my cheeks. "Thought I saw someone I knew."

Trent raised an eyebrow, shared a look with Maya. "It's senior year. You know everyone."

I smirked at him. "Hardly. I'm not captain of the surf team or in the summer's hot new Disney release."

Trent slung an arm around my shoulder. "Nope. But you are my best friend."

"Oh. My. God." Maya squealed. "He just said something mushy! Did Trent just say something mushy? Say something mushy about me!"

Trent slung his other arm around her. "Fine, I'll sprinkle some fairy dust on this moment. Our friendship is like a mermaid's book club—a mix of deep discussions, questionable choices, and always better with a splash of sarcasm."

"Mermaids! You said *mermaids!* I knew you believed really!" Maya poked him and wriggled out from under his arm, leading the way to our first class.

After a morning that crawled by, Trent nudged my shoulder as we made our way to the cafeteria. "I meant to say to you earlier, I was worried you might have seen the news this morning?"

I faced him. His tangled surfer hair fell over his forehead. He stared at me with those damningly emotional eyes of his which almost convinced me to start spewing the details of my nightmare and everything I'd found online about sharks. But then, he was a surfer, he probably knew most of it. And he still went out on the waves every day. I shrugged it off and looked away.

He touched my arm. "Sorry, I didn't mean to..."

"S'okay," I replied.

Maya bounded toward us, her hair and books both caught up in her exuberant stride. "Study Skills after lunch."

Trent huffed. "What is the point of that damn class anyway?"

She laughed. "Study Skills and How to Apply to College? I think it says what it does on the can."

"I don't even want to go to college."

"So drop the class," I said.

He puffed out his cheeks. "It's compulsory."

"What are you going to do if you don't go to college?" Maya asked.

I laughed at her gaping mouth. She was going to be one of those studious, innocent college types who spent her life in the library, unaware of her beauty, naively fending off propositions from a line full of guys. And girls.

"We can't all be geniuses," he said. "I'm going to surf. Or act. Or both."

"Lucky for some," I muttered.

"I'll get you a role anytime you want," Trent said.

"Yeah...all those people watching you kiss someone on screen..." I grimaced. "No thanks."

"Who said you had to be in a romance?" Trent asked. "You can be a badass action woman."

Neither of us mentioned surfing. I'd have to go into the water for that.

"But what about your brains?" Maya tossed a hand in the air. "I can't imagine anything more exciting than furthering your knowledge, learning more about the world, what secrets it possesses waiting for you to discover. It's so exciting." Maya rubbed a hand across one of her books like it was the Holy Grail.

Trent and I both rolled our eyes.

"Does she get how nerdy she sounds?" he asked.

"It's Honor Roll blindness," I replied. "And those thick framed glasses. What happened to your contacts?"

"Stupid foster siblings ran off with them again," she huffed. "As soon as I'm eighteen I'm going to get laser-eye surgery. I've almost got enough saved from my tutor money. Then I'll be able to see a mermaid properly."

"This again." Trent winked at me as he held the door of the cafeteria open for us.

Maya paused on the threshold and lowered her voice, "I know you don't believe me, but I did see one."

"It was probably a swimmer with one of those pull-on mermaid tails. They're all over the place at the moment," he said, passing out trays as we joined the line.

She slammed a plate onto her tray. "*At the moment* being the operative words. They weren't around seven years ago."

"Prototype." He grabbed two burgers and a large scoop of French fries.

"Maybe we should agree to disagree," I said. "We're all entitled to our own opinions."

"Exactly!" Maya and Trent said at the same time, then both cracked up.

We sat at a table together, and I'd barely taken a bite of an apple when I felt the hairs on the back of my neck stir.

I looked up and, across the cafeteria, saw him again—the guy from this morning. His handsomeness was almost offensive: the groomed sandy-brown hair that begged to be tousled, the chiseled lines of his jaw that screamed strength, the toned muscles rippling under his T-shirt, and those dimples that could make anyone's heart flutter. It was a face so captivating, so arrestingly beautiful, that I found myself completely unable to look away.

An overwhelming sense of déjà vu struck. I knew this guy. He was part of my past. Tangled in it. How could I have forgotten him?

I shook my head. I hadn't forgotten him. Not really. He'd been pushed into the box of forbidden memories along with everything else. The same box that kept unlocking itself and dousing me with regular nightmares. And now here he was, in the flesh, bringing with him so many of the things I'd thought I'd buried.

"I'm afraid, Cordelia, that I can't let you win this one."

My heart rate increased, and I grinned. "You can try. But don't feel bad when you lose."

He stepped onto the diving block and flashed me those adorable dimples. I climbed onto the block next to him. Hanging my toes over the edge, I waited for the whistle to blow. The smell of chlorine surrounded me. I knew I could take him. I knew I was faster. And it wasn't my style to let someone win.

Wade Waters sat in the middle of a hubbub of swirling activity; giggling cheerleaders, a couple of jocks clowning around, and two basketball players engaging in a playful wrestle. But amidst it all, he lifted his head and stared at me. The star quarterback socked him on the shoulder and he didn't flinch. He kept his gaze on me and gave me the faintest of smiles.

"Who is that?" Maya asked. "That guy staring at Cordy?"

"Huh?" Trent swiveled his head to follow my eyeline.

"Him, over there?" She pointed toward Wade with less tact than I would have liked. Heat crept up my neck. He ignored the bustle of activity around him. His eyes never left mine, not for a single moment. The intensity of it made me feel...I didn't know what, but I didn't want it to stop.

"Well, I'll be damned," Trent said.

"Who is he?" she asked again.

"You don't recognize him, Maya?"

She narrowed her eyes through her glasses. "Yes, I do. That's what's driving me crazy."

Wade moved his head to engage in conversation with the head cheerleader—Babette, one of those girls with a glossy, high ponytail and perfectly pert b-cup breasts and legs that went on for miles.

I cleared my throat. "It's Wade."

Maya's brows furrowed. "Wade?"

"Wade Waters," Trent said. "I heard he was back." He twisted in his seat to get a better look.

We stared at Wade. He was still listening to Babette, but he turned in my direction once again and winked.

"Did he just wink at you?" Maya asked.

"Uh...I'm not sure..."

Wade Waters. A long time ago that had been a very

special name. He'd been on the school swim team with me, and we'd often competed for times. He'd been the object of my first crush. Then everything happened with my family, and when I emerged from my cocoon of misery six months after the tragedy, Trent informed me Wade and his family had moved to San Francisco. I'd assumed he was going to be my first kiss. I was pretty sure he'd liked me too.

But he'd moved away, and I never saw him again, until today. And my first kiss? That didn't happened for another two years during a game of truth or dare.

"I'm sure he winked at you," Trent said. "Looks like you'll pick up right where you left off then." He made a hole with the thumb and forefinger of one hand, then stuck the forefinger of the other through it, a devious grin on his face.

I balled a napkin and threw it at his nose.

Only Dylan, Trent, and Maya had known about my feelings for Wade.

"I'm not sure...it's been so long...we were thirteen..."

"Are you blushing, Cordy?" Trent asked, the corners of his mouth curling into a smirk.

"Maybe?" I asked, as if it might be possible that the current heat on my neck and face might be attributed to something else. Like the weather. Or a weird adverse reaction to the air conditioning.

"He's pretty hot, Cord," Maya said. "You're one lucky girl."

I hid my face behind a hand. "Stop it! Both of you! I am so out of here." I picked up my tray and headed to the exit of the cafeteria. Maya and Trent followed suit, chattering about birthday plans and the next big wave he planned on conquering that afternoon. As I left the cafeteria, the prickle of Wade's gaze on my back made me turn my head.

He smiled, his dark eyes locked on me. Dark eyes that made me never want to stop staring at him. Dark eyes full of mystery and lost time.

CHAPTER THREE

The waves roared, crashing to the beach, bringing whispers and taunts I didn't care to listen to.

"Please be careful out there." I touched Trent's arm, pressing my point. An ocean breeze wound between my legs, irritating my shins.

"I always am."

I shifted my weight to my other foot and dug my toes into the sand. "Considering what happened yesterday."

"I know, Cordy. I know. But I can't stop living my life because of one shark attack."

"It's not just one."

A flush crawled up his neck. "I know it's hard for you. I get it. And I'm sorry. But I'm not going to stop surfing."

"I know. I don't want you to." That was a lie. Could I put all my friends in a padded room and lock the door so I knew they'd be safe?

He held my gaze. "I wish there was something I could do to help you."

I stared at my sand-encrusted feet. "Me too. I know I need to...get over it...but I don't know how."

"More people get eaten by hippos."

"Remind me not to visit Africa."

He tugged on the end of my hair. "It was miles away in San Francisco."

I poked a finger into his chest. "Sharks can swim fast. Especially ones that aren't normal and attack people on purpose."

He raised a blond eyebrow. "You don't know that."

I crossed my arms. "Yes, I do."

"Maya and her mermaids, you and your sharks." Trent looked over his shoulder at the glistening ocean. "And now you're freaking me out. But I have to go into the water. I've got the competition to practice for."

I gazed out to sea. A few sailboats interrupted the straight line of the horizon, and the unobstructed sun made a mirror of the surface. "I know. I wasn't trying to scare you. I just want to you to be careful."

I squeezed my eyes closed as a memory assaulted me.

THE SHARK SHUNTED against the boat. Dylan and I gripped hard to the grabrails. The boat rocked and spun, and waves splashed over us, drowning the deck in frigid saltwater and seaweed. With my teeth chattering and my legs trembling, I tightened my life jacket. Dad reached for the flare gun and managed to fire one shot into the sky before the next wave ripped the gun away and sucked it into the churning infinity below.

But no one was going to see a flare on such a sunny day.

No one.

It would do nothing to save us.

TRENT SMILED as he rubbed sunblock onto the back of his neck. "If I get into trouble, you can save me."

"Uh-uh." I wagged a finger. "You're on your own. I'm not setting foot anywhere near the ocean."

His hands flew to his chest in mock horror. "Even for me?"

"Argh! Go!" I pushed him away. "Before I have to tie you up and forbid it."

"I'll be off to Maverick's soon," he called as he splashed into the water.

He was referring to the most dangerous beach on the Californian coast where his hero, Mark Foo, had lost his life. Actually, it wasn't a beach, it was more of a craggy line of hideously sharp rocks known for its big waves. Although Trent could perform a number of tricks on his short board, the long board excited him more and the search for the biggest wave. While the rest of us went running for cover during an earthquake, checking our survival packs were up to date, hiding in door frames, he would grab his surfboard and head to the beach to inspect the subsequent swell of waves approaching the coastline.

Now, he dove under the water with his board, plunging under each swell until he passed the break line and could paddle on calmer water. Waves rolled toward shore. White crests formed green rooms, and the water's foaming tongues licked the beach. My toes twitched, desperate to edge closer to the water, but I couldn't allow it, no matter how strong the ocean's magnetic pull was.

"I promise you, mermaids are real," Maya said, rubbing sunblock into her skin. We went through a bottle of factor fifty every week. She was almost as fair as me. "I saw one right off that pier." She pointed toward the towering concrete structure. Waves lapped at the stone support pillars and seaweed floated in large swirls in between. A gentle offshore breeze played with the ends of my hair, and I tugged my cap lower to ward off the afternoon sun.

"I know that's what you believe..."

Maya tutted. "Why can't you take my word for it? I would believe you."

Smiling, I unfolded my beach chair and plopped into it. "It's not that I don't believe you, per se. But we're talking about mermaids. *Mermaids.* If they really existed, we'd know about it. The whole world would."

She sank into her own chair and a large frown crept across her forehead. "I am not happy with your response."

I chuckled. "I know."

"There are weird things in the water you know." She flexed her wrists and then rested them on the ends of her armrests.

"I know," I repeated.

Maya patted my hand. "Are we far enough away from the water for you?"

"Considering we're almost butting up against the beach wall, I'd say so. Unless you want to walk to Shades and get a shake and watch Trent from the upper deck?"

She tipped her face toward the sun. "As long as you're happy, I cannot be bothered to move right now."

I sighed. "Me neither."

I slid my sunglasses into place and shielded my eyes against the sun to watch Trent. He soared in the distance, careening across his first wave of the afternoon. Maya chattered on about birthday plans. I leaned back against my chair and fell asleep for a few minutes, the effects of the nightmares and missed sleep finally catching up with me.

Maya poked me. "I asked you a question."

"Sorry," I said. "I haven't been sleeping well."

"You okay?"

"There was a shark attack in San Fran."

"Oh, shit." Her hand flew to her mouth. "Sorry, I didn't hear. Stupid foster siblings hid my car keys too. I didn't go anywhere near the news this morning. Was everyone okay?"

I shook my head. "Two."

"Jesus H." Maya looked at the ocean, leaned forward until she'd located Trent, then relaxed back into her chair. I wasn't the only one edgy about sharks. "I'm sorry, Cordy."

"It's not your fault." I clenched my fists around the armrests.

"You know what I mean."

"Thanks."

I turned my attention back to the waves and Trent.

"Ouch," I said, as he fell off the board and landed on his back. "I think I could hear the impact."

Maya laughed. "He's going to be sore."

"And pissed." I smirked, accepting a fist bump from her.

An hour later, with his wetsuit dangling around his waist,

Trent arrived on the beach. "Sorry, Maya, I didn't see any mermaids today."

"Ha, ha!" she said. "I'm surprised. I was sure during that colossal wipeout you might have encountered something interesting."

Grabbing a towel from the sand, he blotted his dripping hair. "Nope. Only creature I saw in the water today was a stingray I almost stepped on."

We sat thirty feet away from the lapping waves, but my uneasiness remained front and center. I wondered where the shark was. Not the one from the news this morning, but the great white who'd stolen my family. Was it still alive? Was it responsible for this newest attack in San Francisco?

"Poor stingray. Sure you didn't land on it with your back?" Maya asked. "With that backward belly-flop thing you did?"

"Ouch. Touché." He tickled her ribs, and she fell off her chair.

The three of us gathered our belongings and headed to our separate vehicles. Trent drove the notorious VW minivan all surfers seemed to have. With a bedroom no bigger than a box and his garage stuffed full of his dad's car parts, he claimed he needed the space to store his five surfboards. Maya drove a VW too. But hers was a sunshine-yellow bug. The old style. Bought from the money she earned tutoring. I dumped my beach bag onto the passenger seat of my red jeep and put the key in the ignition.

"Where's Cordy gone?" Trent feigned a hand over his brow as though looking for a small object. "Maya, can you see her anywhere?"

"I'm here, you ass."

"Oh, yeah." He looked in my direction. "Couldn't quite make you out with all that red hair. Don't have an accident or anything, the first responders won't be able to find you."

"Jerk," Maya called as I gunned the engine and drowned him out.

He turned away, walking backward toward his van, and held his index fingers in a cross resembling the shape to ward off vampires. The rebuttal was one of his favorites and always signaled to him that he'd had the last word on the matter.

My laugh and hair were caught by the wind as I left Maya and Trent behind and headed for my house on Del Monte, only four blocks from the beach. After parking in the drive, I listened to the engine tick over for a minute before getting out, then I entered the house.

The quietness unsettled me while Dad was at work. I wandered from room to room, turning on lights as night approached. With no homework yet assigned, I pulled a feather duster from under the sink and attacked the various knick-knacks in the house that hadn't seen a good cleaning for weeks. My thoughts tumbled—dancing between the past, skirting around college brochures, and settling on Wade. The strangeness of seeing him again after all these years created an uneasy lump in my stomach. He reminded me of another time, when my mother and brother were alive, and life was happy and uncomplicated. As I dusted, a rush of new memories and emotions surfaced, and I wasn't sure how to deal with them. Wade had approached me after the attack, sincere and caring. But I hadn't been able to look into his eyes; I hadn't been able to respond. And he'd walked away.

I finally settled on the couch in front of the TV, but I didn't switch it on. Instead, I grabbed my iPad and loaded the YouTube app. I tapped on the first video. It was from my thirteenth birthday party. Mine and Dylan's. And there was his smiling face. We'd had a beach party with our friends. There'd been hotdogs and hamburgers and Dorito chips and my favorite song playing in the background; Train's *Mermaid* song.

"Catch it, Cordy! Catch it!" Dylan's voice called from the screen. He threw a football in my direction.

I'd caught it, but then fumbled it, and it fell to the ground. Trent had arrived and tackled me. The clip lasted five minutes. Mom had been behind the camera and I could hear her laughter. I watched it sometimes, when I needed to be close to Dylan, when I wanted to hear his voice, or when I wanted to expel the nightmarish image of his screaming face being yanked away from me and remember him in a less gruesome manner.

THE THIRTY-SIX-FOOT SAILBOAT lay almost horizontal, sails skimming the ocean and collecting water like buckets. Dylan screamed. Mom yelled at us. But none of us could move. My head snapped from side to side, following the fin. My own urine warmed the frigid water around me. I panted for air. The shark flew out of the water and chomped a chunk out of the hull. I caught the briefest of glimpses of a white underbelly, serrated dorsal fin, and three lines of violently jagged teeth. A primitive animal built for one purpose only.

To kill.

And kill it did.

LEANING my head back on the couch, I closed my eyes and let out a long, exasperated sigh. I missed him. I missed my brother every day. He was always the one who could make everyone laugh, like Trent. When the two of them were together there wasn't a person in the room not holding their sides with the agony of prolonged laughter. My father was right. Dylan would want me to be happy, he'd want me to enjoy my life. He'd want me to face my fears.

So would Mom. She was the one person who always made me feel brave. Who calmed me down before a big swim meet, who wrapped me in a towel after a race. I missed her touch. The way she would squeeze my shoulder when she walked by, just letting me know she was there. Her summery perfume would trail behind her, and I'd inhale deep to make it last longer.

I opened my eyes and glanced at the TV.

"Okay, Dylan, Mom. Here goes nothing." I thumbed the remote and the TV winked to life. Straight to the news channel where my father had left it.

I waited for the one story that had occupied my mind all day. *"Shark attack in San Francisco—two killed."* I watched the report on the missing child at Disneyland who'd been found in the staff changing room, the account of the latest suicide bombing on the other side of the world and of the celebrity who'd secretly undergone his nuptials in Las Vegas. I waited, but I wasn't prepared for it when it came on.

"A mother and her sixteen-year-old son were taken by a great white shark off the coast of San Francisco."

My hands turned clammy as the video footage of the mother and son playing Frisbee on the beach minutes before played out. I bit down on my knuckles to suppress a welling scream.

"Reports say they entered the water intending to go snorkeling and within moments were attacked by the shark."

My finger hovered over the power button on the remote. I couldn't bear more people dying in the same way as my mother and brother. The paused iPad screen showed Dylan's smiling face. No. I could do this. It was exposure therapy. The more I watched about sharks the more accustomed to them I would become.

"I'm home," Dad called from the front door.

His footsteps tapped down the hall and around the corner. He inhaled sharply as he joined me in front of the TV.

"Cordy..." He took the remote from my lap, thumbed it, and the screen went black once again. "Cordy, why are you watching that?" He sat on the wood coffee table in front of me.

"I'm trying to get over my fears. I need to put the nightmare behind me. I need to face...the shark." I drew my legs to my chest.

"I'm not sure that's the right way." Dad sighed and pulled at his thickening beard. "I didn't want you to see it. I was worried how it would affect you, that you might start thinking vicious sharks were everywhere."

"It could be the same one."

"No," he said automatically. "No." Softer the second time.

"I'm worried about you, Dad. You're in the water all the time. What if the shark came back? What if it wanted to finish what it started?"

"That's nonsense. Sharks don't have intent. They don't have specific targets." He held my forearms and made me look at him. "Cordy. I'm perfectly safe. I promise you. And most of the work is being done in the lab now anyway. We've caught the specimens we need; my job is running the tests."

I glared at him. "Why does it have to be sharks that have this stupid hormone thing? Why can't it be another animal?"

"Cordelia." He gave me a sharp look. "It's important work. We've started first stage trials." His gaze fell to his lap for a moment. "Your mom was so scared. I need to do this. For her. To help other people like her. And it could help you."

"Like me?"

"People who struggle with anxiety." Dad rubbed his thumb against the back of my hand.

But I didn't struggle with anxiety. I struggled with sharks murdering half of my family. A few beats of silence passed.

"She was afraid when Dylan and I were in the water too, wasn't she?" I remembered. "And she feared the sailing most, being over deep waters."

"Yes, that's right. Her anxiety was always worse on the ocean, but she forced herself to endure it. She was a strong woman, your mother."

But not strong enough to defeat a twenty-foot great white shark. "If she hadn't gone sailing that day, she'd be alive." I pressed my knuckles into my eyes as if I could deter the gathering tears by sheer force.

"Don't go there," he said. "It only ends in misery. You have to put the 'what ifs' behind you."

I lowered my hands but couldn't unclench them. "I'm trying. I'm really trying."

"I know." He stroked my hair. "But, Cordy, I don't think watching the news about shark attacks is the right way to go. If you really want to address your fears, then I'll get you whatever help you need. But watching that..." Dad hiked a thumb over his shoulder at the blank screen, "isn't going to help."

"Okay, Dad."

"I'd suggest starting with a bath."

He was right. The shark's slash of a mouth and jagged teeth appeared in my mind. All it had taken was a thirty-second news report to bring it flooding back.

"And let me reiterate, shark attacks, despite this latest report, are extremely rare."

Why did he sound like he was trying to convince someone other than me?

CHAPTER FOUR

I stared at the image of a boat sailing across a sparkling ocean that I'd taped to the inside of my locker for some form of exposure therapy. My stomach roiled and I broke out in a cold sweat. I slammed the locker closed.

"Cordelia?"

I turned from my locker to find myself face-to-face with Wade.

Wade.

Oh my God, it was Wade.

My heart leaped into my throat and nerves fluttered in my stomach. He was so close, his arm almost brushing mine. An electric charge formed between us, one I had no control over, even though I knew I was acting like an idiot with a first crush.

Oh, for goodness sake, Cordelia!

"Hi," I managed.

A surge of memories swelled in my mind as I stared into his deep blue eyes. The color of the ocean. The color of sapphires. The color everything should be. Eyes that had been staring at me all week. But he hadn't approached me. Until now.

He shoved his hands into his pockets. "It's been a long time."

"Five years."

He tilted his head "*That* long, huh? Seeing you now, it feels like only yesterday..."

"I know. Me too."

He smiled. I smiled right back.

"I can't believe your hair. You let it grow. It's more beautiful than I remembered."

I blushed and fidgeted with the end of a curl. "Thank you."

I wanted to say something nice in return, but every thought racing through my mind was wildly inappropriate. I couldn't tear my gaze away from him, mesmerized by how his once-blond hair had deepened into a rich, golden brown, catching the light of the late afternoon sun like strands of spun gold. His blue T-shirt clung to his body in the most tantalizing way, highlighting pecs that seemed as sculpted as a Greek god. The color of his shirt did something magical to his eyes, making them blaze with an intensity that left me breathless. A thousand forbidden fantasies danced in my mind, like the overwhelming desire for him to sweep me into his arms and whisk me away and ravage me in a hay pile in a barn like I was a maiden from long ago. Nope. No way could I voice any of those thoughts.

"Did I say that out loud?" Wade slapped his hand on his

forehead, a blush crawling up his neck. "Stupid. My approach was much more polished in my head."

I laughed. "Approach? You have an approach?"

"It would appear not." He managed a sheepish grin. "How are you, Cordelia Blue?"

I liked the way he used my full name. We started walking to the parking lot together and I practiced stringing a coherent sentence together in my head.

"Um...good...thanks...you?" So much for a coherent sentence. I took a breath. This was Wade. *My* Wade. "Well, apart from the fact that I've had a nightmare every night this week."

Now why did I say that? My whole first week at school had been plagued by the awful, repetitive nightmare of losing my brother and mother, which I hadn't yet confessed to anyone.

"I'm sorry to hear that." A little furrow broke the smoothness of his forehead above the bridge of his nose as his gaze swept over my face, drinking in every detail. He raised a hand, briefly brushed his thumb over my cheek, igniting a thousand fires on my skin. "I remember one time I had a dream every night for two weeks. It was about a big green monster with three eyes and a jagged tooth who would chase me around school. It was only when I dove into a swimming pool that it would disappear." A faraway look appeared in his softened eyes. "It was because of a big swim meet a couple of years ago. Man, I was nervous."

"You've always been an excellent swimmer."

"Not as good as you, Cordelia Blue. You were always my main competition."

"Competition? I thought we were teammates?"

Smiling, he cocked his head, his eyes narrowing playfully. "Are you trying to tell me that it wasn't your number one mission to break my records, despite us being on the same team?"

I grinned. "Of course it was. And I did too."

"Yes, you did. Don't think I've forgotten..."

Wade paused to pull his vibrating cellphone from his pocket. He glanced briefly at the screen and then returned the phone to his pocket. "Sorry about that. Family stuff. Anyway, where were we?" His gaze raked over my face, dipped lower for a few seconds, causing a new flush of heat to erupt over my skin. "Swimming. That's right. You still smashing records? I bet you're the fastest in San Diego, California even."

"I...actually no," I said, bracing myself for another flashback. "Not since...not for...almost five years."

The look of horror on Wade's face was too painful to watch. "Shit! Cordelia, I'm sorry, I didn't realize. I am the biggest ass ever..."

And on he went, apologizing and re-apologizing and offering to carry my books to my car for me.

"Wade," I said, as I climbed into my jeep. "It's okay, you can stop apologizing. I've spent the last five years shackled by memories and trauma and I've recently decided...no, not just decided, but I am determined to face my fears and get my life back...and I'm not sure why I'm telling you this as I haven't seen you in just as long, but...there's something about you I feel I can trust—"

"You can. Anything. We've always been a good team."

Team? Is that what we were? If the electricity still hovering between us and the way he was looking at me was anything to go by, we were going to be a hell of a lot more than a good team. The thought almost made me lose the path of the conversation. I'd had a crush on Wade five years ago, had almost forgotten about his existence, and yet he'd walked back into my life only a week ago and now I could barely think of anything else. When I wasn't obsessing over sharks. "It's time I got over my fears and started embracing life again. I don't know when I'm going to be able to get back in a pool, but it's something I want to try."

"You can do it, Cordelia." The tenderness in his voice softened the anxiety I felt at facing my fears. With him standing there, concern emanating from his eyes, I thought perhaps I could make progress. "And if you need any help with it...I'd be happy to."

"Thanks, Wade." I buckled my seatbelt. "It's good to see you again." Understatement of the fucking year.

"You too." He turned to leave. "Oh, and Cordelia? If getting in the water is too much for now, why don't you try being around it? You could come and watch the swim meet next week. It's against San Diego High School."

I raised my eyebrows. "That's quite a meet."

"Our biggest rivals." He tapped his hand on the door frame. "I could use all the support I can get. Will you come?"

"I'd like to." He smiled at my response. "I can't promise anything, but I'd like to."

"That's good enough for me." He waved and turned toward the school.

Swim practice. What I used to do, a long, long time ago.

What we used to do together. Competing for times. One-upping each other and grinning triumphantly when we beat the other. But I never minded when Wade won. He was a superb swimmer, and I was content just to watch him part the water.

My good mood died when I turned on the car radio. There was a breaking news report.

Another shark attack.

Santa Barbara.

Three killed.

The smell hit me first.

The acrid scent of chlorine rushed up my nose, swarmed down my throat, surrounded my mind, and evoked the past.

CLINGING TO THE SINKING BOAT, *my father, brother, and I could do nothing but watch in horror at the inevitability and cursing randomness of my mother's death.*

Mom hung from the mast. The shark's jaws wrapped around her waist. She released her grip. It dragged her beneath the surface. A pool of red appeared and quickly dissipated on the churning ocean.

My mother was gone.

Just like that.

I screamed until my throat turned hoarse, but the shark wasn't finished.

· · ·

I stood in the entrance of the school pool, causing a bottle neck, unable to move.

"Cordy?"

Steam rose from the Olympic-sized swimming pool and swirled toward the open windows. The crowding spectators raised the temperature further. I struggled to breathe, and beads of sweat prickled my hairline. I could dive into the water and get away from it all, but then I'd have to actually dive into the water.

"Cordy?"

Maya and Trent flanked my sides.

"You don't have to do this," Maya said in my ear.

"Get a move on." Babette nudged me as she shouldered by. "What are you even doing here, you don't swim anymore?"

Ignoring the toxic cheerleader, Maya and Trent eased me away from the doorway and toward the bleachers. But one look at the towering benches and my legs turned to mush.

"We can go back to yours?" Trent suggested. "Watch a movie? Make popcorn? Ignore the fact that swimming pools exist? You can even talk about Wade's manly pecs, and I will promise not to barf. Well, I promise to *try* not to barf."

I cracked a smile, then shook my head, my first conscious action since I'd entered the pool. "I need to do this."

I pushed my shoulders down and dragged in the over-whelming scents surrounding me. Memories swirled around me. But they weren't all bad. The feel of water slipping over my skin as I dove into the pool. It's velvet coolness supporting me as I sped along the lane, arm over arm, zoned out, completely in my own head, not thinking, just being, just existing, everything else so far, far away. The hit of chlorine at the back of my throat, the smell of it on my skin two days later, the feeling of victory.

I smiled. I'd totally forgotten that feeling.

Maya grabbed my hand and gave it a gentle squeeze. "Let's sit here." She gestured to the end of a bleacher about halfway up.

"You're doing well, Cordy," Trent said.

"I'm not an invalid." But I was panting and glad for the seat. I sat on the bench and crossed my arms. "Sorry. I guess I'm a little nervous." I picked up the race schedule and fanned my face. The waft of cooler air calmed me enough that I could breathe again.

"S'okay," Maya said, sitting next to me. "It's to be expected."

Trent pointed toward the changing rooms. "There's the wonder boy himself."

My pulse quickened as Wade emerged. I'd seen him in his swimming gear countless times before, but that was five years ago. And now he was...well, a man. There wasn't a single part of his body that wasn't toned to perfection and my eyes didn't know where to settle. As I took in the power of his arms, the chiseled hardness of his abs, the protective wall of his solid chest...a warm flush erupted over my skin, and I couldn't deny the ache settling between my legs.

Wade jumped on the spot a few times and circled his arms.

Maya nudged me. "Nice shorts."

Wade wore the prerequisite Speedos. They didn't hide much.

"How can he have any self-respect touting himself in a pair of..." Trent shook his head. "I don't know *what* that is."

"I'm not complaining." I laughed and waggled my eyebrows.

"Oh Lord!" Trent sunk his head into his arms. "Let me escape now please."

"You promised to not barf," I reminded him.

"I didn't think you heard that," Trent replied.

I ignored him and focused on Wade heading to his lane. Standing on the block, he scanned the crowd. Back and forth, once, twice, and then his gaze settled on me. He smiled and waved. I gave him a lame thumbs-up in return.

"Smooth," Trent said.

I elbowed him in the ribs.

The whistle blew, and Wade dove into the water, leaving barely a ripple. Arm over arm, he tore through the water. He made it look effortless, natural, as though he'd never done anything else. The longing to be in the water and swimming beside him pulled at me. Intensely. I shifted on the bench and clamped my hands together to stop myself from standing up and diving in.

When he climbed out of the pool, the crowd roared. He'd beaten his opponents by a whole body length. He'd also set a new high school one-hundred-meter freestyle record.

"I'll be damned," Trent said. "He's really good."

I smiled. "He is."

"Hey, Maya." Trent looked over my head at her. "Maybe he's a mer*man*."

"There's legend about them too you know," she replied.

"That'll be the day." He chuckled and flicked her on the nose.

She swatted him away. "You can't have one without the other. They need to procreate."

Trent pulled a face. "Ew. Mermaid sex. I don't want to know."

"Cascadia would not be happy with you."

"Cas...*who?*"

"The first mermaid."

He snickered.

Maya pointed a finger at him. "She was a goddess, Vortex's sister. One of the original three water deities. The first shapeshifter, able to shift between any ocean creature at all—"

"What, she could shift into a plankton? Wouldn't she be eaten by a whale?" Trent could barely breathe for laughing so hard. "Then, poof, no more goddess."

Maya raised her middle finger. I chuckled under my breath.

The crowd roared again as Wade won another race. Babette erupted from the first row of bleachers and threw herself at his chest, effectively using her body as his towel. He frowned, removed her arms from around his neck and placed her a couple of feet away. I allowed a small smile of triumph to play across my lips.

Wade looked for me and waved again. Babette put her hands on her hips and marched back to her seat. But not before giving me a scornful look.

The rest of the night passed by in a blur. No one was able

to out swim Wade in any of his races, and with each win, the crowd grew wilder and the applause more thunderous. Only when the swimmers retreated to the changing rooms did the crowd disperse.

"I think I'm going to wait for him," I said to my friends as we loitered outside the pool.

"Cordy and Wade, sitting in a tree—" Trent began the childhood taunt.

"Grow up." Maya socked him on the shoulder. She reached for me as Trent dragged her away in a fireman's lift. "Good luck!" she called.

"Corade, or perhaps Wadelia," Trent continued, amusing himself at my expense all the way to his van.

I hovered by the entrance to the changing room, not entirely sure if Wade was expecting me to wait, if he wanted me to wait, if it was the right thing to do. I jostled my weight from one foot to the other, was thinking maybe I'd missed him, when he emerged from the building.

"Hey." He spoke only one word, but it melted me completely.

"Hey, yourself."

"How did it go?" he asked, coming to a stop only a couple of feet in front of me.

"I'd say you broke every record there was to beat, will have your face plastered across every local newspaper and are probably now, if you weren't already, the most popular guy in high school. I'm going to have a fight on my hands with Babette now." A fair assessment of the evening.

"I meant for you." He dropped his gym bag at my feet.

His gaze raked over my face, dropped to my neck, my throat, lower. He didn't raise his eyes again until he'd performed an entire loop of my body. Every single nerve ending was a blazing fire. "How did you feel being so close to the pool?"

"Oh, I see." I shuffled my feet, unable to tear my eyes away from him. The sight of his biceps straining against the fabric of his shirt sent a shiver down my spine. His damp hair, tousled and curling in the most enticing way, begged for my fingers to run through it. My gaze lingered on him, drinking in every detail, every inch of his striking form. "It was good. Better than good. I realized I miss it. Really miss it."

His grin widened as he took a step closer. So close. But not close enough. "I'm glad."

"Thanks to you, it was the right idea."

He touched my arm. An inferno erupted over my skin. "Maybe you'll come watch all of my meets?"

The moonlight did something to his eyes. They darkened to almost black. There was so much mystery locked in his dark blue irises and I longed to discover every one of his secrets.

"I'd like that." My voice was barely a murmur. I couldn't seem to manage any more volume.

"What was that about having to fight off Babette?" He closed the gap between us, and his breath swept against my cheek. I drowned in his smell. Chlorine and soap and something musky I couldn't put my finger on. Was it seaweed?

"She's got some nerve."

He dipped his face toward mine and whispered into my ear, "Cordelia Blue, can I take you on a date?"

"I'd like that very much." My nose was in the crook of his neck. The smell of him intensified. The feel of him almost undid me.

I grabbed his arm to steady myself, and when I was no longer in danger of nose-diving the concrete path, I left it there, tucked in his elbow, wrapped in his warmth.

His lips moved from my ear to my cheek, and he brushed them against my skin.

"How did it go?" Dad asked, as I walked through the front door. A football game played on the TV. The Chargers were thrashing the Patriots by a wide margin. Dad sat in the easy chair dressed in sweatpants and a T-shirt, the footpad of the chair launched to max, one hand resting on the crank, the other cradling a bottle of beer.

"Good. It went well." I dumped my bag on the kitchen counter. "So well in fact I think I might try taking a bath."

He sat up, his legs either side of the footpad, one eye on me, the other on the screen. "You sure?"

"Yeah. It's time." My heart skipped a beat, but I was determined.

"Okay, let me know if you need anything."

"Matches? For the candles?"

"I think..." He rose to his feet. "They might be in the junk drawer."

He pulled a kitchen drawer open. Nestled inside was a ball of string, some envelopes, a couple of sticks of Big Red, a lone die, some loose change and my mother's keyrings.

"Look," I said, lifting three keyrings from the drawer. Each of the three keyrings consisted of a chain with a dangling jewel. Two were a cloudy, milky color. "I haven't seen these for…"

"These are opals," Dad said, pointing to the milky colored ball hanging at the end of the chain. "Your birthstone. Your mother carried them around to keep a little part of you and Dylan with her when you were at school and stuff."

"What's this one?" The third keyring was an elongated, rectangular jewel, dark blue and much larger than the opals. I stared at the jewel, then blinked twice. Within its inky depths, ribbons of color moved in concentric patterns, puffs of blue floated from one end to the other, like clouds scudding across the sky. I shook my head and the movement stopped. Jesus. I was losing it.

"I have no idea," Dad replied. "Maybe it's her birthstone. Sapphire is blue, right?"

"I think so. Is that the birthstone for February?"

"I don't know, Cord." He took a swig of his beer. "Pass me the iPad, I'll look it up."

I handed him the tablet, and he double tapped the Google icon. Within seconds he had a list of the months with their corresponding birthstones and flowers. "No, February is amethyst, which is purple. So, it's not your mom's."

"What about yours?"

"April, let's see." He peered at the small screen. "Nope. April is diamond."

"Ha. You always did have expensive taste." I bumped my shoulder against his. "Turning the basement into a high-tech cinema room and putting yourself on the list to test shuttles to Mars. Honestly."

He smiled. "I didn't hear you complaining the other night when you were watching your movie with surround sound and a 3D headset."

"True." I gestured to the strange, blue stone that seemed to lighten under the harsh fluorescent spotlights of the kitchen. "But I wonder what it represents."

"I'm not sure, Cordy." He closed the web page and picked up the tangle of keyrings. "Do you want them?"

I took the keyrings from his hand, feeling the smooth stones. "Let's put them back."

Noticing the matches, I grabbed them from the drawer. I placed the tangle of keyrings at the back and slid it shut.

"Thanks, Dad," I said, and kissed his cheek.

He resumed his seat, then whooped as the Chargers scored another touchdown.

In the family bathroom, I peered into the empty tub, the shiny ceramic reflecting a distorted version of my face. I hesitated at the taps, not immediately remembering which was hot and which was cold. Like muscle memory, the information came back to me. I turned the hot and put a finger under the stream waiting for it to warm up. I mixed in the cold until the water was the right temperature. In went the plug.

The vanilla candles my mother and I had always used were still under the sink. After blowing the dust off them, I set three around the edge of the bath. I struck a match and lit the first candle. When all three were flaming, the smell of vanilla filled the small room. I smiled as I remembered whenever my mother or I had used one of these candles, Dylan would launch a search of the house for a cake, convinced the vanilla smell was coming from the kitchen and the oven. Sometimes Mom would give in and bake him one.

Grabbing my bath robe, I threw in on the floor and then undressed and stepped into the bath. I stood in water past my ankles. This was the first time I'd been in water this deep for five years. My toes twitched against the ceramic, searching for the hot currents. Water ebbed between my toes and lapped gently against my legs. *So good.* I couldn't believe I'd denied myself this for five years.

When the bath rocked like a boat, and the images swarmed into my mind, I focused on the objects in the room —the flickering candles, the cream shutters framing the frosted window, the glint of the chrome taps. After a minute, I was ready for more.

In my mind, my mother urged me on, her voice a whisper of pride. Squatting on my haunches, I eased myself into the heat. Steam rose in front of my face and my skin turned pink. A knot of tension released from the back of my neck as my shoulders dropped beneath the surface. But the fear came, thick and suffocating, taking me back.

THE SHARK APPEARED for a third time and set its dead, primordial eyes on Dylan. We were all bobbing in the waves now. The sails had collected enough water to fill a swimming pool, and now the extra weight pulled the broken hull beneath the surface. The shark clutched Dylan's waist in its mouth and tugged.

"Cord..." he screamed. He reached for me. My younger

brother by thirty seconds. And I could do nothing to protect him.

I DIDN'T GET out of the bath. I sat there and endured. The memories would always be with me. My therapist told me not to fight against them, to let them float through me as if they were nothing more than air. She was right; they *were* nothing more than air, but it jarred the breath from my lungs all the same.

The vanilla candles flickered with my shaky exhales. Heat flushed my face. Water covered my body. But I was okay, there, in the bath, despite the grisly memories. I would fight them. Hard. I was determined to take back the reins of my life, memories be damned.

"Everything okay, Cordy?" Dad called at the door.

"Yep. Thanks, Dad."

"I'm proud of you."

"Is the game over?"

"Yeah. Chargers won by thirty points." He proceeded to give me a blow-by-blow account.

"Dad, trying to relax in here now."

"Um, sorry, I'll leave you alone." His footsteps retreated toward the kitchen, and I heard the clatter of dishes as he unloaded the dishwasher.

I took a deep breath and let my head slip under the water. My hair, now weightless, swirled around my face in a slow, elegant dance and brought pockets of heat closer to my body.

Opening my eyes, blurry images of the window and white ceiling filled my vision. I closed them again and remembered Wade charging through the pool, slicing the water as if it was butter and he a knife. My chest swelled with longing. For the pool. For the water. For record breaking. For Wade.

Without warning, Dylan's silently screaming face appeared before me, shouting my name, pointing desperately to something behind me, trying to get me to look. Stifling a shriek, I erupted from the water.

Fearing a shark would somehow burst through the pipes and explode out of the sink at my back, I glanced over my shoulder. But, of course, there was nothing there. It was an imprint from my recurring nightmare. But he'd never pointed before, and the desperation in his eyes was unnerving. I shuddered, unexpectedly cold and realized the bath had lost its warmth. Time to get out—I'd done enough conquering of fears for one night.

I pushed myself to my feet and readied myself to step out of the bath, and almost fell over the side. I couldn't move. I couldn't separate my legs. Something held them together.

The prickly coat of anxiety covered my skin, thickening as the seconds stretched on, weighing me down as I stood there shivering, unable to move.

The ridiculous idea of insubstantial ghosts surfaced first, their hands reaching from the depths of the drain, their grip hard and real and unyielding, their intent vengeful. I almost yelped as I remembered the terrifying image from a horror movie I'd watched a couple of weeks ago—Trent's choice.

As goosebumps littered my skin, I tried once more to step over the side of the bath. My legs refused to separate. The clamp held strong. Whimpering, I fell over the side and landed on my hip.

"Oof." I knocked the air from my lungs.

Sitting up, I looked at my legs. A flicker of revulsion rushed through me.

Not my legs.

I didn't recognize them.

Stuck together.

Not tied.

Not clamped.

Melded together from ankle to thigh as though I'd been exposed to an intense fire and my legs had simply melted together.

A scream formed in my lungs, tunneled up my windpipe, and devastated the bathroom. I couldn't breathe, I couldn't think. I couldn't stop screaming. Until I had to gasp for breath.

When the world stopped turning and the screams petered out, I dared to touch the skin connecting my legs. I blinked a few times. Held my breath. Then attempted to think rationally. It was like all the other skin covering my body, but pinker, perhaps turning a pale shade of red. The heat from the bath?

"Cordy?" Dad pounded on the door. "Are you okay? What the hell's going on? What's happened?" He turned the door handle, but I had locked the door.

"Don't come in here," I said. "I'm okay."

He must have heard the panic in my voice because he gave the door one good shove, sending splinters flying, and burst into the room. I grabbed my robe and threw myself into it.

"What's the matter?" He scurried to my side and helped me to stand.

"I..." But what would I say? I looked at my feet. I stood on two separate legs once again. Huh. "I must have fallen asleep in the bath. Nightmare. It freaked me out, and I scrambled to get out and I guess I fell."

And that must have been the truth of it. My mind was playing tricks on me. Why on earth would my legs be stuck together? That was the stuff of B-rate science-fiction flicks, not real life. I needed to stop watching those horror movies. And thinking about serial killer sharks. I'd faced my fear, and this was payback. "I'm sorry I scared you."

"It's okay." Dad pulled me closer for a hug. "It's okay. I was just worried."

I stood there, soaking up the solidity of my father's arms and saturating his shirt with my wet hair. I felt like a little girl again, believing my parents were immortal and could kill the monsters of my nightmares with merely a withering glance. If only that were true. If only we hadn't gone sailing that day. My mother hadn't defeated a monster; it had killed her.

"It's getting late," I said when I felt brave enough to move again. "And it's going to take me at least half an hour to dry this." I gestured to my dripping hair.

"You sure you're okay?" He held me by my forearms and inspected my face.

"Yes, I'm sure."

"I'll check on you in a few."

"Dad, seriously. I'm okay."

"I'm still going to check on you."

Like a little kid afraid of the dark. I sighed.

After he released me, I retreated to my room and sat on my bed. Stretching my legs out, I inspected them again. Legs. Just my normal pale, freckled legs. It must have been my crazy, freaked-out mind. My imagination. I was finally facing my demons and my mind over-reacted. Fear can have powerful effects on the mind and body.

That was all it was. Just fear.

CHAPTER SIX

The dark, inky ocean surrounded the ship, tugging it down, down, down into its depths.

The image of the *Titanic* sinking on the poster was enough to give me a shiver, but it stirred curiosity too. There were so many secrets hidden in the deep, dark blue. And I missed the water.

"Shit." Wade stood outside the box office window and shook his head. He stepped closer to the ticket office, until his nose touched the glass, and peered at the poster of the sinking ship. "It's disaster movie weekend. I thought we could watch something old school like *Airplane*."

"Trying to give me a fear of flying too?"

"I...no...I..."

"Relax," I laughed. "I'm teasing you."

"Huh." He turned to face me, a glimmer of amusement in his eyes. "There might be payback for that."

"I'm counting on it."

He smiled, touched the back of my hand. Fire immediately ignited. Every single time he touched me. Which hadn't been that many times and wasn't nearly enough. "I had a whole plan."

I raised an eyebrow. "A plan for what, exactly?"

Wade leaned against the wall, crossed one ankle over the other. An adorable blush creeped up his neck. "I thought if we watched something...scary...it would give me an excuse to get close to you..." His blush deepened. "Too cheesy, right?"

I tilted my head. "Maybe not cheesy enough."

He grinned. I melted. Job done. I was mere putty in his presence.

"But I don't want to put you through an ocean related disaster movie. I'm sorry, Cordelia. I didn't realize—"

"Wade." I closed the small gap between us, put my hand on his arm, soaked up the feel of him, the smell of him, the everything of him. How could one person have this much of an effect on me? Why bother questioning it? I loved it. "It's okay."

I looked at the poster of the sinking behemoth. *Titanic II*. I'd seen boat-related disaster movies before and not been affected by them. The movies were usually far enough removed from the reality of my own ordeal that I didn't stop to compare the two. I actually enjoyed the story of Titanic and found it a fascinating—albeit tragic—point in history.

"Really, it's okay," I said again, taking his hand. "It might be good for me."

Wade glanced at me sideways. "Are you sure?" He frowned. "We could skip it and go to dinner."

"But then you wouldn't have an excuse to get closer to me..." I said, with mock seriousness.

"*Titanic II* it is then." He laughed and threw an arm around my shoulder. "Two for *Titanic*," he said to the ticket lady as he paid with his phone. She handed him the tickets with a wry smile, and he stuck them into his pocket. "Are there any sequels as good as the original?" he asked me as we walked into the foyer.

"The *Jaws* movies?"

"You've watched those?"

"Actually, yes," I said. "Before."

"I could only bear the first one. They're...creepy."

"*Alien, Terminator,* and *Toy Story*," I said. "Their sequels are equally good."

"Yes, yes and, I'll admit it, yes," he said.

We walked to the popcorn counter, and I almost called an end to the date right then and there when he confessed he preferred sweet popcorn to salted. I'm mean, honestly.

"So what is your favorite movie of all time, Cordelia Blue?" he asked after we settled on separate buckets of popcorn. We carried our drinks from the concession stand and found our seats in the darkened theater.

"You'll laugh," I said. "Everyone does."

"Try me."

"*The Karate Kid,*" I said. "The original."

And he did laugh, a great, heaving chuckle that caused him to spew his mouthful of popcorn. He launched into a coughing fit, and I had to pat his back a few times to stop him spluttering.

"Wax on! Wax off!" he laughed.

I poked his chest. "It's not that funny."

"Can you do the crane kick?"

"Only if I'm provoked."

"I'll be good." He raised a hand in surrender. "Why is it your favorite?"

"Because I love a good underdog story. I guess I watched it at an impressionable age. It stayed with me."

"I get that."

"I like it when the asswipes get taken down."

"Unfortunately that only happens in the movies. In real life, the underdogs usually stay the underdogs, and the bullies usually win." Wade sighed, as if remembering a personal experience.

"Maybe." The house lights darkened, and the screen came to life. "Maybe not," I whispered to myself as the movie began.

Wade slipped an arm around my shoulder, wrapped one of my curls around his fingers, the gentle sensation sending shivers to my scalp. He didn't try anything else. Damn him. Sitting next to him, with the weight of his arm across my shoulder, the pressure of his knee pressed against mine, the smell of him so close, I could barely concentrate on the movie.

My head rested against his neck and the scent of his after-shave wound around me, reminding me of last night. Of him, in the pool, swimming lap after lap. Then I pictured myself swimming lap after lap and wondered if it could ever be again.

When the movie finished, Wade took my bucket of popcorn and stacked it inside his, then offered a hand to pull me to my feet. When I stood, our noses were almost touching. He stared into my eyes. A look of such intensity, a look of...I don't know what it was, but I didn't want it to stop. He dipped his head and brushed his lips across my cheek, the promise of more lingering in his tentative contact.

Before I could prolong the moment, we were walking out of the theater and along the beach path to an Italian restaurant.

"Again, Cordelia, I'm sorry about the movie," Wade said as we took our seats.

"It was good exposure therapy," I said, settling into a wicker chair and watching a lone candle flicker in a glass vase. We sat outside, under the twinkling light of a September sky. "Since the beginning of school this year it's occurred to me that I want to try and put it behind me. I've been having nightmares."

"I remember." The soft brush of his fingertips against mine sent a charge through me.

"And I want them to stop. I think the more I can do to face the fears and the memories, the better and the quicker I can put it behind me. It's coming up to five years. *Five years.*" I shook my head at the idea that five years could pass so quickly, but the pain lodged firmly in my chest hadn't diminished one bit.

"I remember when it happened." The flickering candle threw shadows across his face. "We were about to go on a date."

"Yes, we were." I dared to meet his eyes. Darkened in the candlelight, he didn't look away. Neither did I.

"But then, I didn't want to get in your way, I knew you needed space and then—"

"Then you moved away, and I didn't realize until Trent

told me six months later." I re-aligned my silverware as a sudden twinge of nerves made my fingers quiver. The old feelings came rushing back. All of them. More than I'd had before. Was it possible to fall in love this quickly? "I'm so sorry."

Wade enfolded my hand in his. "We got there in the end, didn't we? It's probably better we're a little older this time around anyway. I don't think a relationship would have lasted particularly long at thirteen, do you?" He chuckled, a soft, warm sound that somehow made the tips of my ears tingle.

"Relationship?"

But he changed the subject. "I know how you felt, to lose your mother. When we were in San Francisco I lost my mother too."

"Oh, Wade. I had no idea. I'm sorry." I squeezed his hand back. "What happened?"

"We lost her to the ocean." Pain flickered across dark eyes. "Three years ago now. So, I know what it's like, Cordelia Blue."

"It wasn't a shark, was it? There have been an unusual number of attacks. It's bizarre...I don't get why..." I never talked about this. Not really. Sometimes with Dad. But not to someone my age, to someone who'd experienced the same. The grief rose up my throat, almost a physical thing.

"I'm sorry," I cut myself off. "I shouldn't have asked. I'm dragging everything up again, and that was not my intention."

"There's nothing to drag up," he said. "It just sits there on the surface."

"That's it exactly," I whispered. Someone who understood precisely how I felt.

Wade tilted his head. His features softened as his gaze skimmed my face. "This conversation was not part of my plan either. How am I supposed to make you fall for me if I talk about death and sharks and the horrifying ocean?"

"The ocean isn't horrifying." That's what I chose to focus on?

"It's not?"

"It's our relationship with it that's complicated."

A beat passed before he replied. "I've never heard truer words."

We smiled at each other. And in the brief silence that reigned over the table, his cell phone rang. He pulled it from his pocket, sighed, then punched a rapid-fire message onto the keys and returned the phone to his pocket. "Sorry, got some family stuff going on."

"Your sister?" I remembered he had a sister a couple of years older.

"No. Yes. It's complicated." He picked up his menu. "I'm in the mood for pizza. And garlic bread." He looked at me. "Or should I refrain from garlic tonight?" One eyebrow was raised slightly higher than the other, questioningly.

"It just so happens that I like garlic too, so if we both ate it..." I let the thought dangle.

"I like your thinking, Cordelia Blue."

"Why do you always use my last name?"

"Because it's such an awesome name and deserves to be spoken aloud."

I melted a little then. As if I wasn't already as gooey as the butter on the table.

"Not like mine. When you have a name like mine you

learn to appreciate the beauty in other names. Wade Waters sounds like a porn star, or something from a children's show." He laughed.

"I've always thought it was a very nice name," I said.

"You're just biased, Cordelia Blue."

"That may be true."

After dinner, Wade helped me into my jacket and led me along the torch-lit path. My hand fit snuggly in his, and I relished the warmth radiating from his palm. Maybe when we rounded the corner he would stop and kiss me. Or I would kiss him. Either way.

Unseen waves crashed onto a dark shore on our left and a salty breeze tickled my cheeks. As we neared the end of the path, he smiled at me, and then we ran into a wall of six men.

One man stood in front of the others wearing a hoodie with sleeves pushed to the elbows and ripped jeans. He flashed his teeth into something resembling a menacing grin, revealing a couple of missing teeth.

"Well, hello there," he sneered, shooting a foot in front of Wade, making him stumble forward and land on one knee.

Crouching there, gathering himself, Wade's jaw hardened and something dark and dangerous flashed in his pupils.

"Wade? Are you okay?" Keeping an eye on the thug, I crouched by Wade's side.

Behind the man, five others stood, all in their early twenties and all sporting various ugly tattoos and piercings. And they reeked of fish. They gathered in a semi-circle behind us. As they planted their feet, it was hard to ignore the fact they were wearing steel-toed combat boots. Scuffed and used, I had no doubt they'd been in fights before. The one who kicked Wade glared at us. I spied a jagged scar running the length of his forearm. What kind of gang was this?

"I told you not to come here," Wade snapped as he launched to his feet and rounded on all six of them at the same time. He took a few hurried steps toward the threatening group, hands fisted at his sides and chin thrust forward.

"Wade?" I retreated a step. The car park was deserted. Dark waves crashed onto the empty beach in front of us. There was no one here to help.

"We wanted to make sure you hadn't forgotten," the leader said. "That while you're having fun with your girlfriend here—" He pointed at me.

"Leave Cordelia out of it," Wade barked. "She's got nothing to do with it." A vein throbbed in his temple, and blood dripped from a tightly clenched hand. He raised his fist above his head and took a step toward them. But there were six of them. Six. He couldn't possibly...

"Wade," I looked over my shoulder, desperately seeking a way out of this situation.

"We wanted to make sure you hadn't forgotten what you're supposed to be doing. For the family," the leader said.

Family? What the hell was he talking about?

The leader looked Wade up and down for a full ten seconds. I pulled my denim jacket tighter and prayed I would be good in a fight. Against six men? I'd never been in a girl fight before, let alone faced something like this.

The leader jerked a thumb at the hovering men, and then they retreated, jumping over the low wall into the darkness of the beach and the rolling surf.

"I...what...who?" I didn't know where to begin. "Are you

okay?" I approached Wade and took his bleeding palm in my hand.

He shook his head. "I..."

"I think you need to cut your nails," I said. The flesh wound, while not deep, was long and jagged.

"I do." He pulled a tissue from his pocket and dabbed at the pool of blood on his palm.

I could smell the copper in it. And the salt from the rolling ocean.

"The bleeding has stopped," I said. "But you should bandage it."

He put his hand into his pocket and stood there facing the ocean, seeming to listen to the waves crest and crash on the sand.

"Wade?" I put a hand on his shoulder as my heart rate normalized. "What's going on?"

"I'm sorry, Cordelia." He turned toward me. "It's all this family stuff going on. Believe it or not those guys...they're my cousins." He raised an eyebrow as if he couldn't believe it either.

"All of them?" I sat on the wall.

"Yeah. My mom is the youngest of eight siblings, and her mother is one of eight also. It makes for a large extended family." He dropped to the wall next to me.

"Don't you have any nice, pretty, delicate female cousins?" An offshore wind lifted my hair and whipped it across my face. With a finger, I curled it around an ear and shrugged deeper into my jacket.

"I do." He chuckled. "But those guys were here to send a message."

"What kind of message? Why would they threaten you? What kind of family does that?"

"There's a bit of a feud going on about an heirloom that belonged to my mother, about who should rightfully possess it and, unfortunately, no one knows where it is. I'm sorry to say you got caught in the middle of it."

"Wow."

"I know." A large wave crashed behind us. A few speckles of spray landed on my cheeks.

"Is there anything I can do?"

He dipped his head close. "Would it be too much to ask you to stick around and give me a second chance?"

"You're not the one who needs a second chance."

"Thank you, Cordelia Blue." He offered me his arm, and we walked along the boardwalk back to his car.

At my house, he accompanied me to my door and apologized again. "This wasn't quite the first date I had in mind. Scaring you with sinking boats and threatening cousins." He shook his head and looked at his feet.

"Wade," I said, placing my hands on his cheeks. "You haven't done anything wrong. Being with you is enough."

Leaning forward, I rested my forehead against his. I drank in his smell and caught the strange scent of something like seaweed again. Or was it a memory of our walk along the beach?

Wade's lips met mine with a gentle, testing pressure, and as I surrendered to him, he deepened the kiss. I wound my arms around his neck while he threaded his fingers through my curls. Every tug of hair sent sensations racing over my scalp, streaking across my skin, until a desperate ache formed in the lowest part of my stomach.

I pressed myself against him, drawing his tongue into my mouth, prolonging the kiss. Every part of him was taut against me. His corded arms locked around me, trapping me against him. I allowed my fingers to trace the lines of his chest, the ridges of his abs, the tightness of his ass. All mine. The temptation to caress him everywhere consumed me. But I held back, savoring the delicious tension between us.

I'd been waiting for love for a long time. For someone strong and safe to help me battle my demons. To protect me from serial killer sharks. I couldn't think of anyone better than the best swimmer I knew.

He lifted me into his arms, and I wrapped my legs around his waist, pressing myself closer, feeling every inch of his arousal. His hands gripped my ass, pulling me tight against him, as his lips devoured my mouth, then my throat, then an ear...then he placed me back on the ground, breathless.

"I've wanted to do that for a long time," he said, his fingers tangled in my hair.

"Me too." I kissed his nose, then his lips, then the shell of his ear. "Don't stop."

He kissed me again, long and hard and deep, then pulled away. "If I don't stop now, I'll never leave."

"Who said you had to leave?"

He smiled against my mouth. "Not the way I want to meet your dad."

I slapped his chest. "You're killing me."

"Good night, Cordelia Blue." He tipped a pretend hat at me and retreated along the drive.

Missing heirlooms and nasty cousins sounded like a lot to deal with. But it didn't faze me. I'd take his problems any day over the memories I carried and a paralyzing phobia.

But the grass is always greener on the other side. Until you're well and truly entrenched. Then it's too late to extricate yourself.

CHAPTER SEVEN

I fixated on the ocean, scanned the rolling surf, looking for anything out of place. But so far, it was just a normal sunny afternoon with eight-foot waves perfect for Trent's surf competition. Tell that to the Mom and son who'd died last week on a similar day.

Further along the beach, bleachers had been erected for spectators to watch the competition. Maya and I opted for an area away from squealing speakers and far enough from the water where I could sit without hyperventilating.

Trent skidded in between our beach chairs and covered us in a layer of sand. "I've got ten minutes. You guys didn't leave much time for the well-wishes and pumping of confidence."

"Huh. Didn't think you needed much confidence boosting." Maya rolled her eyes and flicked the sand off her legs. "And I brought something more scintillating to captivate my attention." She plucked a schoolbook from her beach bag.

Shakespeare's *Hamlet* materialized in her hands. Trent grabbed it and buried it in the sand.

"Hey!"

"My moves are way better than anything that Hamlet dude had to say," he said.

"See, don't need much of the confidence boosting, do you?" She retrieved her book from the sand.

"You nervous?" I asked. "I didn't think you got nervous."

A crowd was gathering on the beach. Supporters dug banners into the sand and little kids played in the shallows with ice-cream smeared faces.

"He's only nervous that he's going to come across a mermaid," Maya said as she rubbed sunblock onto her shoulders. "Oh, by the way, I found a new website that details the lore and prophecies."

"Like what, exactly?" Trent asked.

I frowned at him over his surfboard. "Since when are you interested in the details?"

He shrugged. "I want to know how bad Maya's delusions are. Whether we need to buy her a straight jacket for her birthday."

She flicked her hair over her shoulder and started ticking points off on her fingers. "It's known that humans evolved from the ocean, right?"

Trent and I nodded.

"It's not unlikely those ocean creatures we evolved from are merfolk."

There was a beat of silence. Then Trent burst out laughing.

I clamped down on the smile playing on my lips. I didn't want to upset her. "Anything else?"

Her turn to nod. "Look at the French words for sea and mother."

Trent rolled his wrist imperiously. "Which are? We can't all be language geniuses."

"*Mer* and *mere*, respectively," she replied. "Mother of the sea."

"That doesn't mean anything," he said. "A *mere* coincidence, and it doesn't actually suggest the existence of a mermaid."

She raised her hand, signaling there was more. "When the Trojans' ships burned in the war, it was reported the wood transformed into bodies of sea goddesses."

He scoffed. "Transformed?"

"It's not all about the past. There are prophecies too."

"Prophecies? Like the 'chosen one' type stuff in every other Netflix series? I think even I might need to draw the line there," I said.

"Not necessarily *chosen one*, but things that will come to pass. I can't help what's real." Maya rolled a lock of blonde hair around a finger and pursed her lips. "'*The one who walks the land can break the curse*,' that's it!"

"Now what are you talking about?" Trent muttered, coating his board in wax.

"The prophecy," she said. "The one I found online. Oh, and also, a fifteenth century painting of Noah's Ark depicts a mermaid, a merman and a merdog swimming alongside the Ark."

Trent laughed so hard he fell over sideways in the sand. "A merdog? Seriously?"

A hard frown turned Maya cross-eyed. "I can see my intelligence is wasted on you."

"Save it for Harvard," he replied, still clutching his stomach.

"Fine. And if you don't want to listen, then I want to hear about Cordy's date again."

Trent groaned. "From one lame topic to the next."

Six whole days had passed since my first date with Wade and, while we were waiting for him to join us at the beach, I didn't think it would hurt to give them another blow by blow account.

"I can't begin to describe how he makes me feel..."

"But he likes sweet popcorn." Trent feigned being disgusted. "You have to break-up with him immediately."

"I'm not sure we're actually exclusive." Were we officially a couple or was it too soon for such labels?

"Yes, you are." Maya unfolded a beach chair and plopped into it. "Tell me about the kiss again."

"Really? Again?" Trent threw his wax in his backpack. "I think I'm going to barf."

"Isn't it nice to know how much us girls gush over our boyfriends?" I asked.

"If I had a girlfriend...ah...speak of the devil, here comes the man himself."

The three of us turned to see Wade leaping the low beach wall and heading in our direction.

Wearing a pair of jeans and a crisp, white T-shirt, Wade

was hardly dressed for the beach, but I couldn't stop admiring the way his clothes clung to his muscular frame.

"Hey," Wade said as he joined us, then planted a lingering kiss on my cheek. "What's up? What have I missed?"

A blush heated my cheeks. Trent cleared his throat ceremoniously, causing the heat to spread to my neck. "Actually, now that you mention it, we were having an interesting conversation about—"

Stop! I said with my eyes. *Now!*

"About mermaids and merman and the secrets of the deep."

Wade startled, shoved his hands in his pockets, flicked his blue gaze at the ocean. "Mermaids?"

"Don't worry about it." Maya waved a hand dismissively.

"Some of us are believers." Trent nodded in Maya's direction.

"Of mermaids?" Wade coughed, then shook off the sand from his sneakers.

Trent rolled his eyes. "I know, right?"

With a small frown wrinkling the bridge of his nose, Wade turned his gaze toward Maya. "Huh."

"Trent, what time do you need to get in the water?" I cut in before a bickering volcano could ensue.

He glanced at his watch, then eyed the judges setting up under the shady gazebo. "A couple minutes."

"Man, I miss surfing," Wade said.

Trent frowned. "You can borrow a board any time."

Wade chuckled. "Yeah. Thanks. That's not it. Haven't surfed since I was thirteen, since...well, it's complicated."

"You had a virus and lost all sense of balance?" Trent questioned, inspecting Wade's two firmly planted legs. "No wait, that can't be it, you can still walk in a straight line. I know! I got it! You developed a sudden fear of crabs and now can't go anywhere near the shoreline...or you got attacked by one of Maya's mermaids."

Maya slapped Trent's shoulder. "They are not *my* mermaids. And they certainly don't attack."

"Don't they?" Wade asked.

We all stared at Wade.

A flicker of unease cut through my stomach. My head was stuck in the strange experience of my bath the other night. I knew creatures from fantasy novels didn't exist, but if they did...I shook the bizarre thoughts away. Just because my legs had been stuck together for a brief moment, probably from out-of-date bubble bath or another perfectly reasonable explanation, did not mean I had to go looking into the fantastical for answers. Nope. Not me. Mermaids weren't real. Creatures from the black lagoon did not exist. Unicorns did not shit rainbows.

Wade shrugged. "Just, you know, if mermaids did exist, I doubt they'd be all cuddly and cute, you know? I mean, the legends are all about how they lure sailors to their deaths, right?"

"Right..." Trent rolled out the word.

"Pfff." Maya waved a hand. "So misunderstood."

Wade fiddled with his belt loop. "Anyway, surf competition. I came to say good luck. I can't stay. Got some family crap going on." Wade glanced at me and raised his eyebrows. "But I can catch up with you in the evening, if you're free?"

"Perfect," I replied, and leaned into his offered kiss.

The world dissolved around us. There was only the sun heating the back of my neck and Wade's tongue exploring my mouth. His hands on my hips and the electricity dancing between us.

Trent cleared his throat and I pulled away.

"You two," Maya shook her head.

Trent flicked sand at me. "There's a time and a place, you know."

"There's every time and every place," I retorted as Wade swept an arm around my waist.

Wade raised a hand. "My bad. Cordelia is my drug."

Trent pretended to retch into the sand and we all laughed.

"Good luck, buddy." Wade slapped Trent's shoulder as he picked up his board.

"Look out for those nasty mermaids who don't like surfers invading their territory," Maya called after him as he ran down the beach.

"And look out for those sand crabs who steel the books of studious females on their way to Harvard," he called back.

I was about to laugh, when I caught Wade's expression.

"You okay?" I asked.

Wade nodded, kissed the corner of my mouth, and backed away. "Gotta go, but I'll see you tonight."

A horn blasted from the lifeguard station where the surfing judges had set up. *Please God, let there be no sharks today.* Especially murderous ones.

"*Ladies and gentlemen,*" the commentator spoke into his megaphone. "*Welcome to the third heat of the San Diego high school surfing competition. Thanks to the offshore earthquake an hour ago we have some decent sized swells heading our way. Prepare yourselves, ladies and gents, to see some special stunts today. The top three combined scores after today will advance to regionals next week. Currently, in first place, with a total of fifty-five points is Trent Summers..."*

"Whoop, whoop," Maya called from her chair.

"...in second place, with a total of fifty points is Steven Charles, and in third place with a total of forty-nine points is Ray Jackson. Take your places, ladies and gentlemen, any of them could take the top position. Today will reveal all..."

"Come on, Trent." She leaned forward in her beach chair as Trent mounted his board and took his first wave. Hamlet rested in her lap, and she gripped the volume in her fingers, fanning the pages nervously.

My own nerves flamed in my limbs, making my calves twitch. The water crashed onto shore. I struggled to keep my eyes on Trent.

"...and Trent Summers is riding up the lip, ladies and gents...and wow, that was some big air; a frontside air-reverse, and he nailed the landing, followed by a backside three-sixty, earning him seven point five points from the judges..."

"Yes!" Maya clapped and rose to her feet, the book falling unnoticed to the sand. I retrieved it from under her chair and put it back into her bag.

"The waves are huge," I said, scanning the ocean. I stood to join Maya and together we walked closer to the shoreline. The waves hurtled toward the sand, like a giant tongue, stretching, trying to climb farther and farther up the beach and succeeding with the incoming tide. A few feet away, I stopped. I didn't want to get any closer. Anxiety itched the back of my neck.

"*...eight points to Ray Jackson for his frontside roundhouse cutback, an oldie but goodie...*"

"Ten feet, maybe," she said. "Big enough to surf the tube." She clapped a few times in rapid succession. "That'll get him some points."

Trent came on to shore, waved at us, and then turned with his board and splashed his way back into the ocean.

"*...here comes a big one now, ladies and gentlemen...*"

"A twelve-footer at least." Maya jumped up and down. "Go, Trent!"

"He can't hear you." The sun beat down on the back of my neck, but it didn't dissipate the chill on my spine, and I could barely manage more than the odd shallow breath.

"I know."

The looming shadow of the memorial pier to my right offered a sanctuary away from the crowds. I gestured to Maya that we move in that direction where we'd get a better view and I wouldn't feel so suffocated.

Trent popped onto his board and hovered on top of the wave. Then the wave broke, and he slipped down the wall, pulling in under the lip, into the widening tunnel, preparing his entry into the tube.

"Yes!" Maya pumped her arm.

Please God, please God, please God, please God.

Trent disappeared inside the wave, inside the tube. I could make out his shadow as he slipped down the middle of the wave. Clouds rolled in from the ocean. White clouds. Harmless clouds.

"...and the points are racking up ladies and gentlemen, ten points for Trent Summers and more if he stays in the tube for a full ten seconds...he's maintaining his position in the pit..."

Trent remained in the middle of the tube. His board pivoted, angling up the wall—trying for a roundhouse cutback like his opponent?—when he fell off the board and into the water.

And then I couldn't see him anymore. Or his board.

Please God, please God, please God, Please God. My heart beat in rhythm with my prayer.

"Where is he?" The waves continued to roll in. Contestant after contestant performed tricks and drifted on to shore. "I can't see him. He hasn't come up yet."

"Give him a minute," Maya said. "He's leashed to his board, right?"

"Yes," I replied. "But that's not always a good thing. If the board gets stuck on something below, it could hold him down there."

"He's a strong swimmer, he'll be up any second now."

"...and Trent Summers seems to have taken a real tumble; he doesn't know up from down right now, and I'll bet his hair is tangled in the sand..."

We waited. Steven Charles and Ray Jackson rode their waves and strode along the beach. They didn't dash back into the water for the final minute of competition, but stood there on the beach, with their hands shielding their eyes, looking for Trent.

"He should be up by now." I took a few steps closer to the water line. The foam stretched toward my toes. I wanted to close the distance. But then I'd have to deal with my past.

"How long has it been?" Maya asked, her back ramrod straight.

"*...Trent Summers has been under for a full minute, ladies and gentlemen. The lifeguards are going in...*"

I inched forward, watching the clouds, the waves, the other contestants, looking for a sign of Trent. Water lapped at my feet. The ocean inhaled the wave covering my toes, and my feet disappeared into the sucking sand. I was actually standing in the ocean.

Three loud horns signaled the end of the twenty-minute segment.

But Trent did not reappear.

Maya grabbed my hand. "Where is he, Cordy?"

Another step into the water. Then three more and the water was past my shins. The waves buffeted against my knees. I would not let my friend drown in the ocean. I would not let another person I loved succumb to the same fate as my mother and brother. Instinct took over.

I threw my sunglasses at Maya and dashed further into the breaking surf. When the water reached my waist, my legs collapsed beneath me, and I could no longer stand. I fell under the water, under the foam. The cold hit my chest and stomach and stilled the breath in my lungs. Stretching for the surface, I fought for my feet. But they weren't there. I no longer had feet. Perhaps they were numb with cold and shock. My head rose above the surface, and I sucked in a breath of air.

As I went under again, I caught a glimpse of a large, red fish. A rip current yanked at my legs. Strong and insistent, it tugged at my body. Is that what Trent was now fighting? Or was there something else out there?

Saltwater burned my throat and stung my eyes, but I opened them anyway. I needed to see why I couldn't stand. Under the water, fighting the rip current and the foaming white above my head, I looked toward where my feet ought to be. The panicked, red fish flipped around in their place. Transfixed, I stared at the flailing red fish. It took me a full minute to realize it wasn't a fish. It was a tail. And it was mine.

I stared. I had a tail, and it was covered in scales. Beautiful scales of sunset oranges, poppy-reds, deep, mountain-sky purples, and candy-floss pinks. The scales were a kaleidoscope of vibrant colors, a shepherd's-delight sunset, and they shimmered and sparkled as though they were encrusted with diamonds. And there was a tail fin at the end of it, its breadth at least as wide as I was tall. It stopped flapping around and sat on the sand. My head remained under the water, but I no longer experienced the urge to breathe.

A hand grabbed my arm and dragged me out of the water under the shadowy pillars of the pier.

"I knew it!" Maya finished hauling me out of the water and threw a towel over my legs. Tail. "I knew it! Mermaids do exist, and you are one!"

"Did anybody see?" I looked over my shoulder at the horde of spectators gathered on the beach.

"No. Everyone was too busy looking for Trent."

"Thank God. Where is he?"

"He's fine. He surfaced as you ran into the water—what did you think you were doing by the way? Did you think you were going to reach him before the lifeguards on their jet skis?" She wrung her hands at me. "He's coming this way now. But more importantly, what the hell, Cordelia?"

"Maya, I don't know what's going on..." I pushed the towel away from my tail. Legs. They were legs again. And feet. I could wiggle my toes. I could stand. But I didn't feel like it yet. I might faint if I tried. "I'm not a mermaid."

She squatted beside me. "How do you explain it then?"

"I...can't."

"Hey. That was some wave, huh?" Trent flopped to the sand beside me and shook his hair, causing water to fly in all directions.

"Are you okay?" Maya moved from her squat to her knees and placed her hand on Trent's arm.

"I am. All good. Just adding a little drama for the spectators." He laughed, smoothing back his hair. But he didn't look at us. His gaze followed the waves and the horizon.

Maya wagged a finger at him. "Don't scare me like that again."

He buried her feet in the sand. "Thought you were too busy reading *Hamlet* to watch?"

"Hmph," she retorted, kicking the sand at him. "It was hard to ignore the circus, so, you know, I had to see what was going on. When I realized it was just you falling off your board, again, yeah, 'course I went back to *Hamlet*."

Trent chuckled and let her have the final word.

"Looks like you got through." I nodded toward the board with the final scores.

"Ah, second place. I'll take it I guess, considering."

"Why did you fall?" I asked, glancing surreptitiously at

my legs and feet. They remained legs and feet. "You were doing so well."

He frowned. "Something clipped my board."

"A shark?" Maya asked. "Do you think a shark went for your board?"

My stomach clenched. "If there is another shark attack, then I will personally buy a bazooka and shoot them dead."

"You get 'em, Cordy!" She punched the air.

"I didn't see a shark...but I did see something." Trent's eyes clouded, and his gaze went off into the middle distance again. The frown deepened. His tanned skin paled. Digging a hand into the sand, he picked up a shell and chucked it into the water. The waves licked at it, taking five attempts to dislodge it from the wet sand and carry it deeper. "It was just a fish. Just a really pretty fish."

Maya looked at me pointedly. "Maybe it was Cordy's hair. She went in the water to save you."

He took in my soaked bikini and dripping wet hair. "You went in the water, Cordy?"

"Um, yeah. I was worried about you."

"You went in the ocean, for me?" His voice softened, and his eyes filled with admiration.

"I...yes...I guess I did. I couldn't let..." But I couldn't finish the thought because my voice broke, and a tear escaped at the enormity of what I'd done.

"It's okay, Cordy." He put an arm around me. "It's okay. That was brave. I'm proud of you."

"Me too." Maya threw her arms around me too, and then we fell back in a heap and were covered with salt and water and sand. "Yuck."

"Trent! Are you okay? Please don't do that to me again!" His mother approached us and engulfed her son in a bear hug.

"You gave us a real scare, son," his father said, shielding his eyes from the sun.

"I am feeling a little beaten up." Trent winked at me. "I could definitely use a pizza, and maybe some ice-cream."

"You poor thing." His mother played with his hair, running her fingers through it to shake out the sand. He ducked away. "Pizza and ice-cream. That's perfect."

"And maybe a nice hot bath—"

"With bubbles," his mother said, rubbing his arm, patting his back, and parting his hair away from his eyes. "We'll get some of that nice bubble bath from the store on the way home."

"If you'll excuse us, girls," Trent's father said. "I'm going to take my son home before he runs his mother ragged with errands." Mr. Summers held out a hand and hauled Trent to his feet.

"About that ice-cream," Trent said as he walked away with his parents. "I like the little parlor downtown, maybe we could stop by there."

"He's fine," I said to Maya.

"Yes, he is."

We walked to my jeep in an awkward silence. We'd never had an awkward silence before. I dumped my bag and towel on the back seat, slowly, trying to delay the inevitable conversation.

She put the beach chairs into the trunk of my car. "Are we going to talk about it?"

"About what?" My brain had turned to mush. I'd walked to my car in a stupor of disbelief, unable to make sense of my extraordinary experience in the ocean, let alone begun to find the words to talk about it.

"About your beautiful red tail and the fact that you're a mermaid." Her voice was gentle and kind and filled with wonder.

"I thought perhaps I was hallucinating." I looked in a wing mirror. Same face. Same freckles. Same red hair. Human. Just a human. For now. My legs trembled a little. But at least they remained legs.

"Nope," Maya said, shaking her head. "I was there too. I saw it too."

"Shared hallucination?" I threw my damp hair into a ponytail and topped it off with a baseball cap.

"Nope. How long have you been a mermaid?" She leaned on the door of my jeep, settling in.

"I'm not a *mermaid*." I found it surprisingly difficult to say the once innocent word out loud.

She raised her eyebrows at me.

"I'm not!" I took the baseball cap off and chucked it through the open window.

Her eyebrows rose higher.

"I don't know." I sighed, resigned to the inquisition. "That was the first time that's ever happened to me."

"Was your mother a mermaid?"

"I don't know."

"What about Dylan? Your father?"

"I don't know."

"Are there other mermaids?"

"Maya! I don't know! I don't have the answers to any of your questions." I nudged her out of the way and climbed into my jeep. "And you can't tell anyone either. They'll stick me in a lab and poke me with needles, and I'll never see the sun again."

"I wouldn't, Cordy." She opened the passenger door and clambered in beside me. "We'll figure it out together."

"I do have an idea," I said.

"I'm all ears."

"My father's working at his lab. It's Saturday; he'll be the only one there. The tanks will be deserted, we could..."

Her grin stretched from ear to ear. "Let's go. Let's experiment with your tail."

CHAPTER EIGHT

I *am a mermaid.*
A mermaid.
A *freaking mermaid.*

Shock covered me like the ocean's cold embrace and made my thoughts sluggish. I couldn't get my head around it. I had a tail. And scales. And gills.

I am a mermaid.

I shook my head the entire drive to my father's lab at the naval base. After we passed through security, we were escorted to the lab with an ocean view where my father was busy at work, even though it was six o'clock on a Saturday evening.

"Cordy, Maya, they told me you were on your way." He wore shorts and flip-flops, and his thick stubble revealed flecks of gray. "What are you doing here? Are you looking for take-out money?"

"No thanks, Dad," I said. "Is there anyone else here now?"

"No." He offered a sheepish smile. "I came to work on the test results. I work better when it's quiet."

"Frank?" I enquired after the scientist responsible for feeding the sharks.

He pushed back from his desk and crossed his arms. "He went a half hour ago. Why?"

"If you don't mind, I'd like to take a look around the shark tanks," I said.

"If this is about the attacks, I told you I'm looking in to it," Dad said.

"Cordy went in the ocean today," Maya blurted. I stepped on her toe. Hard. "Ow!"

"You did?" His eyes widened as he rose from his chair.

"It wasn't exactly on purpose."

Maya relayed the story to my father, minus the mermaid part.

"I'm glad Trent is okay," Dad said. "And I'm proud of you, Cordy, that was brave, but why do you want to look at the sharks?"

"I want to see how I react. How I feel." It was partly the truth. The sharks were back there in the tanks, and I wanted to know if I would be filled with a sense of dread if I locked eyes with one, even if it was only a three-foot leopard shark renowned for shyness. I wouldn't go anywhere near the dangerous ones. Not yet.

"If you're sure, Cordy," he said. "I'll be locking up in thirty minutes. Is that enough time?"

"Yes." Maya was already backing toward the door.

"Cordy," he called after me. "I really am proud of you. You're taking this facing your fears thing seriously, and I'm glad to see you trying so hard. Your mother, Dylan, they'd be proud of you too."

"Thanks, Dad." I left him alone in his lab before he spotted the tears in my eyes.

The viewing areas were built underground to enable the sharks to remain in their natural habitat. Set on the edge of the ocean, the lab was able to corner off areas for the larger specimens and build channels for ocean water to reach the native inhabitants. Others were isolated in temperatures more suited to their natural environments. As Maya and I walked down the stairs and into the cavernous room, the smell of saltwater hit my nose. That, and fish. Arm in arm, we strolled through dimly lit passageways, coming to a stop at the juvenile leopard sharks.

Their bodies possessed a range of markings, each one unique, from bold, black stripes to the classic leopard spots or sometimes a combination. I watched them for a minute, their upturned mouths sifting through the sand.

Ranging from twelve inches to three feet, they seemed perfectly harmless. And leopard sharks usually were. But I didn't trust any shark anymore. As I stared, their languid movements became uniformed until they were all swimming in a circle in the same direction.

"That's weird," I muttered.

They swam faster and faster, until their tails became frenzied, kicking up grit from the bottom of the tank, their mouths opening wider, their eyes glowing with menace.

Transfixed, I couldn't move away, even though my mouth dried out and my pulse pounded in my ears.

"Ahh!" Maya shouted, snapping my attention away. I

hurried to catch up with her, unaware she had already progressed around the corner, only to find her doubled over with laughter. "It's trying to eat me."

"It's a whale shark," I said, stopping next to her. The whale shark was a gentle giant of the deep, yet its sheer size sent a shiver down my spine.

"It's huge."

That was an understatement. Far bigger than the leopard sharks, it dwarfed other creatures in the ocean. Probably at least fifteen feet long.

"It's a juvenile," I said. "They can grow up to forty feet long."

"I guess that's why it's called a whale shark." The docile shark turned toward us and opened its enormous circular mouth. "Look, see, it's trying to eat us."

"How is it going to eat you?" I asked. "It has no teeth." I tensed against the memory of a vicious shark that did have teeth.

She shuddered. "Its mouth looks big enough to suck me up in one gulp."

"It is." The shark circled around and opened its mouth for another gulp of minute sea life.

"Come on. We should hurry." She grabbed my hand and pulled me through the passageways.

Toward the end of the room, near the empty tanks, I stopped abruptly. "If there's one shark you want to be afraid of." A surge of courage flowed through me, even though my voice was hollow with dread. "It's this one."

Alone in the tank swam a six-foot tiger shark. It circled the tank lazily, but its speed was ten times faster than the whale shark. "Tiger sharks are number two on the list of attacking humans unprovoked." Shark facts reeled off my tongue. Despite being terrified of them, I hunted down information, trying to make sense of what had happened to my family.

"What's the first?"

"The great white."

"The one that...killed Dylan and your mother?" She drifted closer to the tiger shark.

"Yes." Thank God my father didn't have one here.

The tiger shark, with is elongated snout and downward slit of a mouth housing dozens of sharp, triangular teeth, and its dead, unfeeling eyes, was enough to make my entire body tingle with tension.

"Cord." Maya linked her arm through mine. "We're not here for this. Let's go."

"But if I'm going to go back in the ocean...I'm going to have to face sharks."

"Not today, you don't."

The shark drifted drowsily, its jagged teeth spilling out of its mouth like barbed wire, its eyes flat and unemotive. And then it seemed to notice me. My eyes locked with the lifeless gaze of the predator. Swimming toward me, it rested its snout on the glass wall. It appeared to be sizing me up, perhaps considering if it could propel itself out of the tank. I took a step back. Maya mimicked my actions.

"So creepy." She tightened her grip on my arm. Goosebumps erupted over my skin. "It's staring at us."

The tingling tension caused every pore on my body to sting and every hair to stand erect. We backed away. The shark rolled one of its black eyes at me and then streaked toward the other side of the tank.

Maya pulled me around another corner. The area was deserted. Several uninhabited tanks sprawled out before me. If only I could work up the courage to get in one. After that little staring contest with the tiger shark, my heart rate had no interest in slowing down.

"You okay?" Maya asked.

I nodded as I slipped out of my shorts and beach shirt and folded them in a pile at the base of the tank. Mounting the ladder, I stood at the top of the tank in my bikini and stared at the water. I worked saliva into my mouth.

"You don't have to, Cordy."

Oh, but I do. "I have to figure out what's going on with me."

I seated myself on the first rung of the ladder in the tank, under the cool saltwater. Maya's expectant breaths brushed against my shoulder. We waited. We didn't have to wait long.

"Oh my goodness," Maya gasped.

I no longer had knees, or shins, or ankles, or toes. Scales covered my body like an advancing lava, quickly and decisively, and swallowed my legs and feet. In the place of my feet appeared the most enormous and beautiful tail fin I'd ever seen.

A mesmerizing assortment of colors shimmered at me; the oranges ranged from bright pumpkin to the softest of sun-kissed sands, purples from the thistles of Scottish Highlands to the palest of lavenders, and pinks like a child's rosy cheeks on a cold winter's day to the merest hint of a candy floss blush.

But the most overwhelming color, the color which caught the eye and made the tail seem alive, on fire, was a vivid scarlet red. It was the red of a witch's lipstick, or the red I would paint my toenails in the summer, or the red of a London bus. Red, red, red.

"Cordy, you're beautiful." Maya's eyes were as wide as the moon.

The tail fin stretched at least six-foot wide. Thick at its base, where my toes should have been, but as it extended into the water it narrowed until it became nothing but a wisp of color, a mere suggestion of a sparkle. Red fronds swayed from the end, tapering to a burnt sienna, then a sunflower yellow and then to nothing as they came to their willowy end.

"Can I touch it?"

"Yes."

We both poked a finger into the simmering kaleidoscope of color. The scales were tough and resistant to my insistent prodding. As tough as chainmail. Shark proof?

"It's so smooth," she said, stroking me where my thigh had once been.

I laughed. "I'm not a dog."

"No, you're better."

Not a B-rate science fiction movie then. Or a horror flick. Or a trick of my mind. This was real life, and I had a tail. I waved the fin up and down, once, twice, faster, getting a feel for the power in new muscles. The water in the tank bubbled, then churned as my tail sent waves across its diameter. I wiggled it harder. It took surprisingly little effort to turn the tank into a raging ocean.

A wave crested over the side of the tank and soaked Maya. "Hey!"

"Sorry," I called. "I'm going in."

There was no hesitation. There was no fear. There were no images of my mother and brother in death. Instead, as I slipped under the water, I felt I was where I was supposed to be. Connected. Finally.

I dove to the bottom of the tank and worked the tail, propelling myself to the other side in a matter of mere seconds. The power, the strength, like wearing ten pairs of flippers and perhaps jet-propelled boots too.

As I swam and drifted and twirled in circles, the scales extended above my waist. They crept up my sides and came to cover my breasts in imitation of a push-up bra. An exceedingly sparkly push-up bra. Suddenly I had a cleavage. Twirling and circling and diving, I giggled with delight. The scales along my ribcage revealed a line of gill slits. The transformation wasn't merely about looks. Underwater, I no longer needed to breathe.

"Cordy?" My father's voice.

"Quick." Maya tapped on the glass wall of the tank. "Get out."

I swam to the edge of the tank, to the ladder. I looked at my tail. "How?" I said. "I don't have any legs to climb the ladder."

"Cordy?"

"Here." She offered her hand. Clutching it, she put an arm under mine and heaved me out of the water, out of the tank, and we landed in a heap on the floor. "Ouch!" She sat up, rubbing an elbow.

"Sorry." I scrambled to my feet. Feet. My tail had disappeared and my bikini was back. "Quick, help me." I grabbed my shorts and shirt. Maya snatched a towel from the rack along the wall.

I managed to slip into my clothes and was toweling my hair dry when my father rounded the corner.

He pulled up short. "Did you go in the tank, Cordy?"

"I..." I glanced at my friend for help.

"She..." Maya looked from my father to me and shrugged helplessly.

"You know, if you wanted to try swimming again, I could take you to a public swimming pool," he said.

"I know. I'm sorry. I wanted some privacy."

Maya shot me a that-was-close look.

"Okay." Dad shoved his hands into his pockets. "But let me know next time."

Beep beep. My phone sounded from my pocket. I removed it from my shorts and looked at a message from Wade.

Family situation running longer than expected. Doesn't look like I'll be able to come over tonight. Sorry. X.

I sighed.

"Everything okay?" Dad asked.

"Wade," I replied. "He can't come over tonight."

"I was looking forward to meeting him," Dad said. "Perhaps the three of us can grab a pizza instead?"

"Yes please," Maya said, always eager to delay her return to her foster parents. "That was awesome," she whispered to me as my father led the way out of the building.

I smiled. It really was awesome. But even better, I was no

longer afraid of the water. Sharks—yes, water—no. I certainly could never drown. I had gills.

DAD KNOCKED on my bedroom door just before midnight. "There's a rather beat-up looking young man in our kitchen asking for you."

"Beat up?" I climbed out of bed.

"See for yourself." I followed him into the kitchen.

Wade, dripping wet hair onto his jacket, sat on a kitchen stool, holding an icepack to his head.

"Your father was kind enough to get this for me." He pointed to the icepack.

"I'm going to leave you two alone," Dad said.

"It was nice to meet you, Mr. Blue."

My father looked Wade up and down, took in his battered appearance and the obvious fact that he'd been in some kind of fight. "I haven't made up my mind about you yet. And it's *Doctor* Blue, by the way." And then to me; "Cordy, don't be too late." Then he disappeared along the hall.

"What happened?" I removed the icepack from his head and examined the swollen red welt that looked in danger of bleeding again.

Wade winced as I touched his head. "Things with my family didn't go well."

"So you resorted to fist-fighting?"

"It got out of hand. We're not normally like this. Emotions are high right now."

"That must be some heirloom."

"It's valuable," he said. "But that's not why I'm here."

"It's not?"

He shook his head, then winced. "I don't want to think about my family right now."

"I wish I could help."

"You do." Dropping the icepack on the counter, he tugged on one of my curls. "Just by being here."

I took his hand in mine, kissed his knuckles, one at a time.

"That's what I'm talking about," he murmured.

"You're here for a booty call?"

"No!" Wade shot off the stool, and when he saw me laughing, sat back down with a sheepish grin. "I don't think I'm your dad's favorite person right now. The last thing I want to do is make it worse by being caught in your bedroom."

I cocked an eyebrow, trailing my hand across the kitchen counter. "Who said anything about a bedroom?"

Wade blushed. "You are killing me right now." His voice was low, teasing, but there was an underlying tension, a magnetic pull drawing us closer.

He smiled when he took in my oversized men's pajamas. Then he gently held the collars of my shirt in one hand, balling them into his fist, and inched me toward him until I was standing between his legs.

"Now who's killing who?" I muttered as the heat of his touch erupted over my skin.

He held me against his chest, his thumb tracing patterns on my arm as he dipped his head to capture my lips in a hungry kiss.

"I needed to be with you," he said when he came up for air. "I couldn't be anywhere else." He shivered.

"You're soaking wet." I rubbed his arms with rapid strokes.

"I took a shower, before I came. I didn't want you to see me bloody."

He smelled of saltwater. It wasn't an unappealing scent. "In the ocean?"

"No, that must be my new Cordelia-won't-be-able-to-keep-her-hands-off-me shower gel."

"I see." But he was right. All I wanted to do was touch him. And kiss him. Lose myself in him.

His hand drifted to the small of my back, his thumb tracing circles through the thin cotton fabric. With his other hand, he reached into my hair and entwined his fingers at the nape of my neck, pulling me closer until there was no space left between us. Enticing shivers ran down my spine, tickling my skin, making me want him. Want him in ways I'd never explored before.

I helped him out of his jacket, which landed in a heap at our feet, and then I let my hands roam under his shirt, exploring, greedy to touch him. Wade's hands floated to my face, and he cupped my chin. He kissed me, his tongue sweeping past my lips, devouring me. When he pressed my body against his, that's the moment I gave myself to him. That's the moment I knew I was falling in love. Properly. Irresolutely. No going back. But perhaps I'd always been in love with him. From the time I was thirteen, and ever since, I'd only been waiting for his return to evoke passion in me again.

"It's working, isn't it?"

"Don't stop," I whispered.

His lips went to my neck, my collarbone, his kisses blazing against my heated skin. He pressed his body tightly against mine, and I could feel every part of him yielding to accommodate my shape.

My hands roamed his back possessively. He belonged to me now. I yearned to consume every inch of him, to explore every part of his body, to get it know it as well as I knew my own. My fingers brushed over a jagged line.

"What's this?" I touched the length of a six-inch long wound. It was bulbous and rough.

"Nothing," he said. "An old injury."

Old? It felt far from old. A warning bell went off in my head. But this was Wade. *Wade*. There was no reason to have warning bells.

"Cordy," Dad called from the hallway.

"Just leaving, Dr. Blue," Wade called back. "I should go, before your dad locks you away and never lets me see you again."

"Okay." I sighed and rested my forehead against his.

"Ow."

"Sorry."

"I'll see you at school, Cordelia Blue." He retrieved his jacket from the floor, slipped it on, then walked to the front door. Pausing to wrap his fingers in my hair once more, he gave me one more light kiss, and then he was gone.

CHAPTER NINE

Eyes watched me.

Did they know my secret? Could they tell something was different about me?

I'd never been so glad to leave school at the end of the day. And as soon as I threw the front door open, Maya screeched to a halt in her yellow bug on my driveway.

"I've got it!" she called through her open window.

"Got what?"

"The book."

"What book?"

Rolling her eyes, she climbed out of the car with a huge book in her arms and followed me into the house.

"Is that why you weren't in first period this morning?" I asked.

Maya smiled as we entered the kitchen and she set the book on the counter, causing a plume of dust to rise and make us sneeze. Hoisting herself onto a stool, she flashed a Cheshire-cat grin in my direction.

The ledger-sized book was hardback and brown with age. The front cover portrayed a faint picture of two mermaids. To clarify, one mermaid and one merman with faded blue tail fins swimming round each other. Between them, an embossed symbol—orbs of different colors circling a large blue sphere in the center.

The Mermaid Chronicles

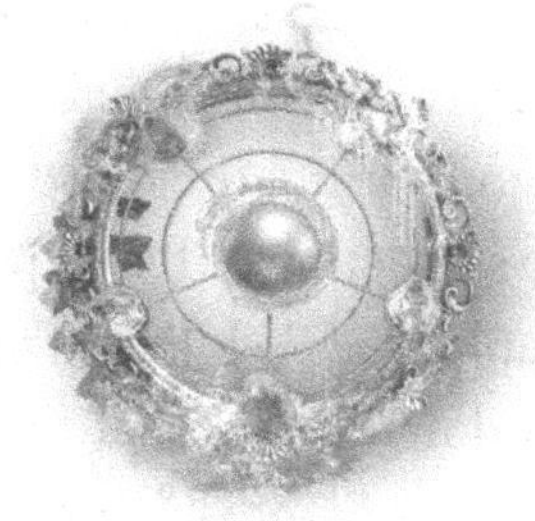

"WHAT DOES IT SAY?" I pointed to the title, which was obviously written in a foreign, ancient language.

"'*The Mermaid Chronicles*.' Right here." She stuck her finger in the middle of the strange markings which I assumed must be the title. "Can't you read it?"

I frowned and shook my head. "I'm not a linguist like you."

She gaped at me. "It's in English. I admit, it's a little dated and the writing is an old-fashioned cursive, but it is English."

I raised an eyebrow. "No...it's not."

We stared at each other, and then the cover of the book.

"What's going on?"

"I have no idea," she replied.

"Is there something wrong with me that I can't read it?" I asked. "I'm a mermaid, surely I should be able to read a book about my ancestry?"

"I would agree," Maya said, flicking through the pages. "But I don't have any answers."

I glanced over her shoulder at the turning pages. "What does it say?"

"The book is divided into sections. From what I've been able to decipher, there is information about merfolk history, a reference section, significant figures, and a list of prophecies. And at the end there's a section of blank pages."

"Prophecies? Blank pages?" I flicked to the end.

She shrugged. "I don't know what they're for. Maybe for us to record what happens next." She took the book and turned back to the beginning, the history section. "So far, I've been able to learn a little about the origins of merfolk and other sea creatures. Want to know where you come from, Cordy?"

My breath stilled. I never believed a book like this would exist. Let alone have any tangible information. "I'm not sure."

Maya droned on with animated hands punctuating her every word, choosing to ignore my hesitation. "They're as old as humans, older actually. While land animals emerged from the sea and grew legs to walk—primates, then cavemen, then us— merfolk evolved at similar times, but they remained in the water with their tails. About the time we started walking on two legs rather than four, they also evolved legs, able to go back and forth between the two. And that's where things get hazy. The book alludes to an event in the merfolk's past, some cataclysmic occurrence, which took away their ability to walk. Almost as if they devolved."

I prodded the rough page with a cautious finger. "And you think this is real?"

"Yes, I've spent a long time tracking this book down. I'm sure it's real." She turned the thick pages, examining the cursive script.

"Look here." She pointed at a particularly curly looking word. "Atlantis."

"Really, Maya?" I dropped my head into my hands. Nothing about this book was real. "Really? Atlantis? As in the lost island of...wherever? The sunken myth that no one has been able to prove? The utopian society that Plato told stories about?" Countless myths surrounded Atlantis, its origins and subsequent disappearance. *Myths* being the operative word. I slipped off the stool and slunk away from the kitchen.

"Where are you going?"

"I'm going to have a bath and play with my tail."

"Good idea. I'll let you know when I find something useful." Oblivious to my sarcasm, she turned her attention back to the book and the fantasy world she was living in.

I woke early the next Saturday as dawn peeked between the hills. The building desire in my chest had me popping antacids left, right and center, but I knew they'd never cure the unquashable urge to swim. It had been there all week, ever since I discovered my tail, and now I needed to stretch my wings, so to speak, and swim where mermaids were supposed to swim. The ocean.

Pulling on a beach dress over my bikini, and then a cream cardigan that reached my knees, plus my adopted Navy cap, I left the house. Walking along Niagara Avenue, I bought a powdered doughnut from OB Doughnuts and munched it on the way to the pier. I sat under the concrete pillars, in the shadows, away from the rising sun and early joggers. After wiping the sugar from my lips, I dug my hands into the cool sand and sprinkled it over my feet. I stared at the ocean. Mesmerized, I watched as the waves approached the beach. Endless. Eternal. My heart beat in a rhythm that matched the pace of the beckoning waves.

The sun rose. Its rays stretched across the water in its early morning greeting, lighting the ocean with glittering sparkles. I stood, threw off my clothes and approached the gentle waves. The sea breezes caressed my bare skin and fondled my hair, whispering at me. The pull was stronger than any magnet, stronger than the tide itself.

I allowed a moment for the water to lap at my feet before I charged in and dove into the frigid waves. But I wasn't cold for long, because as the scales covered my body, they did something to the way I felt temperature, and I was no longer cold.

I flicked my tail and found myself past the end of the pier and out in the ocean as fast as any fish, or shark. Floating on my back, the sun's rays warmed the human areas of my skin. My hair drifted under me, around me, and I thought I must look like Maya's Ariel.

An unexpected splash sent me diving under the water for cover and looking in every direction. I clamped my mouth shut and let my gills do the hard work. But I needn't have feared. Coming toward me was the smiling face of the friendliest mammal on the planet—a dolphin. The animal, with a scar on its flank, approached and click-whistle-squeaked at me as if it expected me to understand. I laughed. My new status certainly didn't extend to communication with animals. That would be weird. Although my eyesight underwater had increased dramatically. Despite the cloudy depths, I could see the ocean floor.

The dolphin poked its snout into my chest and then gripped my hand in its mouth, gently, pulling me farther out to sea. Was I supposed to follow? Did it just nod at me?

Why not?

I swam with the dolphin. We dove into the depths, deeper than I'd ever gone, where the sun didn't shine. The ocean was different down there. Shapes darted and weaved before me. Any one of them could be a shark. *The* shark.

My heart knocked against my ribs. But the dolphin led me closer to the surface and, when the other shapes followed, I realized they were dolphins too. There must have been six or seven, diving and leaping and twisting before me, over my head, splashing me with obvious amusement.

I grabbed hold of one's dorsal fin, and it took me for a ride in twisting circles, faster and faster, and my hair became tangled around my arms. Several more shapes darted toward us, and I hoped more dolphins were coming to join the impromptu party. But the six or seven I was already with became agitated, and the original one with the scar on its flank click-whistle-squeaked at me again. A warning this time. I could decipher that much.

As the other dark shapes approached, I trailed the dolphins back to the beach, toward the shallows, where I would be safe on legs once again.

"*Cordelia.*" The wind whispered my name.

I swam across the surface, propelling myself away from those looming shadows. As I reached the beach, my tail gave way to legs, and I scrambled up the shore, under the pier and fell back in the sand, panting for air. I looked back at the ocean, and there, in the distance a shark leaped into the sky and gnashed the air with its jaws.

"*Cordelia.*" Softer this time, but no less urgent. With goosebumps erupting over my skin, I pushed myself straight. The voice was familiar. *Dylan.* I'd know it anywhere. It was firmly etched in my memory, and I watched the video of our thirteenth birthday party at least once a month.

Perhaps it was the whispers of his ghost. He hadn't died far from here, and now that I'd dared to enter the ocean again, maybe his essence remained here, waiting for me, welcoming me back to the one place I should never have left. His voice, pure and clear, echoed in my head.

But what about Mom? Why didn't I hear her too?

I closed my eyes against the sudden wave of loss. A brief

but intense swell of emotion sent something thick and hard shooting up my throat and it lodged over my voice box. I clenched my teeth together, trying to bite the memories back down. My stomach rolled. I drew my knees under my chin and waited for the moment to pass.

Gradually, like the stuttering of a wind-up toy in its last few seconds of power, the stabbing pain of grief leached out of my body and I was able to open my eyes again. There was nothing to see or hear or feel except the ocean, the sand, and the whispering wind.

"You've barely said a word the whole way here," I said.

Wade stared through the windscreen of his car at the brick wall surrounding the car park. The lights of the swanky restaurant spilled out of the large glass windows but didn't illuminate our dark corner.

"Is there anything I can do?" I peered into his distracted face. Although a yellowing bruise remained on his forehead, the swelling had reduced.

"I'm sorry, Cordelia." He sighed and drummed his fingers against the steering wheel. "I'm supposed to be making up for that terrible date when my cousins accosted us, and now I'm distracted and not giving you the attention you deserve."

"We're a long way from Ocean Beach. I don't think your cousins will follow us here. Let's put the enigma of your missing family heirloom behind us for one night and try and enjoy this fancy restaurant you're taking me to."

"What would I do without you, Cordelia Blue?" Wade

asked as he opened my car door. Although his smile was forced, there was genuine warmth in his eyes.

"Lead a far less exciting life and always wonder what it would feel like to kiss me."

"That," he squeezed my hand, "I already know."

Wade plucked me off my feet and lifted me into his arms. Burying his head in my hair, he stayed there, breathing me in. He kissed me, briefly, the promise of more hovering on his lips, and then escorted me into the five-star restaurant with a view of the ocean. Delicious smells weaved out of the kitchen, and my stomach rumbled in response. As we were led to a table, the sun set over the water, turning the sky from blue to a combination of fiery reds, deep pinks and soft oranges that reminded me of my tail.

The evening was glorious. The food was divine, and Wade sat close to me, on the same side of the table, insisting we share our dishes. After we had eaten, we moved outside to the terrace to enjoy a pot of green tea and see if we could spot any shooting stars.

"Here you are," a voice said. The gray-hoodie cousin, the one with the scar. He appeared in front of us after having climbed the rocky beach path. At least this time he was alone.

"Jordan." Wade remained in his seat and pressed his lips into a thin line. He reached a hand toward me and laid it in my lap, squeezed my thigh. "As you can see, I'm a little busy here."

"You forgot something." Jordan's mouth twisted into an ugly sneer. His teeth were no longer missing. Perhaps he'd had them fixed. "It must have come loose during our scuffle last week." He threw something in Wade's direction that clinked against his teacup. "I don't want you to forget your heritage."

Wade picked up the item and held it within a clenched fist. "It couldn't have waited?"

"Do I need to remind you how important family loyalty is?" Jordan crossed his arms and leaned against the balcony.

"No," Wade whispered, looking away from his cousin to his clenched hand.

"Good." Jordan jolted forward and slapped Wade on the back. Hard. "Keep looking." And then he left.

Wade let out a whoosh of air. "I'm sorry. Again."

"Wade. What's going on?"

When he wouldn't look at me, I placed my hand on his jaw and turned his face toward me. Tears glimmered in his eyes, in danger of brimming over. "Tell me what's going on, Wade. If I'm going to be a part of your life, and I hope I am, then I need to know what's going on."

"You're right." He blinked twice, and the tears vanished. "The heirloom. It's my fault."

"What is it?" I pulled my cardigan tight to ward off the evening chill.

"It's a jewel that's been in my family for over a thousand years."

"You can trace your ancestry back that far?"

A fragile smile lifted the corners of his lips. "Further."

"Where are they from?"

"An ancient island." He toyed with his teacup, running his finger around the rim. "It was destroyed a long time ago. Anyway, I knew my mother had the jewel, and she entrusted it to me before she...left us," he stumbled. "But I lost it."

"Where?"

"That's the problem, Cordelia Blue, I dropped it in the ocean." He swallowed the rest of his tea and placed the cup back in its saucer.

"In the ocean? How on earth does your cousin expect you to find it? Scuba dive every inch of the seabed?"

A bitter laugh ripped out of Wade's throat. "Actually, yes. I dropped it in an area protected by rocks and unaffected by currents." His gaze swept out across the ocean, as if he might be able to spot the heirloom from here.

"So it shouldn't be so hard to find, right?"

"Wrong. I can't find it anywhere. I've been in the ocean every day." Wade ran a finger along my cheek. "That's why I smelled like the ocean last weekend, at your house. It wasn't my new Cordelia-won't-be-able-to-keep-her-hands-off-me shower gel. I was diving for the jewel."

"At night? Are you insane?" I poured us both more tea, wishing for something stronger.

"It glows in the dark. It's easier to find at night."

"You do know how many shark attacks there have been this year, right?"

He laughed again. A raw, miserable sound.

"I'm not joking."

"I know." He squeezed my hand. "But I have no choice."

"Fuck the jewel," I said. "No heirloom is worth your life."

His eyes brightened as he searched my face, his expression softening, his hand gripping mine. "You are quite something."

"It's just a stone. Just an expensive glow in the dark rock

that doesn't have any bearing on your future." I kissed the back of his clenched fist. "You don't need it."

"*I* don't." He sighed. "But it's not up to me."

"What can I do?"

"You are not to involve yourself with this."

It was my turn to laugh. "Too late."

"Maybe you should run while you can."

I shook my head. "I repeat. Too late." I nudged his loosely curled fist. "What's in your hand?"

Wade unfolded his palm to reveal a leather-strap necklace with a shark's tooth pendant. "It's the tooth of a blue shark. I found it on the beach when I was a kid and my sister made it into a necklace for me. It came off in my fight with Jordon last week."

"At least he returned it to you. That's got to mean something, right?"

"Maybe."

"What did he mean, about your family's heritage?" I gestured to the jagged white tooth.

"My family are fishermen. Always have been, probably always will be. We're all expected to go into the family business. It was his way of underlying his point about family loyalty."

"If I were you, I'd be tempted to flee the country to a remote island and forget my family ever existed. You could lie on a beach all day and carve wooden statues out of driftwood for tourists and then spend your hard earned cash on cocktails served in coconut shells with little umbrellas in them."

"And sleep on the beach and fish for food." Wade mustered a smile. He pulled the necklace over his head and let the tooth dangle at his collarbone. "Only if you came with me, Cordelia Blue."

"That can be arranged," I said, taking his hand.

I glanced toward the beach path, wondering if Jordan or another cousin might come back. How easily they slipped into the darkness and shadows.

CHAPTER TEN

The idea of Trent surfing alone filled me with dread.

"How long is he going to be?" I asked Maya as she tugged the ancient mermaid book out from under my bed. She'd decided my house was the safest place to keep it; away from the prying eyes and scribbling fingers of four younger foster siblings. As a result, she'd been at my house every afternoon this week, pouring over the pages, and rifling through the larder for snacks.

She shrugged. "He'll be here soon. He knows I'll choose a Disney movie if he doesn't get here on time."

"He shouldn't complain. There are some pretty badass Disney movies."

"What about Wade?" Maya asked as she heaved the book on top of my bed.

"I'm seeing him tomorrow night."

"We like Wade. We don't mind if you invite him to movie night."

"I know. And thanks." I sat on the bed next to her. "What happened to your contacts?" I gestured to the thick-framed black glasses she'd recently pushed up her nose.

"Stupid foster siblings hid them again when I was sleeping. I'm lucky I have the glasses. I can't see anything without them."

Even though the black frames were too big for her narrow face, there was something about the contrast with her blonde hair that leant her a striking, intelligent beauty.

"I think they suit you."

"Here it is." She stuck a finger in the middle of a page. "This is the bit I thought was curious." She continued to read from the yellowed pages. "Merfolk aren't the only humanoid water species. Apparently, there is a second species, but..."

"But what?" I asked, trying to read the cursive words even though I didn't understand a word of it.

"I can't see anymore; the page is damaged, and that's all I can figure out. But further down here." She pointed at a word I recognized. "It says both species came from the land of Atlantis. Atlantis!" She threw her hands in the air and almost fell off the bed.

"Maya, Atlantis is a myth." I went to my bay window that overlooked the beach. A sliver of ocean sparkled at me. If I went too long without seeing it, I became agitated.

"That's what you said about merfolk."

True. Could Atlantis have been a real island, a real place? Were there truths behind the ancient legends and myths?

"What did you say about a prophecy?" I asked as I plopped into an armchair in the corner of the room.

Maya had been insistent all day at school that she'd found evidence that supported the prophecy she'd found online.

"Ah." She flicked through the book a few more pages. "Here. It says *'the one who walks the land can break the curse, united.'*"

"What does it mean?"

"What does what mean?" Trent asked as he walked into my bedroom. His hair was wet from the ocean, and he wore a surfing T-shirt and board shorts.

Maya slammed the book closed and then attempted to sit on it, succeeding only in drawing more attention to the fact she had something to hide.

"What does what mean?" Trent asked again, taking a couple of steps toward Maya and me. He frowned. "What are you guys doing?"

"Nothing," Maya squeaked. I glared at her.

Trent took two more decisive steps toward the bed, lifted Maya off the book and dumped her on the floor. He lugged the volume closer, and his brow wrinkled as he glanced at the cover.

"Mermaids?" he asked, looking from Maya to me. "What's this about?"

"Research," Maya said, getting to her feet. "For my English paper. I managed to track down an old book about the myths of mermaids."

"I can't believe something like this exists." He flicked through the pages. "Is this supposed to be real? What language is this?" He turned toward me.

"You can't read it either?" I asked.

He shook his head. "It's gibberish."

Trent had a photographic memory, had studied Latin in Freshman year. If he couldn't make any sense out if it, then I was sure this was a 'Maya' thing and not a 'me' thing.

Maya hugged the book. "I guess I was meant to find it."

"Why?" Trent asked. "What's going on?"

"He's going to find out eventually," I said to Maya, "and he's our best friend."

Trent sat on my bed and looked between the two of us as if he was watching a tennis game. "Care to enlighten me?"

"Cordy is a mermaid," Maya blurted. She really had to stop doing that.

Trent didn't laugh as I'd expected. He continued to look from Maya to me, back and forth. He was going to pull a muscle if he kept it up.

"What you learn here today," I said, getting to my feet. "Stays between the three of us. No one else can know."

I stood in front of Trent and stared at him, making it clear something momentous was about to be revealed.

"Okay..."

"Promise," I said.

He chuckled. "What, with a pinky swear?"

"With your life. If they find out, then I'll never know normal again."

"Who are *they*?" he asked. "Some secret government agency?"

"Maybe. Anyone out there." I waved my hand at my window and the world beyond. "Follow me, Trent."

I led my friends into the bathroom and shut the newly repaired door behind us. As I ran the bath, I slipped my shorts off. I was about to remove my top when Trent cut in.

"Girls, while I'm a warm-blooded male and I love a little ménage-a-trois as much as the next guy, I'm not sure I want one with my two best friends. It doesn't feel right somehow."

"Oh, relax." I threw my top at him. "You see more of me when I wear a bikini."

Maya flicked him on the back of the head. "In your dreams, buddy."

I was poised to jump into the bath when I turned back to Trent. "Prepare yourself for this, Trent. Seriously."

"Come on, you're not actually going to turn into a mermaid."

I jumped into the bath and submerged myself under the water. My tail rose and displayed itself in all its glory.

Trent turned as white as the bath under his suntanned skin and looked in danger of passing out. Maya smiled smugly at him as his jaw worked up and down.

"I..." he managed and then sat on the bathmat.

Maya clapped with child-like glee. "Cordy is a mermaid."

"How long have you known? How long have you been like this?"

"Since you fell off your board in that surfing competition and I dove into the water after you. I didn't get far because the tail appeared, and I freaked out a little."

"I bet you did." He rose to his knees and peered into the bath. "This actually explains a lot."

"How so?" Maya said, joining Trent at the edge of the bath.

"That day, when I was under the water and the current mistook my head for a drill, I thought I saw something. Now I realize what it was; a mermaid, but it wasn't you, Cordy, because its tail was blue. It got between me and something else. Something big. A shark, I think." He shuddered.

"Then what happened?" Maya asked.

He splayed his hands. "They both swam away. I didn't get a good look at either of them; it was more of an impression. It happened so quickly." He opened his mouth to say something more and then stopped, looked at my tail again and stroked it with a gentle finger. "That's amazing."

Maya touched my arm. "Cordy, you might have a family out there."

Did the voice that had called my name at the beach belong to another mermaid? Or had it merely been the wind and my imagination?

"You can't tell anyone," I said, as I flicked my tail and sprinkled Trent with water.

He wiped an arm across his face. "Who would believe me?"

He had a point.

I climbed out of the bath, and Maya handed me a towel. Trent turned his back when my underwear turned see-through and waited until I was dressed again.

He held the bathroom door open. "What were you talking about when I came in? You were trying to figure something out."

The three of us went back to my bedroom, and Maya flicked the book open to the relevant page. "*The one who walks the land can break the curse, united.*"

"What does it mean?" Trent asked, sitting beside her.

"That's what we were trying to figure out," I said. "Maya insists there's a whole section of prophecies that have come and gone, while some are still to pass, and that this is the latest one."

"Are we sure this book is authentic?"

"Yes," Maya said. "I've spent hours locating it and paid a small fortune having it shipped here. I'm sure."

"But you're the only one who can read it," he said.

"I know," she replied.

"Why?"

"That, I don't know. Hopefully I'll figure it out soon."

Trent stared at the strange markings in the book. "Okay, so the one who walks the land must be a mermaid, and it suggests not all mermaids can walk."

"I think so," I said.

Trent continued with his train of thought. "So the curse can, or will be broken by a mermaid who can walk the land, like you, Cordy—"

"It doesn't say mermaid," Maya said. "It only says *the one who walks the land*. There are two humanoid water species, but we don't know what the other is."

"I think we need to stop getting ahead of ourselves." I slipped my arms into a sweatshirt. "Being a mermaid is one thing. But prophecies? Really? I'm not some kind of underwater Percy Jackson."

Maya nudged me. "Maybe you are."

"Back to the prophecy," Trent said. "So Cordy, or something like Cordy can break the curse. What's the curse?"

"It doesn't say." Maya tapped the arm of her glasses. "I've spent hours examining this book, and I can't find any mention of what the curse actually is."

An ominous silence descended on the three of us as we

contemplated Maya's words. I fiddled with the cushion on my lap, winding the tassels around my finger. It was a needle-point Mom had completed of dolphins swimming in the water. She'd had it made into a pillow for my tenth birthday.

"Oh well." Trent rose from my bed. "Life goes on as normal then."

"I guess. Apart from the whole I-have-a-tail thing now."

"No," Maya shouted, surprising both Trent and I. "Life does *not* go on as normal. We need to break the curse." She waited for us to agree with her.

"Why?" I asked. "The curse, whatever it is, might be there for a reason, and unless you can figure out what it is and how it can be broken, then there's not much point in thinking about it."

"What? No! No, no, no, no!" She threw a sock at me and then stuck her nose back in the book. "I'll find something," she whispered. "I'll figure it out."

"Let us know when you do," Trent said. "And in the meantime, Cordy, I think you should try out for the swim team. You'd be awesome. Better than before. And you and Wade can do a whole Bonnie-and-Clyde-in-the-water thing."

"And how would I explain the tail every time I dove into a pool? I'm aiming for a low profile, not the cover of National Enquirer. And I don't plan on robbing any banks."

"Your tail won't appear in chlorine," Maya said, from her cross-legged position. "I read in the book your tail will only emerge in pure, natural waters. Fresh water or salt-water, not water with chemicals."

"But there's chlorine in the water system. How come my tail appeared in the bath?"

She tutted. "Actually, the water system around here is pretty pure. Most of San Diego's water treatment facilities pride themselves on not using chlorine in their processes. So maybe whatever chemicals they do use are so low it doesn't affect your tail?"

I cocked my head. "I guess I should test that before I try it in public."

Trent had planted a seed. Ever since I'd been back in the water, ever since I discovered my tail, I had an unending urge to swim, fast and hard and far.

I woke with the yearning in the pit of my stomach every day. "But I'd like to, if not join the swim team, be in the water again at least."

"In that case," Maya said, bouncing on the bed. "I know just the thing to do."

The three of us waited for the evening to turn to night and my father to go to bed. For once, none of us paid much attention to the movie. I had a vague impression of a war scenario, soldiers and guns and bullets flying, but as for a plot? My head was stuck in the plot of my own life. For once, Trent didn't go near the popcorn or drink any soda. Maybe the existence of my tail had affected him more than he let on.

When the clock signaled an hour late enough and my father was snoring sufficiently loud enough, we crept out of my house and piled into my Jeep.

"Where to?" I asked Maya.

"School," she replied with a wicked grin.

Trent and I looked at each other and burst out laughing.

"The school swimming pool?" I asked.

"Yes." She rolled her eyes, as if we were stupid not to

understand. "I have a copy of the key for the fire escape door. I've been at school after hours lots of times. It's deserted so no one will see us."

"What for, Maya?" Continuing to laugh, it took Trent three attempts to buckle his seatbelt. "In case you have the urge to raid the library?"

"Maybe." She narrowed her eyes at him. "Just drive."

Maya was right. After we arrived at the school and broke in using her spare key with the stealth of a marching band, I jumped in the pool and nothing happened. I swam, arm over arm, with kicking legs, not a flipping tail. When I stopped and concentrated and tried to will my tail into existence, nothing happened.

"Okay," I said. "Swimming pools are safe, but I need help with something if I'm going to try out for the team."

"What is it?" Maya asked.

"I need to cut my hair." I gestured to my flaming-red hair which tumbled past my waist. "It keeps getting in my way when I swim, and I certainly can't pile it under a swimming hat."

"I'll do it," Trent said.

We drove back to my house, and I settled myself on a kitchen stool. Trent took the scissors in one hand, my hair in the other, and snipped. The first clip of the blades sounded loud in my ears. But he was gentle and surprisingly skilled, and my red hair quickly covered the kitchen tiles.

Trent was quiet as he piled my cut hair into a bundle and handed it to me. "Are you going to tell Wade?"

"No," I said. "God, no. What would I say?"

"It's a hard secret to keep," he said.

"That's why I have the two of you. I can talk to the two of you." I slid off the stool and stuffed my hair into a baggie.

"Of course you can, Cordy," Maya said.

Trent shrugged into a surfing hoodie two sizes too big. His curls fell over his face, but his eyes didn't leave the floor. He opened the door.

"You'll keep my secret?" I asked him. His eyes locked on me. "Of course."

Without any further words, I knew he was thinking about Dylan. About whether Dylan might have been a mermaid, or merman too. He'd died without ever knowing. And what about my mother? Where had my tail come from?

I was back on the swim team.

I'd begged and pleaded and insisted I should be allowed on the swim team, in senior year, even though I missed the tryouts and even though Coach Ford had never seen me swim before.

It had only taken a minor demonstration of my skills to prove to Coach I was worthy. After spending a calmer hour convincing him I was no longer crippled by the horrifying nightmares of my mother's and brother's death—which had stopped ever since I'd discovered my tail and embraced being in water once again—he agreed to give me a place on the team with my first meet for this coming Friday night.

"Congratulations!" Maya threw her arms around me on Monday afternoon.

Trent elbowed her out the way to give me his own hug. "Well done."

"By the way," Maya said. "About your tail." She mouthed the last two words, and Trent and I huddled around her.

"Yes?"

"You can control its appearance. In the book it says you can control when the tail emerges."

"That's good to know. Maybe I won't end up in some fisherman's net thinking he's caught a whole new species of weird," I said.

"You can protect me when I'm surfing." Trent parodied balancing on a surfboard. "Or flick your tail a little and give me an extra push."

"Protect you? I'm still scared of sharks. One thing at a time."

"I just heard the news." Wade appeared. "I'm proud of you, Cordy." He wrapped his arms around me and hugged me fiercely, his lips lingering on the shell of my ear. "Now we can spend more time together."

"Strange," a rather piqued voice interrupted.

Babette stood behind us, an unsettled expression on her face like she'd swallowed a fly. She wore her cheerleading uniform and her shiny, high ponytail swung back and forth like a pendulum, emphasizing her every word.

"I can't say I ever took much notice of your hair before, Cordelia, but now it's gone I kind of miss it." She gave Wade one long, lingering glance before she pivoted on the ball of her squeaky sneaker and marched off down the hall.

"That was a bit of a backhanded compliment, I believe," Maya said.

"I can't believe she bothered to talk to me directly," I said.

"She doesn't take rejection well, does she?" Wade dug his fingers in my hair and brought my red locks toward his face. "I think it's beautiful. I love it."

"Where do I get me some of that?" Trent asked.

"Some of what?" Maya asked.

Trent put both hands over his heart and fluttered his eyelashes. "True love."

The bell rang and Maya grabbed Trent's hand and pulled him along the hallway.

As Wade leaned in for a kiss, I noted the dark circles under his eyes, deep purple bruises. The whites were bloodshot and the pupils watery.

"Are you okay?" I asked. "You look exhausted."

"I'm not getting much sleep."

"Are you getting any?" I took his hand and laced my fingers through his. "Or are you spending all your nights diving for the heirloom?"

"I need to find it."

"Can I help? Do you want me to come with you?" But was I ready for it? While it was all well and good for me to swim laps in a safe, chlorinated swimming pool, was I ready for the ocean at night? And what about my tail? Could I really learn to control its appearance?

"No, Cordelia Blue." He placed his hands on my shoulders. "I would never ask that of you. I think it's great you're back in a swimming pool and you're making progress, but I'd never ask you to swim in the ocean with me, especially at night."

It had been a few weeks since the last shark attack in Santa Barbara, and I hadn't thought much about the shark responsible since I'd discovered my tail. But it was out there. Somewhere. "I don't like the idea of you being alone out there."

"My cousins are with me. My sister comes down at the weekends to help. It's under control. Really." He cupped my chin. "And the last thing I want to do is re-traumatize you." And then his eyes did something freakishly weird. They turned black, both of them, even the whites. Like a shadow had passed through them. It was only for the briefest of moments and for a second, I thought I imagined it. But the surprise had me stumbling backward, and when I looked again, the black disappeared and Wade's normal, although painfully bloodshot, blue eyes stared at me again.

He frowned. "Cordelia?"

"What's wrong with your eyes?"

"My eyes? Nothing." He stepped toward me. "As I said, I haven't been sleeping well."

"They went black and..." I wasn't sure how to describe it.

"Black?" Wade's frown deepened. "I think the high of getting onto the swim team might be getting to you." He smiled, slung an arm around my shoulder and kissed my cheek. The late bell rang. "Come on, we better go."

Maybe he was right. My life, the other life I simply couldn't share with him, had been turned upside down. I certainly couldn't claim my head was screwed on properly right now. Life was a jam-packed rollercoaster; the tail, the swim team, the anniversary, being with Wade. The highs and lows and emotional swirls were playing with my mind.

Later that night I locked myself in the bathroom and stepped into the full tub.

"If you're going to continue taking these exorbitantly long baths, I might need to increase the water bill payments," Dad commented when I locked the door.

I lowered myself into the bath and the tail popped out. Leaning my head back against a towel, I closed my eyes.

Concentrate.

The effort strained the muscles in my face as I fought for the reappearance of my legs. It took ten minutes. As I was about to give up, I opened my eyes. The scales chased each other along my legs, down to my toes, leaving in their wake the pale, pink skin belonging to my legs and feet.

I stayed in the bath for another hour, periodically topping it up with hot water and dodging the odd sarcastic comment from my father. But, after an hour I mastered control over my tail. I could will its appearance at the merest thought, and I could also will it away again.

Phew. I'd been worried I would never be able to swim at a public beach again or go for a walk along the shore with a special someone because a wave might lap at my feet and send my tail shimmering into existence. Now I had control, and with control came the confidence that I could carry on with the pretense of being normal. I was also relieved I could now shave my legs.

"HAVE you thought any more about your birthday?" Maya asked, handing me my swimming cap.

I stood in the changing room, slipping off my sweatpants, revealing my brand-new school swimsuit. Predominately maroon, bright red slashes decorated each side. Like gills. How appropriate.

"No," I replied, tucking my hair into the cap. "I've had other things on my mind." I gestured toward my legs.

"I thought you might say that." Her lips curved into a huge smile. "I've spoken to your father, and he's happy for me to arrange it for you if you're okay with that?"

"Maya," I said, pausing in my hair tucking to hug her. "That would be great. As much as I want to celebrate, my mind is a little preoccupied with other things right now, and I can't escape the fact I should be sharing it with someone who isn't here anymore. So, it would help to know you're planning something and also that I don't have to think about it. I won't have to dwell on the other implications."

"Leave it to me," she said, rising from the bench. "Good luck with your race."

"Thanks."

I left the changing room with my teammates, many of whom I'd swum with in middle school and were glad to have me back, and went to line up for my race. Wade and the other guys sat on benches lining the end of the pool. The girls were competing first. He stood and walked toward me.

"You can do this," he said, as I took my place.

I searched the crowd for Maya and Trent. They sat halfway up, smiling, giving me a thumbs-up. Next to them my father gripped Maya's hand. His face was pale and pinched, and he was probably worrying I might freak out. No. There would be no freak-outs tonight. Right now, the need to feel the water caress my skin outweighed any nightmarish memory. But I did wish my mother was there sitting next to him. I wanted her to tell me how proud she was.

Before I had any more time to contemplate my father's state of mind, the whistle blew, and I propelled myself off the starting block and into the waiting water. My first race was the fifty-meter front crawl. It had always been my best stroke. I flew through the water. Arm over arm and kicking legs. No tail. I'd barely had time to adjust to the glorious feel of my body carving through the water when I reached the other side, and Wade held out a hand.

"You won," he said. "By four seconds."

The rest of the evening went by in much the same way. I won all my five races, as did Wade. It was like I'd never left. Like the last five years of abstinence had been nothing more than a vivid nightmare and now I'd awoken again in my real life, in my real place in the world, doing what I should be doing.

"This calls for a celebration." My father approached me with my towel. Maya and Trent climbed down from the bleachers, grinning stupidly as though I'd won the lottery or something.

"That was a truly magnificent comeback," Wade said, wrapping his own towel around his waist.

"Everyone back to our house for pizza, and maybe a beer if you're lucky." My father glanced toward Wade and looked him up and down. "You too, Wade.

"Thank you, Dr. Blue. I wouldn't miss it."

"Yes, I can see you two are rather wrapped up in each other." Dad smiled kindly. "And it's nice to see your...injury is looking better too."

Wade's hand went to his head, where the yellow bruise stubbornly remained. "It's feeling much better. Thank you."

"You two get changed, I'll take Maya and Trent, and we'll meet you back home, Cordy."

"Thanks, Dad."

"What's with your toes?" Wade pointed at my feet.

I glanced at my feet to see my toenails glisten in a pale pink color, and then they darkened and turned a scarlet red. Then they reverted back to their normal translucent pale pink.

"Um..." Although my tail was inhibited by chlorine, my body wasn't completely safe guarded against the effects of water.

"It's the new nail polish," Maya said. "The color changing one when it comes into contact with water. It's all the rage right now."

The five of us looked at my feet and waited to see if there would be any further displays of color. Nothing. I breathed a sigh of relief.

After we got changed, Wade and I met outside and walked toward his car.

"If it isn't the fish-people," a voice shot out from the dark of the parking lot. "You two must be mermaids, or something, to swim like that." Babette appeared around the side of a car with a couple of her ass-kissing minions. She stood in the cone of a streetlight, center stage.

My gaze snapped toward her at the mention of the word. Did she know my secret?

"Tell me," she said, the sarcasm dripping. "Have you made any fish babies yet?" Then she laughed, actually it was more of a cackle, and threw her chin toward the sky.

Wade narrowed his eyes. The black flashy thing flickered

across his pupils. Blinking, I cleared my eyes, and the effect was gone, whatever it was. His eyes were blue. Of course they were.

"Don't listen to her," he said to me, and then addressed Babette. "When we decide to—"

"Oh!" Babette interrupted. "You haven't done it yet? If you'd chosen to be with me Wade, I wouldn't have kept you waiting so long." She winked. "It might not be too late."

I prayed it was sufficiently dark enough for the night to be covering the heat in my cheeks. My tongue appeared not to work, despite the thousands of retorts tumbling through my mind. And then I got angry at her audacity to come on to my boyfriend while I was standing right there. I had a strong urge to slap her right across her smug little face.

"When Cordelia and I decide to take our relationship to that level." Wade took my hand, making his stance clear. "You can rest assured you won't be involved in that discussion or with any of the events that might happen afterwards. And if you must know, Cordelia and I haven't been together that long yet, and I would prefer to let things evolve naturally, organically. Otherwise, I think it would turn me off a little. It would deaden the anticipation somewhat. There would be nothing to wait for."

The smile slipped from Babette's face and took up residence on my lips instead.

"Babette," he said. "It's time you left Cordelia alone and accepted not everyone wants to be your boyfriend. I know that's not something you hear often, but if you keep bothering Cordelia, or cracking on to me, you're going to hear it a lot. I don't want to be your boyfriend. Get over it."

Her mouth closed into a tiny 'o' shape, and for once she had nothing to say. Her minions held their sides, trying not to laugh. Wade pulled me away from her and toward his car, leaving her staring after us.

Climbing into his car, the sense of being loved filled me up. Here was a guy, sitting next to me, gazing at me adoringly, making me feel I could do anything. If only I could introduce him to Mom. She would love him as much as I did.

"That was impressive."

"I'm tired of her games, Cordelia Blue."

It was a full five minutes before I let him drive away. Maybe it was because I knew Babette was still watching, maybe it was because I was feeling emboldened by the swim meet, or maybe it was because I was just so damn head over heels for Wade, but I took my time kissing him.

His eyes gleamed with a primal hunger. As my lips brushed against his, a surge of desire coursed through me, igniting a fierce longing I couldn't deny. With a daring confidence, I took control, pulling him closer until our bodies were pressed together in an intoxicating embrace. My hands roamed eagerly, tracing the lines of his jaw, tangling in his hair, guiding him with a hunger that matched his own. The kiss was a spell, weaving through us like a wildfire, consuming every doubt and hesitation, inciting an addiction neither of us could pull away from.

"We should go," Wade said, gasping for air. "Before your father thinks I've kidnapped you."

"I could stay here forever."

Wade put his hand on my thigh, immediately turning me

to mush. "After I've found the heirloom, after graduation, let's do exactly that. Let's go away together."

I grinned as a myriad of images tumbled through my brain. Wade and I together on some far flung beach. No, not on the beach, but in the hotel room, wide double doors open to a patio, a beautiful sunset spilling muted light into the room. A room which we never left.

"I'm going to hold you to that."

We drove back to my house and ate pizza with my father, Trent, and Maya, and drank a half bottle of beer each. Wade and I recounted each of our races a dozen times, and I reveled in a foreign state of happiness. I was actually happy.

Yes, I had a secret life; I was a mermaid, and it wasn't something I could share with my boyfriend, but I was swimming again. I had overcome my fears, and I had two close friends who supported my every endeavor, and a father who would do anything for me. Now, his eyes shone so brightly, that it occurred to me, for however briefly the transient moment might last, that my world was simply perfect and perfectly simple.

My father went to bed, and the four of us headed downstairs to the basement room for movie night. There were four of us now. We were a group of four. I liked the way that sounded.

Maya watched the action movie totally engrossed in the hero's story while Trent made sarcastic comments, as he always does, about the impossibility of muscles being that big, or that no one could jump off a building without breaking a leg, or that the hero and heroine wouldn't actually stop in the middle of an exchange of bullets for a passionate kiss. All the time I sat with Wade's arm around me, and our thighs pressed tightly together in the mutual need to be close to each other.

Maya and Trent left around midnight, and I took Wade to my bedroom. We didn't do the things Babette had callously mocked us for. Instead, we sat bundled in each other's arms and talked and kissed and came to know one another's bodies. My hands drifted to the small of his back and the rough scar. I was about to ask Wade what it was, but he'd fallen asleep, and I was content to watch him breathe.

CHAPTER TWELVE

The ocean called to me. The whisperings I'd heard the last time I'd swum echoed in my mind. There was something out there. Maybe someone. Something I needed to do.

I pulled on my bikini and beach dress, grabbed a towel, and headed to the pier to meet Trent. He preferred to surf in the early morning, and Maya would be along as soon as she could escape from helping her foster siblings with their homework. With foster parents who both worked crazy hours, her siblings would never get their assignments finished if she didn't get involved. As much as she complained about them hiding her contacts and scribbling in her textbooks, she loved them with all her heart.

"Will I be seeing you out there?" Trent asked as he rubbed wax on his board.

My legs itched to turn tail. I needed to swim in a big expanse. I needed to be in the ocean. "I'm going out now." I dumped my towel on the sand next to Trent's backpack.

"Be careful out there." He chucked the wax on his towel and stood with his board under an arm. "There haven't been any more attacks recently but..."

"I know. You too." I scanned the water. The waves were calm today. Gentle ripples lapped at the shore. But farther out, the ocean became a vast no-man's land. An image of the one-dimensional, black eyes of the shark who took my family flashed through my mind. "But I'm a mermaid. I can't stay on land forever."

Together, we charged into the water, Trent remaining above the surface, paddling through the waves, and me diving below, flexing my tail, propelling myself past the end of the pier and into the great, blue beyond.

I lost sight of Trent as he mounted his board and took his first wave of the morning. I dared to venture further out, past the windsurfers, past the sail boats, past the point of good sense. But mermaids were made to explore the depths, and even though a thrum of edgy anticipation streaked through my veins, the pull to continue was too strong to ignore.

I turned my face to the sun and floated on my back, using my tail to stay balanced. It was a glorious October day and my chest filled with the rightness of that moment.

"Cordelia." Someone whispered my name, a feminine voice which floated across the water.

I pointed my tail down and inspected the calm surface. Left, right, circling, I saw no one.

"Cordelia...*pssst.*"

I looked beneath the surface. Under the gently rippling current, a pair of brown eyes, framed by a nest of wild dark hair, stared at me. I startled to the surface and sucked in a lungful of unnecessary air. I wasn't expecting to meet anyone this far out to sea. Beneath the water, a tail emerged. A blue mermaid tail—hard to define against an ocean of the same color—broke the surface of the water. A hand beckoned me to swim deeper.

I stuck my head under the water and strained my eyes to see the undulating fronds of my mermaid sister as she dove.

She waved again. "Follow me."

How could I possibly hear her? More than ten feet below me her words should be indecipherable at best.

"We speak using telepathy. We move our lips because it's what the human side of us has always done, but mostly we communicate through telepathy when we're close enough to each other."

That explained why her voice drifted into my head. She beckoned again. "You need to come with me."

"Who are you?" I asked, as I swam to meet her.

"My name is Nerida." She smiled, revealing a dimple in her chin.

"Nerida?" The word formed on my lips and travelled effortlessly from my mind to hers.

""It means 'sea nymph.'" Bubbles escaped her mouth, rising to the surface. "I don't think my parents were feeling particularly inspired." She laughed, the bubbles increasing in size and effervescence. And then she gasped as my red tail floated around her. "It's as beautiful as they say. I've never seen anything like it."

"What's beautiful? As who says?" I asked, sensing eyes on me.

"Your tail. It's been spotted by many. No one who hasn't

seen it believes it. I've never seen a red tail." She swam in circles around me, inspecting my tail, catching the delicate fronds in her hands.

"How many people have seen it?"

"A few," she murmured. "Most of us have blue or green or sometimes a dark purple. But never this." She ran a finger along my scales.

I examined Nerida's tail. While it glistened and sparkled in much the same way mine did, it didn't have the same eye-catching vibrancy. Her tail was blue, from steely grays to the aqua of a Caribbean Sea and merged well with the water around her. I guessed that would be the point. She blended in. I did not. I glanced nervously around. I was like a red flag to a bull. But for sharks.

"You're fine," Nerida said, having heard my fearful thoughts. "Nothing will attack you."

"How do you know?" I turned in circles, wishing I had three-sixty vision.

"Because it's not allowed," she said, curling into a slow dive. *It's not allowed?* "You need to follow me."

As I swam after her, we were joined by six or seven dolphins. I recognized the one with the scar along its flank, and it whistled at me. Their presence calmed me. Dolphins were known to protect humans— perhaps mermaids too?— from shark attacks. There were many reports of them coming to the rescue.

We swam deeper into the ocean, I suspected, but in truth I had no idea whether we were going up or down or along the coast or further out to sea. There weren't many landmarks to mark my path. Fearing I might not be able to find my way back to the beach on my own, I kept close to Nerida's sparkling blue tail and trailing dark hair. The dolphins swam and leaped around us, clicking and whistling and squeaking at each other.

"Where are we going?" I threw the thought in Nerida's direction.

"It's not far now."

Following Nerida and the dolphins, I flipped my tail and propelled myself through the water faster than any human could. I reveled in the feeling of using my tail, of my muscles working and being stretched to their limits. For the first time in years, I felt connected. To the ocean. To myself. To the world around. And most importantly, to my past. I'd found my calling, and I wasn't alone. There was at least one other mermaid in the world besides me. And Nerida had alluded to more.

The water dimmed; the sun no longer able to penetrate the depth of our dive. I blinked several times to clear the looming shadows from my peripheral vision. Shivering in the colder water, I raced to keep Nerida in sight.

"We're here." Nerida led the way to the surface.

I broke through the water, expecting to be bathed in a warm ray of sunlight, but instead, darkness remained, disorienting me. Gentle waves lapped against the side of something.

I blinked as my eyes adjusted to the gloom. "Where are we?"

"Mermaid Lagoon," Nerida said. "This is our home. I took you through a secret entrance. It's an underwater cave known only to us."

Jagged rocks formed a cavern above our heads. Gentle currents rippled at the surface but strengthened in the depths where the water was exposed to the secret entrance. To my left lay a rocky ledge, relatively flat, and big enough to rest upon. Flickering lights dotted the ledge and craggy rocks, casting large shadows on the uneven walls.

"Our home?" I asked. "How many are there of you?"

"*Us.* How many are there of *us.*" Nerida smiled. "Many. Not as many as before, but we're still a large number, and we live in all the oceans of the world."

"Cordy!" A voice shouted from the other side of the cave. Tumultuous splashing ensued.

"Cordy!" The voice became urgent. And it was familiar. Achingly familiar. Impossibly familiar. I closed my eyes against the unexpected hallucination.

"Cordy!"

I shook my head.

It wasn't possible.

I remembered the last time I saw him.

MY NAME FORMED on his lips. Panic widened his eyes. Bubbles escaped his mouth as he screamed. Blood circled his head, and his eyes grew impossibly wider.

The water thickened with foam and blood, and I couldn't hold my breath any longer. A dorsal fin flashed by, dangerously close.

Dylan screamed again. Then he sucked in his first watery breath. Bubbles streamed from his mouth and nose. With jaws wrapped around his waist, the water took him deeper and faster than I could follow. Kicking after him, I reached for him. Panicked, he wrestled against the violent grip, but only his blood was released.

Dylan's real, alive arms wrapped around me, and he dragged me under the water and shouted my name from his mind, so loudly, so clearly, I knew it must be him.

I opened my eyes, afraid this delicate dream would dissolve with the merest shake of my head, like a cloud in a storm-tossed sky.

"Cordy," Dylan said. We swam to the surface, and he tugged me to the edge of the cave. He anchored his hand on a rock, and a green tail undulated beneath him. "Cordy. It's really you."

"It's really me. But how is it really you?" I whispered, afraid to speak aloud.

I looked him up and down, not daring to touch him, lest he evaporate into thin air. His hair was darker and his body more mature, but his hazel eyes hadn't changed. They remained the color of a budding acorn, a color I'd once thought nondescript, but now, in his impossible presence, I cherished more than my own soul. Hot tears streamed down both our faces.

My gaze wandered to his tail. Green; the color of olives and seaweed and the occasional bright glint of emerald and jade. He hugged me again, held me tightly in his arms, squeezing and squeezing until I had to rely on my gills for oxygen. But when he disentangled himself, I wasn't ready to let him go. I had five years of hugs to make up for, and I wasn't entirely sure this whole thing wasn't some incredibly vivid dream. He might disappear with one flick of his impressive tail.

"It's a long story, Cordy, you might want to climb out for a bit." He wiped his cheeks and gestured to the cave floor strewn with towels and pillows. After he lifted me out of the water, I crawled, on legs, toward the towels and fell back against a pillow, spent and bewildered.

"Aren't you coming?" I settled on the rocks and blotted my eyes with a towel.

"I can't." He leaned his elbows on the cave floor, at the rim of the lake, and rested his chin on top of them.

I sat up. "You can't?"

"None of us can. None of us have legs." He gestured to Nerida and a few other merfolk who'd appeared without my noticing and splashed about in the water. I counted six. Two males and four females. Myself. And Dylan.

"But the towels, the pillows?"

"They're for you."

He'd obviously spent a great deal of time setting things up to make me comfortable. I couldn't imagine where he'd acquired everything and how he'd brought it here.

"Tell me, tell me everything," I said as I blotted my hair with a towel.

He smiled. "We're merfolk."

I laughed. "That much I know." Leaning forward, I socked him on the shoulder—how quickly and easily we fell back into sibling banter. "How are you alive? I saw you. I saw your...dead body." I shuddered at the memory.

"You're right." His smile slipped away. "I did die, as a

human. But the merfolk saved me. They rescued me. Although I was always destined to be a merman, I hadn't yet gone through the transformation that occurs at puberty, so effectively, when I died, I was still very much human. Merfolk who aren't born into it can be transformed through a resuscitation ritual when they are drowning. That's what happened to me. That's what happened to many of us here."

"I don't understand."

"Only those born of the original bloodline can use legs. That's you."

"It should be you too."

"Shit happens."

A laugh burst out of me. "You haven't changed."

"Those who are resuscitated don't have the ability to transform to legs. Nor do those not from the original blood-line. So I'm stuck here in the water," Dylan said. "All of us are."

An idea prickled at the back of my mind. "Original bloodline? Mom was...is she alive?"

"No." His pupils glimmered with pain. My heart sank. "She didn't make it. The merfolk could only save one of us."

I let out the disappointment on a shaky breath, my chest deflating as suddenly as a popped puffer fish.

"Besides, she was already a mermaid. The ritual wouldn't have worked on her."

My thoughts spun. Pictures of my mother cycled through my head, mostly of her sailing and the anxiety that would line her face. If she was a mermaid, why had she been so afraid of water? I pushed the disappointment away and faced my brother. "Why didn't I know you were alive?"

A sad smile twisted Dylan's lips. "How could you, Cordelia? You haven't been near the ocean since the accident. Until now. If you had, I would have found you long ago."

All that lost time because I couldn't face the ocean. Damn. Emotion shuddered through my torso and lodged a lump in my throat.

"It all came from Mom?"

"Yep."

"Does Dad know?"

"I don't know. I don't think so."

"I don't think he does either." Nope, no way. He would have said something. "Why has my tail only just appeared if it's supposed to happen during puberty?" I picked up a tealight and held it in my hand, letting the small flame warm my fingers.

"Your tail won't transition unless there is enough water, and so you never knew, until now."

Tears pricked my eyes. I'd been through five years of mourning because I wasn't brave enough to take a bath.

Dylan rested his hand on mine, and as if sensing my thoughts, said, "It's not your fault. You weren't to know. I don't blame you for not wanting to go back in the water. Hell, I hung out near the rocks for a whole year, terrified the shark was going to come back and finish me off."

I tensed at the image of the wide gaping jaws. "Where is it now?"

"It's around." He passed a hand over the flame. A water droplet fell from his finger and sizzled into the hot wax.

"Have you seen it again?"

Splashes of water sounded at the other side of the cave. The other merfolk. I'd forgotten about them. They swam together, ducking and diving under the surface, their tails shimmering in a kaleidoscope of ocean colors.

"Now and again." Raking his fingers through his hair, he raised his eyes to mine. "There's a lot more to this story, Cord." He paused to watch the other merfolk in a game of water polo. Nerida waved from the center of the game and then dived under the water and booted the ball with her tail. "Sharks aren't allowed to attack merfolk."

"They're not *allowed*?" I stifled a laugh. "I hate to break it to you, Dylan, but I don't think anyone has told the sharks that. They *are* attacking people. There was one in San Francisco not long ago. A mother and son died. Then another in Santa Barbara." I jabbed at his shoulder.

"I heard," he said. "The sharks sometimes attack *people*." He brushed a hand over mine, squeezing my fingers. "But they don't attack *merfolk*. It goes against the truce, however tenuous it may be."

"You have a truce with sharks?" I bent forward until our noses were almost touching, peering into the hazel eyes I'd desperately missed.

"With the selachii, yes. They control the sharks. And they can turn into sharks."

"The second water species." Pieces of the jigsaw fell into place. Maya's book. It was all real.

"Yes. How did you know?"

"Maya, she has a book about merfolk, and it mentions a second humanoid water species."

"Of course she does." He smiled, a faraway look in his eyes.

"The selachii?" I reminded my brother.

"This is complicated, Cordy. Put your listening ears on."

This time I punched his shoulder. He pushed back, and I toppled into the pillows. Smiling, I flicked his nose. He threated to splash me, and I ducked out the way.

"You ready?"

I nodded.

"Much like you and I are from the original line of merfolk—thank you, Mom—there is an original line of selachii who can also go on land. But the bulk of them are confined to the water, like us. The problem is the leader of the selachii likes to *rescue people* when they're in trouble."

"Why the air quotes?"

Dylan snorted. "There's been less rescuing of late and more enforced transformation."

"San Francisco," I muttered. "Santa Barbara."

"Correct. Bang on. You are now entitled to the supersonic washing machine, the one thousand dollars cash, or the stingray swimming experience. What will you choose?"

"Ha, ha."

The glimmer of humor faded from Dylan's eyes. "I believe the selachii's original bloodline lives here in San Diego."

"Who?"

He shook his head. "I don't know. Yet."

"So San Fran, real shark or selachii?"

"Hard to say. The selachii control the real sharks. They swim with them and use them to do their bidding. But they can also turn completely into a shark, and they often do. We," he gestured to his body, "can only ever be half human and half fish. But we get the dolphins as our friends."

"But Mom was a mermaid and a shark attacked her."

Dylan propped his chin on two fists and stared at the small flickering flame of the candle. "The great white that attacked our boat was after Mom. Broke the truce to get to her because he thought she possessed a relic from another time. Merfolk wanted to fight back, but...well...we have spears and they have teeth. So that never happened. But he's confined to the water as he's not from the original bloodline."

"He's still a great white shark."

"Indeed."

One of the dolphins brought some relief to the atmosphere as he performed a succession of somersaults in the air above our heads and then stole the ball from the water polo game.

"That's Flipper."

"Flipper? Seriously? How original."

He raised his hands in mock surrender. "I didn't name him. And he does like to flip."

"Hey!" Nerida charged through the water after him.

"Merfolk and selachii used to be friends. But they fell out centuries ago. The truce came about a few decades ago when both our numbers started dwindling. So we stay away from each other. No more fighting." Dylan raised his eyebrows.

"Apart from Mom."

"Apart from Mom," he echoed. "But tensions are coming to a head."

"Because of Mom?" I dipped my legs into water. They immediately turned red, then into my tail.

"Partly, but also because—"

"It's time." Nerida popped above the surface next to Dylan. "Cordelia, I was hoping we would have more time to introduce you to everyone." She nodded toward the merfolk chasing Flipper, trying to regain their ball. "But we need to get you back to land before night. The ashrays..." She looked at Dylan.

"I'll have to explain the rest another time," he said. "But before you go. I have a favor to ask. From all of us." Stress, poorly masked, strained his voice and tightened the skin around his eyes. Whatever it was, it was serious. Dylan was never serious. "We need you to keep something safe for us, out of the water, at home. Away from the selachii."

I looked from Dylan to Nerida. Twice. Their solemn expressions didn't change.

"Okay..."

Dylan placed an object in my hand. About the size of a large egg, it possessed layers of such milky beauty I was mesmerized and couldn't pull my gaze away from it. A pearl. An enormous pearl.

"It tends to have that effect on people."

I rolled it in my hand, and whispered, "It's beautiful."

"It is," Dylan said. "The merfolk are the rightful keepers of the pearl. It was stolen by the selachii and in their possession for many years, but we've recently managed to take it back."

I raised my eyebrows. "Hence the high tensions."

"Yep. But I don't think it's safe for us to merely have it in our possession. We need to keep it out of the water, away from the majority of selachii. Then I think it will be safe."

"What is it?" I raised the pearl to my nose. No smell, and it was cool to touch.

"It's the purpose of the merfolk to be the guardians of the pearl—"

"Dylan, Cordy, we're running out of time." Nerida patted the rock, urging us to hurry.

"Why me?" I asked.

"You're the only one left who can walk," she replied.

The pearl dropped from my hand, and I caught it with the other. "I'm the only one left from the original bloodline?" I searched my memory for family gatherings over the years. Mom didn't have any siblings and her parents had died when I was young.

Dylan nodded. "You're the last one. Unless you want to pop out a baby or two. Which may be required, to be honest—"

"Time to go." Nerida offered a hand and helped ease me back in the water.

"I'll escort you as far as I can," Dylan said, and then dived under the rippling current.

I held the pearl clutched in one hand and swam after my brother. He led the way back to land, back to Ocean Beach.

"I have to leave you here." We were a mile offshore.

"Dylan, wait." I reached for his arm. "You haven't told me what it does."

"There's no time. I'm sorry."

"What about Dad?" The thought shot to the surface. "We have to tell him you're alive."

"What good would it do? I can't leave the ocean."

And then he was gone. I circled twice, but I couldn't pick out his green tail in the surrounding water and tangles of seaweed. Other shapes approached. At first, they appeared to be the dolphins, coming to escort me for the remainder of the journey, but I didn't hear any of their clicks, whistles, or squeaks.

The pearl vibrated in my palm, its milky opaqueness deepening, swirling, drawing my eyes. A wealth of emotions flooded through me—a burgeoning protectiveness of this flawless jewel, an exquisite sadness, but also a mounting sense of hope. Realizing the looming shapes had drawn closer, I turned, flicked my tail, and swam toward the beach.

I daren't look over my shoulder for I was terrified I might see a shark, a selachii, angling toward me with wide jaws and gnashing teeth, having decided the fight over the possession of the pearl was worth breaking the tenuous truce for.

I emerged from the water beneath the pier. As I surfaced to knee-deep water, I willed my tail away and my legs into existence. A gull cried in the air, and the smell of fried fish wafted from the lone restaurant on the pier. An offshore wind gusted across my shoulders and tugged at my dripping hair.

I walked along the beach to the point where I'd left my clothes. Maya and Trent shared a towel, shoulders pressed together. Maya threw her head back and laughed at something Trent said. The sun set as I approached them, the last of its warmth caressing my cold limbs.

"Hey," Trent called. "Where have you been? You've been gone all day."

"We've been worried." Maya held her hand to brow to see me against the setting sun. "Cordy, you're freezing." I was shivering and goosebumps lined my skin. "Here." She handed me my towel, and I folded myself into it.

"Sit down," Trent said. "Tell us everything."

"My brother is alive." I gazed at the ocean. I had many questions. He was out there somewhere and I wanted to know every detail of his life. "My brother is alive."

Those four words were the most beautiful and most meaningful I had ever uttered. I said it three more times, the last time rising to my knees and shouting it into the sky. "He's a merman too, but he can't walk on land."

Trent followed my gaze out to sea. "He's out there?" His face leached of color, and his pulse sped up in his throat. "Really? He's out there? My best friend is alive?"

I squeezed his hand. "He's alive."

Maya's eyes brimmed with tears. "I can't believe it."

I smiled at them. "I talked to him, touched him, hugged him. He's alive. And even I can't quite believe it."

"You're sure it was him?" Trent asked.

"Yes," I replied.

"I don't know what to say."

"Me neither," I said.

Trent leaped to his feet and then dove into the sand. He rolled over and over again until he got hit by a wave and scrambled back to us.

I told them the whole story; Nerida finding me, seeing Dylan, about the original bloodline and the resuscitation ritual, and the selachii and how they attacked Dylan and my mother.

"When can we see him?" Trent asked.

We'd made no plans. "I don't know. I don't know how to find him."

Hopefully, I could wade into the water again, and he would be there. Or would I spend my days swimming up and down Ocean Beach, forever searching for my brother and the other merfolk? No, he'd given me the pearl, he'd entrusted its safety to me. He would find me again. I wouldn't have to wait another five years.

I couldn't believe I'd let him go, when he'd been right there, close enough to touch and hug and laugh with. But he hadn't given me a choice. He'd pointed me toward the shore and abruptly disappeared beneath the waves.

"He gave me this." I held up the pearl. The three of us huddled together, heads bent, creating a private circle.

Trent swallowed hard and reached for the pearl. I was a little reluctant to release it but after a brief hesitation I let him take it and hold it up to the light.

Maya gasped. "It's the pearl."

"That's the biggest damn pearl I've ever seen," Trent said, rubbing its smooth surface. His curls fell over his forehead and covered the unreadable expression in his eyes.

Bringing her nose close to the pearl, Maya inspected it through her thick glasses. "I read about it in the book."

"Good, you can tell me what it does. Dylan gave it to me and said it had to be kept out of the water and away from the selachii, but he didn't explain why, or what it does."

"In the book," she tapped the arm of her glasses—her thinking pose, "it says the merfolk are the keepers of the keys.

The pearl is one of these keys, and it's extremely powerful if you know how to use it."

I covered my cold toes with warm sand. The questions tumbled through my mind. It seemed there was a whole lot more to this merfolk world than merely swimming with a tail and my brother's miraculous resurrection. I wished I could ask my mother. Although I had mourned her absence over the last five years, her loss now felt more desperate as I was sure she held many of the answers. "What is it a key to?"

"I'm not sure." She swiped her glasses off her face and cleaned them with the edge of her towel. "There are many different types. But I think the white ones have something to do with gaining access to the High Council."

"The High Council?" Trent transferred the pearl from one hand to the other and back again, measuring its weight.

Oh, Mom. Where are you when I need you? I felt enormously out of my depth. A heavy sense of anticipation skittered across my shoulders.

"Yep. They started *The Mermaid Chronicles* to keep an account of events." She moved into studious mode. With her words speeding up, she was obviously pleased she'd remembered the details. "They rule over the water species, and they are the ones who decided the merfolk should protect the pearls."

With the sun almost gone, the anticipation I felt deepened into a chilly foreboding. "From what?"

Maya shrugged. "From being used for the wrong reasons? I'm not sure. It doesn't say."

I gestured for Trent to return the pearl. When he didn't, I

plucked it from his hand. I frowned at the jewel, willing it to reveal its secrets. "But how do you use it?"

"It doesn't say that either." She put her glasses back on and examined the pearl for herself.

"I'm going to keep it safe in my room, away from the selachii, until I get more information from my brother."

"Sounds like a plan." Trent stood and tied his sweatshirt around his waist. He tucked his board under an arm and turned back to us.

"Coming?" He paused for all of two seconds before marching along the beach toward his van. Maya and I followed him to the parking lot.

"Will you look at the book again?" I asked. "See if you can find any more information about this pearl?"

"Sure." Hefting her bag onto the opposite shoulder, she glanced at Trent. "What's with him?"

He hadn't waited for us to catch up with him and was now throwing his board into the back of his van. The board was caught along its length by a screw, creating an ugly three-foot scratch before it slammed into the front seats. Trent didn't seem to notice, or care, and closed the back doors with enough force to make the whole van shake and a hubcap to come loose. It rolled two feet into the road and spiraled lazily before coming to rest with a clanging flourish. Trent stepped over the hubcap and into the driver's seat. He gunned the engine and sped away. Maya retrieved the hubcap from the middle of the road and frowned at the disappearing VW van.

"I'm not sure," I said. "Maybe it's the news about Dylan. He was his best friend."

"There was something else in the book, Cordy." Maya

chewed on her bottom lip. "I know you don't believe in the prophecies, but there was one that worried me. It said," she closed her eyes to remember better, *"the journey to the sunken land will be filled with heartache and loss. The fire mermaid must be determined."* She snapped her eyes open. "Something like that."

"There's already been loss," I said, thinking of my brother and mother. "I've got Dylan back now. There's no way I'll lose him again."

CHAPTER THIRTEEN

 $\mathcal{E}$ very mile Wade drove inland increased the knots in
my stomach.

It was obvious we weren't going to a water park or swimming pool—a chlorinated body of water that would protect
my tail—and panic started to build as a stiffness in my throat
and an edgy restlessness in my limbs.

"Where are we going?" I asked for the third time.

Wade gave me a sidelong glance and a crooked grin as he
steered with one hand. The other was resting on my thigh.
"You don't do well with surprises, do you?"

"I like to know what to expect." I gazed out the window.
We'd been driving for an hour, through the city and out the
other side, and now we were ascending the foothills, the
foliage deep and green and the road narrowing to a single
lane.

"It won't be long now." He squeezed my thigh, sending
involuntary but welcoming shivers through me. Could I get
him to pull over to the side of the road so I could kiss him?

What were the laws on indecent exposure these days? Mind you, if we got arrested, then I wouldn't have to worry about my tail appearing in front of him.

Twenty minutes later he pulled off the road and into a car park where the bays were marked with felled trees and the loosely rectangular area was filled with gravel. A gentle breeze ruffled my newly shortened hair and tickled the back of my neck. The inland heat pressed in around us, and I took a swig of water from the bottle Wade had brought with us.

"You wore your swimsuit, right?"

"Yes..." As I followed Wade along a narrow trail, pushing away branches and swatting mosquitoes, my anxiety heightened. I'd only spent one night controlling my tail, and I suspected it would be a lot harder when I was with Wade and in such close proximity to his lips...his hands...his chest... his everything.

"I think we've driven sufficiently far enough away from home that your cousins won't bother us," I said. "Have you found your family's heirloom yet?"

"Not yet." He swiveled back to me, brushing my cheek with his lips as he spoke. "But they've quit giving me a hard time."

"I hope you find it," I said.

He stood in the middle of the trail, looking into the trees overhead as if the heirloom might magically fly from the ocean to the leaves above his head, and fall into his waiting palm. "Me too," he said, and took my hand.

The trail dropped away, and we descended a steep gradient into a cool gloominess where birds flapped high above our heads and large insects scuttled across our path. The air vibrated with humidity.

Wade smiled and kissed my cheek. "Here we are."

We arrived at a natural spring with a towering waterfall. The cascading water acted as a prism to the sunlight and cast rainbows in every direction. I waited for fairies and sprites to appear. Perhaps, I mused, considering recent events, I should give the fairytales of my childhood a second look.

"They're usually closed on Sundays, but my father knows the guy who runs the place, and I pulled a few strings and managed to wangle us some privacy."

The waterfall flowed into a deep, deliciously cool-looking pool. Surrounded by moss-covered rocks, the swirling water bubbled and rippled gently toward the edges. I frowned. Keeping my tail hidden was going to be a challenge. But how could I refuse to go into the water when he was determined to help me conquer my now, non-existent fears?

"It's too much, isn't it?" Sighing, he set his backpack on the ground. "I'm sorry, Cordelia, I thought with the progress you've been making in the water, this would be fun for you now. But I seem to have underestimated your fears."

"No, it's okay. It's not that," I replied, squeezing his hand. "I was surprised, that's all. You definitely get points for originality and romance." Unable to bear his crestfallen look, I decided I would just have to make sure the tail didn't appear. It would take concentration. A lot of it.

We walked to the water's edge, and he kneeled and dipped in a hand. "Perfect."

He yanked his T-shirt over his head, revealing his broad

shoulders. His triceps rippled with toned muscles, and the delicious hollow of his back begged for my lips.

Stop drooling, Cordelia! I actually had to wipe a hand across my mouth.

After kicking off his shoes, he dove into the water. He swam a lazy front crawl to the middle of the pool and then turned to face me. "Aren't you coming?"

I couldn't stop staring at him. He was even better when he was wet. His two-day stubble appeared darker, more pronounced, and his skin glistened with beads of water, catching the attention of the filtered sunlight, like he'd stepped out of an aftershave commercial.

"Coming," I called, removing my clothes. I inched toward the water's edge and curled my toes around the rocky lip. My toenails glittered in reds and pinks, excited by the proximity of the water.

Concentrate. I squeezed my eyes shut.

"Come on!" Wade laughed, splashing me.

I tensed. My legs, now soaking wet, trembled. I opened one eye. My legs remained. My toenails returned to their normal fleshy pink. Sitting on the shaded rock, I slipped my legs into the water. The urge to transform hit me as forcefully as a wave crashes onto shore.

"Just a minute." I held up a finger as he swam toward me.

He couldn't be here if it went wrong. I needed a moment to gather myself and then I'd be okay. He stopped, treaded water, and waited for me. The desperate urge to convert to my water half subsided and I pushed away from the rock into the water. It was cool and welcoming and soft, like I'd been wrapped in the finest of velvet.

He held me in his arms. "Is it okay for you?"

"It's beautiful. It's perfect." I leaned into him for a kiss, deep and hard and indecent.

We raced against each other from one side of the pool to the other, and we followed each other under the water to see who could hold their breath the longest. It ended in a tie. And when we were tired of that Wade led me behind the waterfall, into the echoing privacy between water and rock, and kissed me deeply, until I was in danger of melting into the water forever.

Dragonflies skimmed the surface and bees droned in the flowered foliage lining the secret pool. The branches of two intertwining willow trees drooped over the water, losing their leaves to the surface. The sun shone down on us, filtered by the surrounding trees, turning the water an aqua blue.

"That tickles." He laughed around the edge of a kiss and kicked his feet. "Stop it." He flinched, pulling his lips from mine.

I looked at our legs. His legs. My tail. My tail had emerged, and its fronds gently undulated over Wade's toes—the source of the tickling.

"I..."

Don't look down. Please don't let him look down. Too late.

Wade released me from his arms and gasped.

"I..." But were there any words that could explain?

"You're a mermaid. An original."

"I..." Words eluded me. Maybe I could dive into the depths and find a rock to hide behind.

"...I had no idea. I've never seen a red tail...but I've heard about it..."

"Wade, I can explain..."

Wait...*what*? He'd never seen a red tail? Had he seen mermaids before? I blew bubbles in the water as I spluttered for words.

Looking up, he took in my stricken face. "You've been keeping secrets."

"I—" Shit. He was furious. "I didn't mean to...I only recently found out...and it's just such a weird—"

"I get it." He laughed. Not furious then. "Maya and you aren't the only ones who know about merfolk. I just didn't realize you were one. But I guess it kind of makes sense, considering you can keep up with me in the water—

"Keep up with *you*? I *thrashed* you..." And then I realized there was another point in there somewhere. "Wade? What aren't you telling me?"

His gaze skimmed my face as he treaded water. "I guess I have a secret of my own."

I waited while the smile slipped from his face and he raked a hand over his wet hair. "Are you going to tell me what it is? Are you going to tell me how you know about merfolk?" The first inklings of alarm crawled up my spine.

"All the selachii know about merfolk."

"You know about selachii too?"

"Yes, Cordelia." He paused, took a breath. "I am one."

My tail flipped unconsciously, and I found myself on the other side of the pool. I grabbed at the sharp, jutting rocks, trying to heave myself up and out of the water. But my tail wouldn't accommodate my wish. My legs refused to materialize, and I hung onto the rock. It scratched and gouged my arms and chest as I attempted to scramble onto the bank.

Wade is a selachii. I shook my head. *Please don't let it be true.*

I lurched toward a different rock. With the surface covered in slippery moss, I couldn't find purchase.

I felt him behind me before he spoke. His shadow loomed over the rock. "Cordelia, what's the matter?"

Resigning myself to a confrontation, I stopped fighting to get out of the pool. "My brother warned me about you."

"About me?" His eyes flew wide, and he pointed at his chest.

"Not you, specifically." I turned to face him. "Selachii."

Treading water, his gaze swept over my tail. A concerned shadow passed through his eyes, and my heart squeezed with longing. What did he look like as a shark? A terrifying image filled my mind.

I clung to the rocks. I willed my legs to appear, but I couldn't seem to shed the tail.

"Your brother is alive?"

"Yes, he's a merman. I found him yesterday." I backed into a crevice. He was only three feet away and drifting closer.

Wade is a selachii.

His flashing black eyes now made sense. It hadn't been my imagination; it had been his shark side appearing.

"I wondered..." he muttered.

I dared to slip away from the shadow of the rock. "You knew?"

"I...no...I wondered if he had been rescued...I heard a

rumor." He drifted a little closer, and I shrank further into the shadows.

My grip tightened on the rock. "Why didn't you tell me?"

"I haven't seen him, Cordelia, and I didn't know, not for sure." He was within touching distance now. "Would you have believed me anyway?"

I examined his face for a hint of a lie. "Probably not."

"Cordelia." He extended his hand toward me. I flinched, but I was out of retreating space. His eyes widened, and he let his hand drift back to his side. "I would never hurt you, Cordelia."

"But the merfolk and selachii—they have some battle going on." I leveled a cold stare at him.

"I'd hardly call it a battle. We don't always see eye-to-eye, but that doesn't mean we hurt each other." His frown grew deeper and his tone insistent.

"One of you attacked my brother! That's why he died!" I shouted, my voice rebounding off the rocks, bouncing off the trees and causing the birds to take flight.

"Easy." He held out his hands as though I was the dangerous one. "Take it easy. I don't know anything about that. Could your brother have it wrong?"

"I was there!" The violent image of his death filled my head. The eyes were the worst. Those dead, emotionless eyes haunted all my dreams.

"Okay, okay," he said. "Maybe you're right. I wasn't there, I don't know what happened. Maybe there is a rogue selachii. Like a psychopathic human. We don't all know each other, and we certainly don't control each other's actions." He offered me his open palms, an honest gesture.

I emerged from the flimsy protection of the rocks and crossed my arms. "Have you attacked anyone?" I demanded.

Wade gasped, and his voice pitched up half an octave when he said, "Of course not! I would never hurt anyone. What on earth has Dylan been telling you? We *save* people, like the merfolk. We rescue those who are drowning and turn them into selachii."

I smacked the water with my palm. "That's not what I've heard."

"I don't know what you've heard, Cordelia, but I've never and would never attack anyone in my shark form. Never. Ever." His anxious eyes never left mine, and his voice thickened with the weight of his convictions. "Ever."

"Show me," I said. "Show me your selachii side."

"Are you sure? You look terrified enough as it is."

I nodded.

"I'm not sure this is a good idea—"

"Do it."

"Cordelia—" A panicked wince crossed his face.

"Now, Wade."

"Okay. Okay."

I stuck my head under the water and watched his legs disappear. The smooth gray skin of a shark transformed his lower half, followed by a vertical tale.

I raised my head above the surface. "What kind of shark are you?"

"A blue."

"That's a rather aggressive species." I narrowed my eyes.

He shrugged. "I can't choose what kind of shark I am. It just is."

Something in the shark tooth hanging at his throat caught the light and emphasized what he really was. It dangled there, blunted with age, and I wondered if it was one of his own. "But you're right, many of the selachii are an aggressive species because we've had to be. Traditionally our role was one of protection and security."

"Ha!"

Wade passed a hand over his brow and rubbed his temple. "I'm serious."

"I don't consider killing my mother and brother part of a 'protection and security' job description."

Wade splashed the water with a jerky tail fin. "I don't know who that was."

Emotions churned inside me. I wanted to believe him. He meant everything to me. But could I trust him?

He hadn't told me about his selachii side. But then, I hadn't told him about being a mermaid. I hadn't kept the information from him because I didn't trust him, but because I didn't know how it would be received. A sane person should run from this, and I hadn't wanted to lose him. Not when he had given me the confidence to face my fears. Not when I felt so loved. So maybe that's why he hadn't revealed his secret to me. Maybe, eventually, we would have trusted each other with the truth if we'd been given the time to reveal it naturally.

A headache pulsed in my temples. "But they were killed by a selachii."

"It would seem so." Wade's blue eyes filled. "I promise you, I don't know who or how or why."

I dipped my head for a moment as I pushed the loss away.

This was Wade. He would never hurt my family. Or me. But he was a selachii. "Do you ever turn completely into a shark?"

"Not often. I like to keep in touch with my human side, and when I go full shark it's too easy to swim away and leave it all behind." He swept a hand over the water to encompass the beautifully exquisite scene around us—the air thick with heat, the vegetation heavy with teeming life, and the cascading waterfall right out of a fantasy.

I peered beneath the water once more only to see Wade had regained his legs. Looking at him now, it was hard to believe he could turn into a deadly killing machine. How could an animal that wrought so much devastation be the same as the person here in front of me? A person I'd known most of my life? The same person who was tender and gentle and safe and strong?

The sound of the waterfall rushed to the forefront, almost intrusively, until I heard little else. Wade had answered my questions, honestly, and I was sure he was telling the truth. With his deep frown and bunched up mouth, he couldn't be more desperate if he was a homeless puppy. Wade. Wade Waters. *My* Wade. He hadn't changed. Of course he hadn't.

The tension drained out of my tail. Why had I been afraid of him? Of course he would never attack me. Or anyone else. He was Wade. *Wade.* He may be a selachii, but he was also Wade, and I was sure my first instincts about him were right.

I tried on a smile. "You would leave all this?"

He smiled in return, perhaps sensing his words had finally made an impression.

"You've met merfolk before?" I asked.

"A few. Cordelia?" His voice was low, resonating with an intensity that made my heart race. Reaching for me, he wrapped his hand around my wrist, pulling me into his powerful arms and holding me against the unyielding wall of his chest. I couldn't deny how he made me feel. I couldn't resist him. With his chest pressed against mine, his arms holding me possessively, I felt the undeniable pull of desire, the electricity between us crackling like lightning beneath the waves. I surrendered to his touch. He let out a long sigh. "This isn't quite what I had planned for today."

"What did you have planned for today?" I whispered as my pulse quickened.

His brightening eyes locked on mine. "To tell you I'm falling in love with you."

CHAPTER FOURTEEN

*D*id he just...?

Was it possible...?

I'm falling in love with you.

Words I would treasure forever. My world turned upside down, inside out, back to front, and everything in between. My breath caught and I wished I could hold on to the moment, make it tangible somehow.

Wade smiled and kissed the corner of my mouth. "While it's true that merfolk and selachii don't fraternize, that they don't particularly like each other, there is nothing that could keep me away from you." He swept wet hair behind my ear. "But what I said isn't quite right."

"Oh?"

"I'm not *falling* in love with you. I *already* love you. All the way. I think I always have."

"Oh..."

While my brain turned to mush and my heart rate soared, an image of fireworks erupted in my mind. They took off into the sky, glorious, glowing red ones that made a pattern of a heart.

I was about to open my mouth and make some awkward half reply in an attempt to communicate mutual feelings that in no way would measure up to the way Wade had expressed himself, when he put a finger to my lips and carried on. "This doesn't have to be some Romeo and Juliet type situation where it's us against the world. I don't care if you're a mermaid, I don't care that I'm a selachii, and everyone else can go fuck themselves."

I laughed. "I think you'll find that's exactly what happened with Romeo and Juliet." But that was just a story of an incredibly naive couple in a land of long ago. "What about your cousins? Are they selachii too?"

"Yes."

"Jordon's teeth grew back..." I realized aloud. I could imagine them in their shark form. I'd bet the lot of them were hammerheads. Although not a particularly aggressive species, combine that with their human side and single-minded focus to harass Wade, and they'd be a force to be reckoned with. And why were they harassing him?

The pearl.

Wade had lost the pearl.

My pearl. Oh *shit*...

"That truly is a magnificent tail." Diving deep, he caught the fronds in his hands. His fingers swept gently over my scales. He ran his hands along its length, his touch a teasing caress, a gesture far more intimate than if he'd been running his hands along my legs. He followed with his lips, kissing the scales, covering them in the burning fire of his touch. All thoughts of the pearl emptied from my mind as heat curled in my stomach, spread outward, swept lower until I found myself clinging to his shoulders, my grasp tight with need.

"Oh, Wade," I sighed when he broke the surface of the water.

He edged closer, wrapping one arm around my waist and used the other to anchor us against a rock. He lowered his lips to mine, devoured my mouth with a new ferocity, his tongue sweeping hungrily between my lips.

"I love you," he whispered against the shell of my ear.

I wanted to say it back, but my tongue was tied in knots and all reason had left my mind. The only thing I could feel were the delicious sensations sparking on my body in every place Wade made contact. And then an image of the pearl slammed back into my mind. Along with a heavy vat of guilt.

Wade pulled away, searched my face. "I'm sensing you're not all right yet. Shall we get out and talk?"

"That's a good idea." Finally able to will my tail away, I scrambled out of the water after him.

Wade opened his backpack and removed a picnic box. As I dressed, he laid the food on a towel—grapes and strawberries, French bread, and expensive cheese. He placed a paper plate and a cup in front of me. I fiddled with them in my lap.

"I'm worried, Wade." I glanced at the now calm pool of water, felt his eyes drifting over my face. "I hear one story from my brother and a different one from you. How do I know what or who to believe?"

And what about the pearl? I had it. Wade wanted it. Didn't it belong to the merfolk?

"You should believe me."

I smiled at the earnestness in his tone, as well as his eyes. "Convince me."

"I've never told someone I love them before." He rested back on his hands. "They are not words I say lightly. And they come with a set of...expectations...I would never lie to the person I love."

I nodded, accepting his words. "I believe you. But I also suspect you don't know everything that occurs within the selachii community...like who is responsible for my mother's death."

"You're right, I don't." Wade's hand drifted to his bare chest to cover his heart. "I can only tell you my truth."

"And Dylan tells me his."

"You haven't seen your brother for five years," he said, placing a tentative hand on my knee. "You have no idea who he is now or what his motivations might be. Just because merfolk look pretty and harmless doesn't mean they are." A black streak travelled across his eyes.

I remembered his comment on the beach, that merfolk weren't cute and cuddly and used to lure sailors to their deaths. "Has something happened?"

"No. I'm just saying."

Did he know my brother was responsible for taking the pearl back?

"Tell me about the selachii," I said, moving to sit next to him so that our knees and shoulders brushed. I needed the contact, the reassurance, and I wanted Wade to feel my love for him. "Tell me how it came to be. If you can be on land, then you must be of the original bloodline."

Wade nodded. "That's right. Just like you."

"But I'm the only mermaid left who can walk. There are loads of you."

He laughed. "Big family."

"You mentioned something about protection and security?"

He drew circles on my knee with his thumb. "Eons ago, the selachii were tasked with being the gatekeepers of Atlantis."

"Really?" I straightened up. "Atlantis?"

Atlantis. Maya's book. Holy shit.

"Really," he said. "The merfolk and other ocean shifters lived on the island happily going from land to sea. But there was a problem. There was another species, the dragon kings, who wanted the island for themselves. Originally there were only four of these dragon kings, or so legend has it, but they reproduced and outgrew their own land. Atlantis was rich in shrimp and crabs and other sea life to feast upon. Now, merfolk are pretty and they have beautiful singing voices—"

"I can't sing."

Wade laughed. "The ability died out, evolved over time. Or devolved. Anyway, merfolk can be pretty hardcore with their spears, but they're not effective against a dragon king twice the size who can breathe fire in both its dragon and human forms."

"Eesh."

He topped up my cup with Pepsi and piled my plate high with bread and fruit.

"As the selachii were a more aggressive species of ocean shifter, they were tasked with guarding Atlantis from invasion. Able to turn into a shark and chase the dragon kings away, we kept Atlantis safe for hundreds of years. But the merfolk grew complacent and the selachii lazy. After many years of peace, another attack was launched. The dragon kings managed to steal Atlantis."

"How do you steal an entire island? Where did they take it?" I bit into a strawberry. Juice ran down my chin, and I wiped it away with my finger.

Crossing his arms over his knees, Wade let his hunk of bread dangle from his fingers. "They managed to come by a key that took Atlantis to another dimension."

"Can't you take it back?"

"No, no one knows how to get to the other dimension."

I rolled onto my stomach and fingered some of the dampness out of my hair. "And they were able to walk off with a whole island? It's like something out of the Bermuda Triangle."

"Exactly. It's based on the same principles."

I snorted out a laugh. "What principles? The Bermuda Triangle stories are unexplained."

"It's about the power of the keys." He tapped the side of his nose conspiratorially. "And before you ask, no one knows exactly how they work."

"Then what happened?"

"The High Council happened." Wade rolled his eyes. The High Council? They were mentioned in Maya's book too. "Up until then, the High Council hadn't needed to interfere in the affairs of the ocean shifters for some time. But the day we lost Atlantis, the council stormed into the ocean and cursed us."

"Cursed you?" I asked, thinking of Maya's prophecy; how

did it go? *The one who walks the land can break the curse, united.* That was it.

"Yes. The merfolk, in my opinion, fared better." He poked me. I giggled and swatted him away. "They were cursed to be unable to walk on land and would have to live in the ocean forever."

"But I can walk," I said, pointing at my toes and flexing them.

"A loophole. The council declared merfolk from the original line could continue to walk. You. Your family. Your mother. Your brother if he had gone through his natural transformation. They did this to give the merfolk a chance to right their past indiscretions."

I rested my chin on my palm. "Which means it's up to me to break the stupid curse."

He gave me an appraising look, examining me from head to toe. "I always thought it was about my family. We're from the original selachii line, and I thought it was us who were destined to break the curse. That was back when I believed the curse was breakable."

"You don't think it's real?"

He shrugged. "The stories are as old as Atlantis itself. Who knows? But that won't stop us trying."

"Enough about curse breaking," I said, as an uneasy shiver raced along my spine. "What happened to the selachii?"

"Ah," Wade said. With haunted eyes he glanced at the water. "It was far worse for the selachii. As we were the gatekeepers, the protectors of Atlantis, our punishment was, is, far worse. We, too, were cursed to live a life in the ocean, but it didn't stop there. In the water we are persecuted by another species, the ashrays."

The name hadn't appeared in Maya's book. "The ashrays?"

"Yep. The ashrays. They're small, but deadly. They're transparent and hard to see in the water, effectively ghosts. Think of them as spectral stingrays. And they move fast." Wincing, the strawberry in his hand turned to a pulpy mess. "They attack us during the night, every night. During the day they can't be in direct sunlight so the selachii stay close to the surface, but during the night..." He shuddered. "Let's just say I'm glad I can escape the water."

"And how are you supposed to escape these horrible creatures?" My touch drifted to his feet, and I pulled at the tiny hairs on top of his toes.

He sighed. "By finding Atlantis."

"Any luck?"

Wade shook his head and wiped his hands on a napkin. "Not for hundreds of years."

"And what do the ashrays do to you?" I kissed his toe.

"Contact with them is the most horrendous experience. It causes an infection on our flesh which grows at night. In the warmth of the sun, the infection subsides but at night, it grows again." He pointed to the wound on the small of his back. "That's the result of contact with an ashray."

"Oh, Wade." My chest tightened, and a surge of anger prickled my scalp. Who the hell did this High Council think they were? "Why? Why did the council feel that was necessary?"

"So we'd never forget what we did and we'd never forget

our responsibilities again." The hard edge in his voice didn't escape my attention.

"Does it hurt?" I asked, peering at the wound. The jagged, raised wound was approximately six inches in length and looked as though it had been inflicted with thousands of sharp teeth.

"On a good day I can forget about it, especially in the sun. On a bad day." His grimace pulled my chest tighter, and pain glinted in his pupils. "I'm glad I haven't had too many of those."

I ran my fingers along the wound, around lumps of scar tissue. "Is there a cure?"

He blew out a 'no' on an elongated sigh. "Each infection lasts for a year before it finally fades away. But we're eternally chased by the ashrays, and new wounds are inflicted."

"How long have you had yours?" I wanted to warm a bowl of saltwater, dip a cloth into it and bathe his wound. For a year. Until he was no longer in pain.

"It's new," he said. "And my first."

"Who is this draconian High Council? Where are they?" I resisted the urge to launch to my feet and demand an audience with these ancient torturers. How dare they inflict such pain on the one I love.

The one I love.

I did love him, despite his selachii side and despite the fact that our relationship had now become extremely complicated.

"There lies the rub." He pulled at his chin. "You know that family heirloom?"

I nodded.

"That's the key to finding the council. The heirloom is a large pearl."

The pearl. *My* pearl.

He hadn't dropped it in the ocean; it had been stolen by the merfolk. And it didn't glow at night, I knew that much, but that had been his explanation for diving into a black ocean. In his selachii form he could see perfectly well without light, but back on our date in La Jolla, he hadn't been able to tell me that.

My thoughts spun. Short, shallow breaths wouldn't move past my chest. I clutched at the rocky surface to feel something solid. Was this relationship going to be *too* complicated? Romeo and Juliet might have had it easier. They'd only had to deal with opposing families. Wade and I had opposing species and a secret jewel we had to keep hidden from each other. And let's not forget hiding our true essence from the rest of the human population. A walk in the park then.

Wade reached for me. He held my hand and kissed my cheek. Tucking his fingers into my hair, he wound it around his fingers and gave it a gentle tug. "We thought the pearl had been lost forever, but then my great grandfather came by it and it has been in my family ever since. Zale—that's our leader—he wants the key to approach the council and plead for mercy. It's been a long time since Atlantis was lost, and we've been persecuted by the ashrays for many lifetimes. I've seen some selachii give up and die with the agony of multiple wounds. We think it's past time to be free of it."

I wanted to give him the pearl right then and there. I wanted to tell him I had it and if we went to Dylan we could figure it out together. I wanted to. But I couldn't. I couldn't hand it over after being warned not to. Even if I did love him, even though I believed every word he said. I couldn't. I couldn't betray my brother or my people. I'd talk to Dylan first, then I'd figure out a way to help Wade.

I set my jaw, trying to suppress the guilt. "How does it work?"

"That's the other problem." Wade lay on the rock and propped his head in his hand. "We're not sure. Since the time my great grandfather found it, no one has been able to figure out how to use it."

"Where is it now?" I kept my eyes on the pool so he wouldn't detect my betrayal.

"Stolen, I think. Either by the ashrays or the merfolk. I'm not sure." He sat up again. "It's a powerful tool, and everyone wants it. I don't suppose you've heard anything?"

My heart knocked painfully against my ribs. I counted to ten in my head. I didn't say no. I didn't shake my head. It wasn't a lie. "The merfolk haven't told me much." It wasn't a lie. Not really. I had to tread carefully here.

It wasn't a lie.

Although they'd given me the pearl, they hadn't told me any of the story Wade had willingly parted with. They'd told me nothing of its origin or power, only thrust it into my keeping with no explanations. They'd put me right in the middle of the battle.

"If you hear anything, would you let me know?" The note of desperation in his voice tugged at my heart. "My family needs to be free of the ashrays; we need the opportunity to prove ourselves. We can't do that without the pearl."

I could only nod in reply because tears welled in my eyes.

Although utterly convinced of his sincerity, I was wary the impact our relationship would have on our different societies. The merfolk and selachii hated each other. How would they respond when they found out about us? Wade may have thought the reference to Romeo and Juliet was funny, a story far removed from our lives, but as I examined the situation, I realized our tale had the potential to be very similar. And perhaps Romeo and Juliet weren't so naive, perhaps they'd just been fiercely in love.

"Come here," he said, drawing me into his arms. I breathed in his appealing ocean, seaweed smell—I understood where that came from now—and pretended I'd made the right decision, even though every fiber of my being urged me to scream into his ear that I had the pearl, and if he came with me now, I could take him into my bedroom and give it to him.

His lips brushed against my ear. "Did you hear me when I told you I love you, Cordelia Blue? I do, I love you."

"I love you too," I whispered, finding my voice again.

"Even if you are a mermaid."

His comment elicited another laugh, one that burbled from my stomach. Then Wade rolled on top of me, and I closed my eyes, anticipating his touch.

His lips met mine, and I melted into the kiss, every fiber of my being craving more. I wanted to drown in the moment, to forget about the dangers lurking in the depths, to forget about the ancient feud between our kind, to forget everything except Wade and me.

When he finally pulled away, I reluctantly opened my eyes, feeling the ache of longing already settling in.

"But what's in a name?" he murmured, his breath warm against my skin." That which we call a rose by any other name would smell as sweet."

I laughed. "A man who knows his Shakespeare. I think I might hold on to you."

"Then all will be right in my world."

If only.

The pearl stared at me as we walked into my room.

Okay, it wasn't really capable of staring at me, but I felt its presence hidden in my bright pink ski sock in my bottom drawer. Wade stood only two feet from it. If he slid the drawer open and rifled through it, he'd find it.

"You're quiet. You didn't say a word the whole way back," Wade said.

"It's a lot to take in."

"It is." He leaned on my chest of drawers and fiddled with my jewelry box. "But I'm relieved to share this side of myself with you. I've never been able to be free with girlfriends before."

I arched an eyebrow. "Girlfriends?"

"Or friends. Anyone. You know what I mean."

"I do."

"Maybe we should stop talking about it," he murmured, setting aside the necklace he'd been tinkering with. He crossed the room in just two strides, his eyes intense as they met mine, and then he kissed me.

The moment our lips collided, it was as if the world ceased to exist, and all that remained was the searing passion between us. With our arms wrapped around each other, we crashed backward onto the bed, the soft fabric welcoming us.

His hands explored beneath my T-shirt, beneath the material of my bikini. Each brush of his fingertips set my skin ablaze. I couldn't stifle the groan that escaped my lips. I tore his T-shirt off and let my hands roam the sculpted contours of his body, clutching him against me.

Lost in him, I forgot everything else—my worries, my fears, the pearl—until all that existed was the feel of his skin against mine, the heat of his breath mingling with mine.

I breathed in his scent, a heady mix of ocean spray and seaweed, and I was intoxicated. His lips trailed a path of fire from my ear to my neck, before returning to claim my mouth once more. He nibbled at my lower lip, igniting a primal hunger within me.

I didn't know where I was anymore. All I could feel was him. His hips fit perfectly against mine, our bodies molding together as if they were made for each other. His hands tangled in my hair, his breath hot against my skin, and I found myself wrapping my legs around his waist, pulling him closer until the hard length of his arousal pressed against me, leaving me gasping for air.

Despite the warnings about the selachii, I couldn't believe they were all bad, not when Wade lay before me, his touch setting my soul ablaze.

Wade untied my bikini top, his mouth descending to

claim a breast, teasing and coaxing with his tongue. Another desperate moan tore from my lips as I arched against him, craving more of his touch.

"Wade, I want you. I want you inside me."

That's when I heard it. A faint, low thrumming sound, like the horn of a distant tugboat. And then it stopped.

Wade lifted his lips from mine, shook his head and then recommenced his slow devouring of my body. Had he heard it too?

His hands and mouth continued to roam my body and I brushed his back, avoiding the tender area of his wound. But I could sense a shift in him; he was distracted, he was pulling back.

The thrumming noise sounded again. Longer this time.

"I can hear it." He sprung to his feet and shook his head again. "I'm sure I heard it." Turning in a slow circle, he examined my room. Then stepped toward my window and looked at the ocean view. "I know we're only a few blocks from the ocean, but I didn't think I'd be able to hear it this far away. We must be close." He threw the curtains wide and stuck his head out the window.

"Close to what?" I asked, lifting the sheet to cover my modesty. I braced myself for his reply.

"The pearl. It makes a noise sometimes. A vibration. It must be nearby."

The pearl thrummed again. I counted five long seconds. Wade turned his gaze into the room, to me.

He stared at me. Long and hard. "You have the pearl." He paled and his eyes flashed black.

"I..." What words could possibly explain that I did

indeed have the pearl and had kept the knowledge from him, in spite of his family's suffering and in spite of his heart-felt pleas for redemption. I sat up, wrapping the sheet around me.

"You have the pearl." Why did that sound like an accusation? Taut tendons stood out on his neck.

Wade sank into an armchair in the corner of my room. "You have the pearl. All this time..." He steepled his fingers under his chin and narrowed his eyes at me.

"It's not like that," I said, moving to the edge of the bed. "Dylan gave it to me, and I want to give it to you, but I can't until I talk to him."

"You have the pearl." He said it slowly, as though digesting the information for the first time. "Everything I told you at the waterfall...you didn't think to mention you had possession of the exact object I've been seeking, that can save my family from a life of hell? You lied to me, Cordelia Blue."

I winced as each jagged word took a chunk out of my heart.

"I didn't lie." But a lie by omission amounted to the same thing, didn't it? "You tell me one thing and Dylan tells me another. I don't want to make an impulsive decision. I need time to think it through. Besides, Dylan says the merfolk are the rightful keepers of the pearl. *The Mermaid Chronicles* says it too."

"*The Mermaid Chronicles?*"

"Maya's book of merfolk history and stuff," I replied. I was tempted to nudge it out from under my bed and show it to him, but something held me back. "It says the merfolk are the rightful keepers of the keys, not the selachii."

As soon as the words flew out of my mouth, a quiver of

doubt surfaced. Had it really said that? I'd had to rely on Maya's interpretation. The pages had been damaged. She hadn't been able to decipher it all, and she herself had admitted the writing was old-fashioned and the vocabulary out of date.

"I don't know anything about any book." His eyes flashed again. "The merfolk protected the pearl when they lived on Atlantis. But not *from* us. From the dragon kings and other enemies. The merfolk protected the pearl, and we protected the merfolk. But there is no Atlantis anymore. What does it matter who holds the pearl?"

"I don't know, Wade—"

"All I know is the selachii had possession of the pearl for generations, and now suddenly we don't." Wade stood and paced the room. He paused to look out the window again. "I know the merfolk seek the pearl too, and the ashrays, and a myriad of other ocean shifters we haven't heard from in centuries. But I also know no one needs it like the selachii. We had it in our possession, and we were getting closer to finding out how to use it, but now it's gone." His lower lip trembled, and then he bit down on it. He swiveled to face me. "Do you have any idea what my family is going through with the ashrays?" He slumped back into the armchair with a hard stare in my direction.

"I do," I said. "That's why I wanted to give it to you."

"You may have wanted to hand it over, Cordelia, but the fact remains you haven't. That speaks volumes."

Tears stung my eyes. "I need to speak to my brother first."

"I told you I loved you. Did that mean nothing to you?" He gripped the armrests and looked at me as though I'd now become some dirty, sticky piece of gum stuck to the bottom of his shoe.

"Of course not," I said, crawling off the bed, the sheet trailing behind me. I wanted to reach out to him, touch him, kiss him, make him believe me.

The pearl thrummed again, and we both stared at my chest of drawers.

"Can I see it?" Desperation replaced the anger in his voice. To deny him was like every ounce of goodness being strangled from my soul.

I hesitated at the edge of my bed, not daring to move toward him, staring at his crestfallen face, his sunken shoulders, the essence of defeat rolling off him and puddling at his feet.

"No." It was barely a whisper. "No." Louder this time but cracked through with emotion at my capacity to inflict such cruelty. I couldn't let him see. Because then I would be tempted to give it to him, and no matter what had recently transpired between us, I needed to talk to my brother first.

"I see." He unfolded himself from the armchair. "How long have you had it?"

"Only since yesterday." I stood limply before him. "Wade." I followed him as he snatched his T-shirt from the floor and made his way to the door. "It doesn't have to be like this."

"That's what I told you." His anguished stare drilled a hole into my heart. "That this doesn't have to be some Romeo and Juliet type situation between the merfolk and selachii. But apparently," he held his hands helplessly before him, "because you've read some book I've never heard of, because

Dylan filled your head with evil selachii thoughts, and because you're not able to see I'm telling you the truth, it does. That's what you're making it."

"What would you do?" I stepped closer to him, so close I could feel the warmth of his skin. "If you were me? Would you hand over the object you'd been entrusted with to the person you were supposed to keep it away from without questioning any of it?"

Wade's shoulders hunched, and his face reddened. Waiting for an indignant retort, I prepared myself for his response, but he dropped his shoulders and blew out an oversized breath. "I guess not. It's just...we were so close. It's our only hope."

Unblinking, he didn't try to hide the emotion pooling in his ocean-blues. We stared at each other, and a single tear escaped and trailed down his cheek.

"I know." I laid a hand on his chest, trying to communicate with my touch what I couldn't seem to with words.

"You're new to this," he said, covering my hand with his. "You don't understand everything yet. You haven't experienced enough of it."

I thought of everything we'd shared at the waterfall, the feelings we revealed to each other. "You're right. And I want it to be over for you too. Please give me some time. Let me figure it out."

He nodded and pulled me against his chest. "Okay," he whispered, resting his chin on top of my head. "Please hurry."

"I will."

"I do love you, Cordelia Blue, and I'm trusting you."

"And I you."

FIVE DAYS. It had been five days of awkward conversations and kisses that only caught the corners of mouths, and long, stretching silences. Things between Wade and I weren't the same. He wouldn't come to my house. He couldn't stand to be so close to the pearl and yet so far away. I couldn't blame him. I held his entire future in my hands.

I tried to find Dylan. And when I couldn't, I sought the other merfolk. I'd even attempted swimming to Mermaid Lagoon but got hopelessly lost.

Wade was suffering, but I couldn't hand over the pearl when I didn't have the full story from Dylan. I'd only just got him back. He'd given me the pearl for a reason, and I needed to understand that before I gave it away. Although I trusted Wade, he was still a selachii, and I was unsure what would happen if the others got their hands on it. I had a deep instinct they weren't all as nice as Wade. I mean, they turned into sharks, they had to have an aggressive streak. And one of them had killed my mother.

Wade skittered from class to class, jiggling a leg through each lesson and staring vacantly out the window. When we stumbled into each other in the hallway, he allowed my lips to find his, but would pull away, always ready with an excuse to be somewhere else. The stress on him took a physical toll too. His tan faded, and the area under his eyes carried deep bruises. He complained of a constant headache. He lost his first swim race. He'd never lost a race before. And when Maya questioned it, I told her and Trent everything.

"But where is your brother?" she asked.

"I don't know." I slammed my locker closed. "I've been looking for him and the other merfolk every day. I haven't seen him in five days. I can only assume that something has happened or they're in hiding. And Wade's been waiting. He promised he wouldn't tell the other selachii, but if I can't get in touch with Dylan...it's not fair on Wade. He asks me to hurry every day, and I have no idea what to tell him."

Concern darted through Maya's eyes. "Maybe you should give it to him."

"My thoughts exactly."

"No." Trent put a hand on my arm.

"Trent?"

"Sorry," he mumbled. "It's just...don't do that. I know Wade's in hell and everything but try and give it another day or two."

"I'm not sure Wade can wait anymore." I rammed an armful of books into my bag.

"I know." He offered me a sympathetic smile. "But try."

Something in the shine of his honey eyes sent alarm bells going off in my head. "You okay?"

"Yeah, just...you know, competition stress. Sorry."

I gave him a hug. "You don't need to apologize."

"And sorry I can't join you at the movies, I really need to get some last minute surf practice in."

Maya touched his arm. "You do what you need to do. We got your back."

"Thanks guys." Trent rallied a smile. "I'm lucky to have you two as my best friends."

I punched his arm lightly. "And don't you forget it."

"And on that note, gotta go." He made a gun with thumb and forefinger and pointed it at me. "But, be patient with Dylan. And the pearl." Jogging backward, he waved at us, then swiveled to face front and ran out the doors.

Maya finished gathering books at her locker and stuffed a couple of files into her bag. "I'm not sure I'm buying into this surf competition stress. Since when does Trent worry about anything?"

"Who knows? It's the biggest one he's been part of yet. He's got a real chance at sponsorship. Or maybe it's something to do with Dylan." I shouldered my backpack. "He wants to see him too. He's been at the beach with me every day."

"Maybe," she said. "Is Wade going to join us for the movie?"

I bit down against the swelling lump in my throat. "I think he's too bummed out."

She rubbed her shoulder against mine as we walked to her car. "Come on. Let's go watch that movie and take your mind off everything."

We ate popcorn and drank soda, and Maya laughed in all the right places as the dimmed lights of the movie theater cocooned me in a numbed silence. An edgy restlessness made my legs jumpy, and every time I looked at the hero on the screen I could only see Wade's face. Which made everything worse.

With music blaring on the radio, Maya drove me home and sang her little heart out to every song. At least that put a smile on my face.

"Big day tomorrow." She grinned at me when she parked in my driveway.

I wracked my brains for a reference I'd missed.

She rolled her eyes. "It's your birthday! Honestly, Cordy."

"I'd kinda forgotten."

"What am I going to do with you?"

"Sorry, Maya. It's all this pearl stuff. And Wade. And Dylan."

She hugged me, and I almost cried on her shoulder. "I know. I get it. Don't you worry about anything. It's sorted. But you have to promise me something?"

Pulling away, I gave her the best smile I could muster and braced myself for her demand, hoping it didn't involve wearing a grass skirt or coconuts instead of a bra.

"Tomorrow, you enjoy yourself, and you take the day off from worrying."

"I'll do my best," I replied, opening the car door.

"It'll be okay. Everything. It will work itself out."

"I hope you're right."

She gave me a quick peck on the cheek before backing her sunny VW out of the driveway. Standing in the drive, an uneasiness snaked through my stomach. As I walked past my dad's car, I ran a finger along its length. I didn't want to go inside yet. And I didn't know why. Like animals sensed earthquakes, I could feel a heavy foreboding oozing from the house.

Finally, when a cloud passed over the moon, and an evening breeze stirred the rose shrub planted near the front steps, I admonished myself for lurking in the shadows too long.

A deathly hush greeted me when I opened the front door. The kitchen clock ticked, louder than it should have. The calendar next to the fridge showed a new scene for October—a swirling waterfall cascading down rocks framed by trees with autumnal leaves. Not California, but close enough to the scene of the private pool with Wade last weekend that a small sigh escaped my lips. My birthday was circled in a thick red permanent marker.

"Dad?" I called quietly. For some reason, even though his car was in the drive, I wasn't expecting a reply.

I closed the door and called again. "Dad?" I stood in the silence of the hallway and listened to the ominous ticking of the clock. The kitchen tap dripped, the overall effect being a drip-drip-tick, drip-drip-tick, causing my nerves to tighten like an overstretched guitar string.

"Oh, Cordy..." Dad emerged from the hallway. "I'm so sorry. It's terrible..."

Drip-drip-tick.

"What's terrible?"

Drip-drip-tick-lurch. That was my heart lurching and throbbing expectantly, waiting for my father to deliver a hammering blow.

"I don't know who would do such a thing." He had his hands on his hips but removed one to block me when I made to pass him. "It's your room, Cordy. I'm not sure you want to go in there."

Ignoring my father's warning, I marched into my room.

The violence of the mess loomed at me. It was unrecognizable from how I'd left it that morning. Completely trashed. The armchair, normally positioned in the corner, was on its side, its upholstery slashed and the seat cushion cut to shreds. It was the chair my father had sat in throughout my childhood, night after night, and read to me about the life of *Winnie the Pooh*.

My bed covers re-carpeted half the room, and my mattress bore the telling lacerations of a hurried autopsy. The drawers in my chest hung open, spilling their contents onto the floor. My closet doors resembled a gaping maw—clothes yanked off the hangers and shoes littering the floor. The curtains lining my bay window had been yanked from their rails and hung askew. The lock on my keepsake box was smashed and its contents dumped in a jumbled pile.

I picked up the medal I'd won at my first swim race and wound its ribbon through my fingers. My Airpods stuck out from behind a garroted pillow. My mother's jewelry box, while disturbed, was not missing any of its contents.

"They didn't take anything," I said.

"Are you sure?" Dad asked, picking up a shredded pillow.

"Yes. Here's my Airpods and Mom's rings."

Dad sat on the slashed mattress, causing a flurry of feathers to fly into the air.

"Who would do such a thing? And why only your room?" Dad looked suspiciously around the room as if the perpetrator might be lurking under a slashed pillow or behind a torn curtain.

"You didn't hear anything?"

Dad shook his head. "I wasn't here all night. Made a quick stop at the lab. Came home to see the back door was hanging wide open, the lock jimmied. Then I started looking around and found this mess in your room. I wanted to tidy it for you before you got back." He placed my ruined pillows back on my ruined bed.

"It's okay, Dad. Nothing is missing." And then I remembered the pearl.

"Are you being bullied or something, Cordy? Is there something going on at school?"

"No, Dad," I said. "I'm fine."

"We should call the cops."

"What good would it do? There's nothing missing."

I spotted the sock—bright, pink, and thick. I'd only worn it once on a weekend ski trip with my father to Big Bear. Neither of us had taken to the skis. Or the ice. Or the cold. The sock lay strewn across the floor in a pile with my other socks and underwear. A wave of embarrassment washed over me as I spotted a black, lacy bra topping the pile.

I picked it up, along with a handful of more virginal styled underwear, and buried it back in the drawer it had come from. The pearl was gone. My hiding place was far too obvious if you'd known where it was.

Wade Waters, how could you?

He was the only person who knew I had the pearl. He knew my father was working, and he knew Maya and I were at the movies. It explained why only my room was trashed. Despite his reassurances to the contrary, his patience had run out and he'd come for the pearl after all. He'd known I'd hidden it in my chest of drawers, but did he have to go and destroy my room, my bed, where only last weekend we'd almost...?

I couldn't say the words. The fact I'd almost let him have me in that way. The fact that I had wanted it, craved it, was worse. The pain of his betrayal stabbed deep into my heart, and the artfulness of his cover-up broke it into tiny pieces.

I turned in a slow circle, surveying the damage, while tears blurred my vision. I tensed against the aching agony setting my heart on fire. I'd never understood girls who couldn't face coming to school after an emotional break-up. I laughed at their obvious stupidity to become so enraptured with a member of the opposite sex that they couldn't seem to function in their lives without that special glance, that stolen kiss, those promises of ever after. No one, I had vowed, would ever make me feel like that.

But this feeling in my chest, this agony burning like a white-hot heat as though I'd been stabbed through with a scalding poker, struck me to my core, and I struggled to breathe. How would I live with this ball of pain lodged inside my chest and stomach?

"Oh, Cordy." Dad pulled on a corner of a photo that had been sticking out from under my keepsake box. A photo of Dylan and me on our thirteenth birthday. "I miss them so much." Dad covered his eyes with a hand and leaned into my offered shoulder. "I wish they were here."

"Me too." Another wave of anger swelled and then gave way to wretched misery. How would I tell Dylan I'd lost the pearl? Especially after the entire merfolk race were relying on me to keep it safe.

How could you, Wade?

I sat next to my father and held his hand. The urge to tell him about my tail, about Dylan and the merfolk, the selachii and the pearl, rested on the tip of my tongue. But I lacked the emotional stamina to start from the beginning—the trip to the bathroom where I'd have to prove the existence of my tail and the look from my father that would reveal whether he accepted me as his daughter or, instead, thought of me as a freak of nature. I couldn't handle that tonight. If ever. So I kept my secrets locked within. And my anger. And the soul-destroying betrayal that scurried through my veins, building in malignancy with each pass though my heart.

But I allowed the sadness to come. The sorrow. I sat and held my father's hand and thought about Dylan and my father's gut-wrenching sense of loss. Together we cried.

It was our birthday tomorrow. Our eighteenth. Thinking of him, I vowed to get the pearl back and give Dylan and my father some peace.

Wade had a lot to answer for.

No one screws with Cordelia Blue.

Blood really does boil when you're angry. I could feel it.

CHAPTER SIXTEEN

My eighteenth birthday brought a medley of emotions. I had expected as much. How could I live through such a milestone without my twin brother by my side?

But now I knew he was alive, I didn't have to carry the sadness.

It wasn't relief I felt though. It was anger. And hurt.

My father and I spent the morning of my eighteenth birthday at a department store where I decided on sheets and a duvet cover in duck-egg blue and pillow slips in a soft cream. We purchased a new duvet and pillows and my father agreed to the latest memory foam mattress.

"Happy birthday," he laughed as the dollars racked up at the till.

"Oh, I'm expecting a lot more than that." I elbowed his ribs.

"Birthday pancakes at Shade's?"

"That'll do for starters," I said, as I carried the bags of bedding to the car. The mattress would be delivered to the house later. I was glad I was getting new sheets, new bedding, new everything. Then I could wipe every memory of Wade being in my room, lying on my sheets, seeping his enticing smell into them and start afresh, with a hardened heart and a determination that I would never trust anyone ever again. Ever.

Dad parked outside the restaurant, and we sat on the balcony overlooking Ocean Beach and the pier. I scanned the distant horizon, looking for Dylan or other merfolk.

The waiter brought a short stack of buttermilk pancakes with a sparkling candle stuck through the middle of the pile, and if that wasn't enough, eggs, bacon and home fries surrounded the wobbling structure. The enticing aromas were too much for my stomach, and I almost drooled on the candle.

"Happy birthday to you," Dad sang as his eyes filled.

"Thanks, Dad." Blowing out the candle, I made a thousand wishes. I wondered if any of them would come true.

"I can't believe you're eighteen."

Both of us glanced at the empty chairs beside us where two other people ought to be sitting. We could never celebrate my birthday without the sense of them hovering between us. Neither my father nor I could face the baking of cakes—that was something my mom had always done. Every year since the accident it was our unspoken agreement to eat a birthday brunch at Shade's. We would order pancakes and stare at the ocean wondering if perhaps they were out there somewhere. This year, I smiled to myself. Although I knew my mother was lost, Dylan was out there, perhaps having the ocean equivalent to birthday pancakes.

"Neither can I," I said.

Dad leaned forward conspiratorially. "I have a message from Maya."

"Oh?"

"You need to be ready at seven o'clock sharp in your best cocktail dress."

"Cocktail dress?" I wanted to put my new sheets on my new mattress, crawl under my new duvet and forget Wade Waters ever existed.

"Yes." Excitement rolled off him like it was Christmas morning. "She's coming to pick you up in a limo."

"A limo?" I choked on my drink.

"Yep." Dad grinned and I couldn't deny his enthusiasm.

"Oh, God...what have you two planned?"

"Nothing but the best for my eighteen-year-old daughter." Dad pushed his finished plate away. "Oh, I almost forgot. It was all those dollars at the department store that distracted me a little." He chuckled softly and then pushed a small, wrapped box across the table.

I tore off the wrapping and then opened the lid of a black, velvet jewelry box to reveal a silver necklace. The hanging pendant was a 'C' for Cordelia, and on the bottom curve of the letter was a single diamond.

"It's beautiful." I pulled the chain from the box and lifted my hair as my father came around the table and fastened the necklace for me. "Thanks, Dad."

"Now it's time to ditch your old man and go do what normal eighteen-year-olds do."

I looked at the ocean again.

"As long as it doesn't involve a certain someone and your new sheets." His eyes twinkled.

"Dad!" Wade Waters wouldn't be coming anywhere near me or my new sheets anytime soon.

"I may be a father, but I'm not stupid. You're an adult now. You've passed the age of consent. I promised myself I wouldn't be one of those overprotective parents who banned boys from the house and made you do pregnancy tests every other week. I want you to be...happy. As a grown up, with grown up needs—"

"Oh my God, Dad, please, stop," I sputtered. "It's not like that." I stared at the napkin in my lap and slowly ripped it in two.

"Is everything okay?" he asked as I proceeded to shred the napkin into tiny pieces.

I nodded. I couldn't speak. Then I shook my head. A few tears sprinkled the torn napkin in my lap. "We're not..."

"It's okay, sweetheart."

It wasn't okay. It wasn't anywhere near the realm of okay. But I could offer no further explanations to my father because I didn't want to cry anymore, not on my birthday, and thinking of Wade and what he'd done would make me spill a thousand more tears.

"I'm going to go for a walk on the beach," I said, in lieu of an explanation.

I needed to be in the water, in the ocean, with Dylan and away from any further questions or kindness from my father. I was afraid I would break. My delicately held together resolve to stay strong and pretend Wade had never been important to me would crumble away, and I would be left...a mess...more than a mess...I let out a sharp, bitter laugh and earned myself a few curious looks from the nearest tables.

Perched on the edge of his chair, Dad frowned, his eyes scanning my face. "If you're sure."

I nodded. My legs twitched. I craved my tail and the simplicity of the water curling over my body.

"Cordy," Dad said, as I rose to my feet. "I'm here if you need me. To talk. Anything."

"I know."

"I'm sure I could manage to put you on my lap and give you a great big bear hug."

"Thanks, Dad." I turned and left the restaurant, leaving my dad staring after me.

I crossed the road and walked along the beach until I drew level with the pier. Beneath it, I stood in the shadows and examined the beckoning waves. I kicked off my shoes. My feet sank into the cool, shaded sand. I removed my clothes and approached the gentle waves. The ocean was calm today, white crests insignificant and insubstantial.

I ducked under the water, my tail fanning out, and weaved through the pillars of the pier. Dylan appeared when I reached the last stone column. He grabbed my elbow and ushered me further out to sea.

"Hey," I called.

"Happy birthday to us," he said in a sing-song voice and smiled widely. "Come on." He turned and dove deeper into the water.

"Hey!"

He popped his head above the surface. "It's our birthday.

There's a party." When he disappeared under the water again, I had to scramble to catch up with him.

"I need to talk to you." I pushed my forceful thoughts into his brain, adding a mental slap for good measure.

He turned his head toward me and smiled mischievously. "Later."

"No, Dylan, now." I stopped swimming and waited for him to return.

I waited. And waited. I peered into the murky gloom and only caught the faintest of shimmers ahead.

"Come on." His voice was faint.

I flicked my tail and hurried after him. Our conversation was obviously going to have to wait.

We swam for miles, past clumps of floating seaweed and enormous shoals of fish. I circled around one to avoid the razor-sharp jaws of a hunting barracuda. Flipper and his friends brought us presents of barnacle-encrusted kelp and mouthfuls of small fish.

The scenery passed me by. I couldn't concentrate on anything except the pearl. How was I going to tell Dylan I had lost it?

After a couple hours, Dylan pointed up. When my head broke the surface, an island shimmered into view. Palm trees grew in abundance with coconuts gathered tightly on their trunks. There was a wide sandy beach littered with seashells, and a coral reef surrounded the whole thing, turning the water a bright aqua blue. Stingrays glided in the shallows, and brightly colored fish darted among the corals.

"Where are we?" I said, turning in circles, taking in this paradise in the middle of the ocean.

"Mermaid Island." Nerida appeared. "That's what we call it anyway."

Flipper and his friends leaped into the air and twirled in circles. Merfolk swam in the protected reef, and a couple hoisted themselves out of the water and lay on the beach.

"Won't they be seen?" I asked Dylan.

"Nah," he replied. "We're far away from any shipping lanes. The water is too shallow and rocky. Come on, let's join them."

Dylan swam to the island and pulled himself out of the water. I bit down on a laugh as he army-commandoed on his stomach to his two mermaid friends. When he reached them, he planted a deep kiss on one and accepted a half coconut shell from the other.

"Come on," he called. "What are you waiting for?"

I swam to the island and crawled up the beach, my legs jelly-like after having used my tail for so long. Sea breezes flowed through the island, ruffling the palms and whipping miniature white caps on the shallow waters.

I plonked myself next to my brother. "Dylan—"

"This is Tammy," he interrupted and gestured to the one he'd kissed, "and this is Jasmine."

Jasmine had short dark hair and dark brown eyes. She handed me a half coconut shell with a sloshing liquid inside. I sniffed at the milky substance. The fumes were enough to knock me out.

"It's coconut magic," Tammy said. Sandy brown curls wound around her face, and when she smiled, her full, red lips revealed a slightly crooked front tooth.

"It's what we drink at a party." Dylan winked. "And

considering it's our eighteenth—happy birthday by the way, sis—we should drink a lot."

"Dylan." I injected more volume into my voice and placed the coconut shell beside me. I was sure I'd be drunk on one sip. "I need to talk to you about something."

"Okay…"

"I've lost the pearl."

He took another large gulp from his shell. "What was that now?"

I stared at my own drink. Maybe a sip would help. The liquid slipped down my throat and ignited a small but uncomfortable fire in my stomach. I coughed.

Dylan laughed. "I bet you haven't had a drink until now."

"I had a beer, the other weekend, with Dad."

"A whole beer?"

"Well, half." I took another sip and found the alcohol slipped down better the second time, even more with the third sip.

"Anyway, what were you saying? Something about the pearl?"

I nodded. "It's gone."

Blanching, his mouth fell open. "Gone? What do you mean, *gone*?"

"It was stolen." A coconut fell from a nearby palm tree, startling us both. It rolled toward Dylan and he pushed it away.

"Stolen? What do you mean, *stolen*?" His voice rose. His gaze roamed the beach and then fixed on me, hard and penetrating.

Tammy propped herself on her elbows and shot a

worried look at Dylan. Jasmine looked back and forth between us.

"The pearl's been stolen," I said again, lowering my gaze to the sand. "Wade took it."

"Dammit!" Dylan made as if to stand, then flopped back onto the sand. "Wade Waters. He's a selachii." He narrowed his eyes.

"I know."

"Why are you fraternizing with selachii?"

"He's my boyfriend. Was," I corrected.

"What the hell, Cordelia? How could you be so stupid?" He slammed a fist into the sand hard enough to draw blood across his knuckles.

"Hey," Tammy said, laying a hand on Dylan's arm. "It's not her fault. You haven't told her the whole story."

"Exactly," I said, launching to my feet. "I've been looking for you every day since you gave it to me, and I couldn't find you anywhere."

Nerida appeared and wiggled up the beach to join our small group.

Dylan sighed and blew his dark hair out of his face. "Okay, we'll save the lecture about dating selachii for another time. Now, why don't you explain what happened."

I sat back down, dipped my head, and drew patterns in the sand. "Wade knew I had the pearl. I had no intention of telling him about it, but he knew. We were in my bedroom, and it started making a noise—"

Nerida's tail flipped. "The pearl only makes a noise when—"

"Not now, Nerida," Dylan snapped.

"And then Wade knew the pearl was in my room. He told me about the persecution of the selachii by the ashrays—he showed me the horrible wound one had inflicted. He explained how Zale, their leader, wants the pearl to plead for mercy before the High Council. And to be perfectly honest," I snatched a coconut shell and took a long sip, "I was somewhat tempted to give it to him. I think he made a good case for it. At least he told me what was going on, what it's for."

I halted, the feel of betrayal fresh and raw. Wade may have told me what the pearl was for, but he'd still taken it. He'd stormed into my room and stolen it, and that was that.

"And did he tell you that only one species can use the pearl?" Dylan asked.

"No." The new information spun in my mind. "But I don't care. His wounds are terrible. His family is suffering—"

"Do you want to see me out of the water Cordy?" He stared at me.

"Of course I do, it just doesn't seem fair..."

"*Fair?*" His expression turned thunderous. "If the selachii hadn't been so fucking lazy and protected us properly, none of this would have happened."

"I don't think the selachii are entirely to blame—"

"Zale killed Mom! He broke the truce."

"Zale? Their leader?"

"Yes," Dylan snarled, his green eyes flaring. "Their leader. And you can bet your ass Wade knew, and he knows the pearl only works for one species too."

"No..." I couldn't believe it. Wade wouldn't...but he'd stolen the pearl.

Wade Waters, you will pay for this. "I feel like a complete fool."

"You said it," Dylan muttered.

"Hey," Nerida said. "Give her a break. She thought she was in love. She's not the only one to make mistakes in love's name." She gave him a pointed stare.

"Whatever," he said. "We're not bringing that up again."

Nerida focused on me. "The problem with the selachii possessing the pearl is that they don't want to use it to get their legs back...I mean, they do want their legs back too, but they plan to use it to attack the High Council."

"Attack?"

"They're furious with the persecution by the ashrays," Nerida said. "And they plan to make their feelings known. They plan to destroy the High Council."

If the High Council were responsible for causing this much pain, then maybe they needed to answer some serious questions, maybe they should be held accountable for their cruel, elongated infliction of punishment. The type of punishment, that in the real world, had been abolished decades ago.

"I'd want revenge too," I said. "If some High Council who never dared to show their faces in centuries of history had subjected me and my family to a life of pain...I'd want revenge too."

"Zale is building an army," Dylan said. "That's why there have been more shark attacks lately."

"An army for what?"

Dylan's eyes dimmed, as well as the green scales of his

tail. "To ensure the selachii are the ones who use the pearl and to keep the merfolk in the water...forever."

Zale. Now I had something to focus my anger on. Now, I too, wanted revenge.

"Don't go there, Cordy." Dylan had correctly guessed at my thoughts. "Things are tense enough as it is. If you attack their leader, it will start a war. One we could never win."

"We need the pearl," Nerida said. "That's the only way we can avoid the selachii. If we can escape the water and be on land, then we don't have to live in fear of them anymore."

"I thought they weren't allowed to attack you...us?" I asked, shivering, despite the heat.

"That was a rule set by the High Council," Tammy replied. "A rule I don't think the selachii will obey for too much longer."

"One they've already broken once," Dylan muttered.

"We used to live in harmony." Nerida collected the coconut shells and poured the contents onto the sand. No one was in the mood for partying anymore. "Back on Atlantis and for years after. But when the dragon kings invaded, the merfolk blamed the selachii for not protecting them. The selachii blamed the merfolk for becoming lazy and allowing the dragon kings to creep onto the island. With nowhere left to live, and the High Council taking refuge in their blue chamber, we took to our separate areas of the water. It's been that way ever since."

"How long?" I asked.

"Centuries," Nerida replied. "Zale has his reasons for wanting the pearl, and we have ours. Not only do I want to use the pearl for the merfolk, but the High Council must be warned. The selachii will stop at nothing to seek revenge for the centuries of ashray torture."

"Wade would never—"

"They're not all bad." She held up a pacifying hand. "But enough of them are. And with Zale as their leader, I'm not holding out much hope for a peaceful conclusion."

Dylan tapped my knee. "Can you get the pearl back?"

"I don't know. I can try. But I don't know how. I don't know where it is." I picked up one of the empty shells, scraping the remaining flesh with a fingernail.

"It's not your fault, Cordy, you weren't to know. But we do need to get it back," he said. "Talk to Wade."

Wade was the last person I wanted to talk to. Was he part of this? This plan for revenge and murder? I thought back to when his cousins had accosted him on our first date. They'd been hostile, tripping him up. He'd fallen to one knee. He'd been angry. No, furious, furious enough to dig his nails into his palm and draw blood.

"What happens if I can't find it?" I asked.

"The selachii don't know how to use it," Nerida said. "That's our saving grace. But neither do we." She sighed, and the end of her tail twitched. "But if they gain access to the High Council, I expect they'll murder them and take the Power of the Sea for themselves."

"The Power of the Sea?"

"Yes." She drummed her fingers against a shell. "The Power of the Sea is held by the council and keeps the world, within the oceans, in balance. If it fell into the wrong hands—"

"The last time was when Tempest tried to steal it from

Vortex—" Tammy stopped when Nerida shot her a warning look.

"Vortex? Tempest? Who are they?"

"The gods of the sea," Dylan said. "Brothers. Vortex gave us Atlantis."

"And we burned it to the ground," Tammy added.

"Cordelia doesn't need to worry about events that were concluded centuries ago." Nerida patted my knee. "Let's concentrate on the problem at hand."

"Find the pearl, Cordy," Dylan said. "*Please.*"

CHAPTER SEVENTEEN

*W*aves of guilt rolled over me, and then resentment. I hadn't chosen to protect the pearl—that decision had been thrust upon me, and it wasn't my fault it had been stolen. I'd done my best, without any answers or explanations. But now everyone expected me to get it back, by myself, without offering any ideas on how to do it.

While I mulled over those thoughts, my father threw five dresses onto my newly made-up bed. I flapped about in my bathrobe, panicking Maya would be there any minute to pick me up. I'd taken a shower to rinse the ocean from my skin and to dispel the dull headache throbbing at my temples. Coconut magic was potent stuff.

"Put this one on." Dad thrust a dark blue, strapless satin number into my hands.

"Okay, okay," I said. "Now shoo, so I can get dressed."

He left my room, and I slid the dress over my head. I peered into the mirror. At least I'd done my make-up already. But all I could see were the dark circles under my eyes and the tightness in my cheeks. It was one week before the anniversary of my mother's death, and the face looking back at me from the mirror matched the horror of my memories.

I closed my eyes and prayed Maya hadn't organized anything too outlandish. As a car horn sounded from the drive, I put on my happy face and grabbed my handbag.

"Have a good time, Cordy," Dad called as I slipped out the door.

The limo was long and black and shiny, and when the driver opened the door for me, soft blue lighting emanated from its depths. The smell of freshly treated leather and an expensive air freshener greeted me as I climbed in.

"Happy birthday, Cordy," Maya squealed, shoving a fake I.D. into my hands. She wiggled like a day-old pup on the polished leather seats, her long blonde hair bouncing around her shoulders. She wore a candy-pink dress, a color I could never pull off with my hair, and strappy silver heels higher than I'd ever dare to attempt.

"Congratulations." Trent was decked out in a soft gray suit, his wild hair tamed, and he held a full champagne flute toward me.

I took the offered drink as I settled on the seat beside him.

"Thanks guys," I said. "Maya, this is lovely."

"Cheers," she toasted.

The three of us clinked glasses and the driver took off. The edge of a smile broke the tension in my lips as I sipped the champagne. Maybe, for one night, I could forget about my troubles. I could forget about Wade and the pearl and instead, concentrate on myself and the most important birthday of my life.

"Here." Maya held a small gift bag toward me. "Open it. It's from both of us."

I removed a small jewelry box from the bag and flipped open the lid to reveal two sparkling diamond earrings.

"Oh, my goodness. You guys, you shouldn't have. It's too much."

"It was Trent's idea." Trent shrugged and pulled at the collar of his shirt. "He needs a girlfriend." Maya rolled her eyes.

Trent held my hair back as I put the earrings in. Maya glanced in his direction, furtively, her gaze traveling the length of his jaw and down his chest. He was wearing a suit. He did look deliciously handsome. I wondered if she was thinking that too.

"They're beautiful," she said, once the earrings were in position.

"Thank you, both of you. I love them." I hugged and kissed them both.

We sat back in our seats, sipping our champagne as the city lights rolled by in a stream of hope and magic. Maya regaled us with stories from my childhood, incidents I'd rather have forgotten about. And once or twice Dylan's name came up. With each mention, Trent would gaze out the window and lose himself in thought until Maya poked him.

"Oh," Maya said, mid-sentence. "I forgot to tell you. Wade's going to meet us there."

I startled, sloshing champagne down my chin. "He's *what?*"

"He couldn't make the limo and said he'd meet us there." She frowned when she took in my displeased expression. "He said he's been trying to call you all day."

I hadn't bothered to look at my phone when I'd arrived home. With Maya and Trent picking me up in the limo, there wasn't anyone else I had needed or wanted to hear from. Apart from my mother, but I buried that wish deep inside.

"What's going on, Cordy?" she asked.

Squeezing my eyes tight, I fought against the overwhelming urge to cry, again. I gritted my teeth and teetered on a fine precipice, not sure which way the tears would go.

Trent rested a gentle hand on my knee. "Cordy?"

"We broke up," I said.

There was silence in the car for a few moments. The limo hit a bump, and we lurched toward each other.

"What happened?" The concern in Maya's voice cracked my reserve to stay strong.

"I..." I took a breath. Trent sat beside me, ankles crossed, fingers plucking at the buttons of his shirt. "I don't think I can do this tonight." I shook my hand at Maya. Maybe the motion could stay the tears. "I can't talk about it right now, not without falling apart."

"Of course." She reached for my hand. "I'm sorry."

Maya refilled our glasses. Sipping at hers, a small frown formed on the bridge of her nose. "Cordy? Does Wade know you broke up? I mean, why would he be coming if you broke up?"

That was a good question. He must have known by taking the pearl he was pointing a large red finger at himself.

Why would he bother showing? Or did he think I was that stupid? "I don't know."

The limo lurched to a halt, and the driver opened the door. We were downtown. Outside the Hyatt.

"First stop, fortieth floor cocktail bar," Maya said. "Do you want to go in, Cordy?"

I nodded. "I'm not going to let Wade ruin my evening. Not when you've tried so hard," I swept a hand across the dazzling building and then toward the sparkling ocean, "to make it perfect for me.

"I thought you might be able to catch a glimpse of Dylan." She pointed to the rooftop bar. "From up there."

I pushed a smile onto my lips. "Maybe."

Trent escorted me through the revolving doors and threw an arm around my shoulders. "I'm sorry it went down like that. With Wade. I'm sorry it didn't work out." It was the most he'd said all night.

"It's not your fault, Trent," I said. "It's Wade's fault. But thanks."

We rode the elevator to the top of the building, and my stomach dropped into my feet. I stumbled as a little ding noise signaled we'd arrived. The elevator doors opened with a *whoosh*.

Maya had reserved a window table, and the waiter set upon us with his notepad before we'd sat. It was a cocktail bar. We had to order cocktails. Armed with our fake IDs, Trent settled on the OB Sun Burn. Maya and I opted for a San Diego Sunset, one of the signature drinks.

When they arrived, Trent gulped his in two swallows and I wasn't far behind him. The sugary sweetness warmed my stomach and helped to deaden my emotions, guarding against the cruel irony that I should have a boyfriend there.

"Let's get drunk," I said, ordering a second cocktail. Perhaps I already was. After the coconut magic, the champagne in the limo, and the stiff cocktail I'd already downed. I pretended not to notice the warning look passing between Trent and Maya.

Train's *Mermaid* song came over the loudspeakers. I was transported to five years ago in a nanosecond. I hadn't listened to the song for five years, and there it was, full of its tropical promise and magical fantasy about mermaids and shipwrecks and sharks, as if they were good things. But the song also brought back good memories, of being with Dylan and Mom, of family days on the beach, of the bonfire beach party we'd had for our thirteenth birthday.

The second cocktail arrived and I inhaled that one too. Trent wasn't far behind me. I stood, not bothering to walk to the dance floor, and moved my body to the music. Maya edged closer to Trent.

"What are we going to do when Wade gets here?" she whispered to him.

Another ding from the elevator followed by the whoosh of the doors signaled a new arrival. Wade Waters stepped out of the cab.

I froze. There he was. Wade, wearing a black suit and white shirt with an adorable red bow tie. His hair was damp and neatly combed and his hands were shoved into his pockets. A red rose bloomed in his breast pocket, and a dazzling smile set his lips on fire.

Maya and Trent stood, wary gazes darting in different directions.

Wade approached me. "Happy birthday, Cordelia Blue." He moved to embrace me and kiss my cheek. I stepped back.

"Not. So. Fast," I ordered.

He frowned. "What's the matter?"

He edged closer, but I stepped back again.

"Seriously? That's how you're going to play it? You're going to deny everything?" Although I wasn't shouting, my voice was loud, and I could hear the slur in it. People were starting to turn and look. Maya and Trent tried to step between us.

"I—" He reached for me.

"You took the pearl!" This time I did shout. Maya gasped. Trent paled.

Our waiter scurried over and exhibited a concerned, disapproving expression. "Is everything okay here, ma'am?"

"Ma'am?" I goggled at him. "Don't *ma'am* me!"

The waiter spent no more than two seconds sizing me up and scurried away again.

Wade kept his blue eyes on mine, a sad smile teetering on his lips. "I don't have the pearl, Cordelia."

I sucked in a steadying breath. Gathering my thoughts, I smoothed my dress, as if readying for a fight. Before I spoke, I willed my voice to sound calm and stable and not like the shrill, bitter woman I felt.

"You were the only one who knew I had it," I said.

He came close, his breath sweeping over my cheek, and his intoxicating scent swarming around me. Maya and Trent edged back into their seats. The other patrons returned to their own drinks and conversation. Wade's gaze stayed locked on me. His jaw was set, cleanly shaven, and I longed to place my lips along its edge, to feel his soft skin.

"Am I?" he asked.

My ankle wobbled in one of my heels, and he caught me before I fell. I shrugged off his grasp, but not before I noticed the warmth of his touch on my arm. No. I would not allow myself to feel this way. He had betrayed me.

"Yes." I brought my gaze to meet his. "You're the only one who knew it was in my room, who had a need for it."

His hand floated to his chest. "But you have told others?"

"Yes." I glanced at Maya and Trent. "No one else needs the pearl like you do, Wade. I asked you to wait. I asked you to trust me. But it was too much for you, wasn't it?"

"It was extraordinarily hard, Cordelia." He exhaled a deep sigh. "But I didn't take the pearl. I wouldn't do that." The last was barely audible.

"Really?" I narrowed my eyes. "Because I can kind of understand it. If I were in your position, I'd probably do the same, to save my family. And now I know the real reason..." I laughed bitterly.

"Real reason?" He extended a hand.

I stopped him with a look. "Yes, Wade, the real reason. That Zale wants the pearl to destroy the High Council."

"Zale wants the pearl to plead mercy before the High Council." His voice rose. "I explained this to you already."

"Is that what he told you? Or is that want you want me to believe?" I asked. Music boomed out of speakers. Colored lights swept around the room. "Only one of the water species can use the pearl, only one can plead before the High Council, only one can be granted their legs again. And Zale has no intention of pleading. He wants revenge. He wants to murder the High Council and take the Power of the Sea for himself."

Wade stumbled as though my words had been physical blows. He grabbed the back of a chair to steady himself. One of the petals from the rose in his breast pocket fell, swirling slowly to the floor.

"No, I can't believe that's true. He wouldn't..." His eyes flashed black. "I only agreed to help him find the pearl to free my mother."

"Your mother? I thought she was dead?"

He leaned on the back of the chair. His face drained of color, and the only hint of a blush was from the wilting red rose. "I never said she was dead."

"Yes, you did. You said she was lost to the ocean." I inhaled sharply. He'd lied to me again. Despite his promises that he never would. Despite his expectations that relationships should hold nothing but honesty. He was full of lies.

Wade plucked the flower from his pocket, pulled off a petal and let it drop to the floor. "She is stuck in the ocean. Zale has been looking after her. She will never be free unless I find the pearl..." He pinched the skin at his throat. "...she has terrible wounds from the ashrays. I'm not sure she can survive them." He leveled his brimming eyes at me. "That's the only reason I want the pearl. To help my mother so she doesn't have to bear these terrible wounds. I don't care much about the High Council, but I thought it was the only way."

"When you said you lost your mother to the ocean, you meant it literally. But you haven't *lost* her, lost her. She's not dead. You can see her whenever you want. You have no idea what it's like to really lose your mother." How could he begin to compare our situations? "And so you took the pearl."

He shook his head. "No, Cordelia, I didn't take the pearl."

"I wish you'd just admit it, Goddammit!" My voice rose again, and I earned another scornful frown from our waiter. Maya hadn't finished her second drink, so I strode swiftly to the table and finished it for her.

"Zale is building an army," I said, my emotions under fragile control. "The increase in shark attacks up and down the coast? He's building an army to murder the council and take the Power of the Sea."

"I don't know anything about that, Cordelia."

I stared at him for a long time, until my eyes blurred with the strain. He stared right back, waiting. I believed him. Deep in my gut, I knew he only wanted to help his mother. He didn't care about the strife between the merfolk and selachii, he didn't care who held the pearl as long as he could help his mother and free her from her painful imprisonment. But the fact remained that he'd taken the pearl, and it didn't seem like he was going to give it back.

"Zale was the one who killed my mother," I said.

"I didn't know that either." He flattened a hand against his shirt and with his thumb, rubbed at a loosening button. "We don't have to fight, Cordelia. I only wanted to be with you...because I love you. I don't care about anyone else, or some ancient prophecy or a dusty old book. It's just us."

"It's *not* just us." I jabbed my index finger in the air. "We are different species. The selachii are trying to tear us apart. And I could deal with all that. I could, if we were on the same page. But I can't love someone who lies to me. You said you would never lie to someone you loved."

Wade placed a hand over his heart. "I never have."

I scoffed.

"Okay, Cordelia, have it your way." He stepped toward me, lifted the rose, and threaded it through my hair, above my ear, gently, tenderly. He fanned my hair back over my shoulders and hesitated. It took all I had to ignore the effect his touch had on me.

"Wade, I need you to give me back the pearl."

"I don't have it, Cordelia." He shrugged, turned, and without a further word, returned to the open elevator doors. Then he was gone.

My heart lurched. Tears ran freely down my cheeks. I collapsed into my chair and let Maya's soothing platitudes attempt to lessen the pain in my heart.

"Are you sure he took the pearl?" Trent asked.

"Who else would take it?" I sighed and looked out of the panoramic window for the first time. The sun had dipped below the horizon and the ocean darkened to the same color as my heart.

"I don't know, Cordy, but it sounded as if he might be innocent."

CHAPTER EIGHTEEN

I slunk into the house trailing a cloud of despair.

Dad glanced at the kitchen clock. "You're home early."

"I know, I'm sorry, I know you and Maya organized a whole thing." I sagged onto the couch, attempted to ignore the heat behind my eyes. After the cocktail lounge scene with Wade, my headache had returned with full force and the celebration had lost its appeal. Maya and Trent had dropped me home in the limo.

"Oh, Cordy, what happened?"

"I'm sorry," I said again, wiping fresh tears away with the back of my hand. "It was lovely, really. It's just...Wade and I broke up." My face crumpled again, and I leaned into my father's arms.

"I'm sorry." He stroked the back of my head.

I sat for a long time relishing the feel of my father's arms around me, until I pulled away a little and noticed one of them was thickly bandaged.

"What happened?" I fingered the white gauze. "Were you trying to cook dinner for yourself again?"

"No." Two little worry lines wrinkled his forehead. "I went to the lab. One of the sharks was going nuts, thrashing around in its tank, so I went to check it out. I put my arm in and it went for me."

"One of the sharks *attacked* you?" I tensed. "Which one?" Could Zale's power extend to the sharks my father kept in his lab? Was he sending a message to the merfolk, to me?

"The tiger," he said. "It's okay, it was only a nip."

"Dad, promise me you won't go diving." I made him look at me. "Only for a little while. The ocean's not safe right now." Until Zale had been dealt with.

"Okay..." he said slowly, searching my face for all the things I wasn't saying. "Most of my work is in the lab at the moment, so, yes, I can promise you that for a little while."

I sighed. "I guess that will have to do."

"I've been a little nervous myself lately." He chuckled, but it was a poor attempt at lightening the mood. "There was another attack off the coast of Baja. And a fourth in L.A. I'm not sure what's going on right now."

I do. "All the more reason to stay out of the water."

"Okay, sweetheart. Okay."

I stood. "I'm going to change out of this dress."

"I'll get the ice-cream. You didn't make it to dinner, did you?"

I shook my head as I backed along the hallway, and now, with my tears dry for the time being, a ravenous hunger growled in my stomach. When I returned to the kitchen, wearing sweatpants and my maroon Point Loma Pointers sweatshirt, a carton of Ben & Jerry's peanut butter cup waited on the kitchen counter.

"Ice-cream is the nectar of the gods." Dad offered me a spoon.

"Not much beats it," I said.

My father and I sat together, eating ice-cream, letting the carton melt on the counter. Our conversation began in safe territories—about the swim team and how good it felt to be in the water again. We talked about Maya and Trent, how long I'd known them, that they'd likely always be my best friends. I managed a little about Wade, without crying, and without mentioning anything to do with merfolk and selachii. We avoided the topic of Dylan, our birthday, but I wondered what he was doing in the ocean right now.

"I'VE BEEN THINKING about the prophecy," Maya said.

My head throbbed from last night's disastrous birthday celebrations. I wasn't sure I was ready to think about more mermaid crap. Kicking off my flip-flops, I rubbed sunblock onto my skin. Trent's final competition was about to start.

"*The one who walks the land can break the curse, united.*"

"I need the pearl to do that," I whispered.

My father and Trent's parents sat nearby. Trent was warming up, doing pop-ups on his board.

"I can't decide if I like him better in a suit or in his shorts," Maya said.

I moved my gaze to Trent again. He was tanned and golden. His hair, bleached by the sun, hung in loose waves past his chin. His strong hands moved rhythmically over the surface of his surfboard, each stroke of wax revealing the power and precision within his sinewy arms.

"I don't think I can take him seriously in a suit." I laughed. "Although he did look rather dashing."

Her gaze continued to loiter over his body, and when I narrowed my eyes at her, she blushed.

"Maya, do you *like* Trent?"

"Shh!" Her blush deepened, and she flicked sand at me. "He can't know. He doesn't feel that way." She averted her gaze to her feet, which were currently buried in the sand.

"Have you asked?"

"No." She growled the word. "*Shh*. And anyway, the pearl. I know you need the pearl—"

"Uh, no, back up a minute, back to Trent." Trent looked up then and grinned at us.

"Shut up, Cordy."

I raised my hands in surrender. "Okay. Okay. But we are going to have this conversation...later."

"Go back to the pearl, please."

I sighed. "If I don't have it, I can't do anything with it. So there will be no talking about curse breaking until I have it back in my possession, if I ever get it back." I took a breath. "Sorry. I think I'm still reeling from seeing Wade last night. After everything he did, I can't believe he decided to show up."

Maya chewed on her bottom lip and gave me a sidelong glance. "I think you might need to talk to him again."

"No."

"Cordy." She leaned in close. "I think you might *need* him."

"I do *not* need a guy in my life. I can take care of myself." My father and Trent's parents paused their conversation to look at me. Dad frowned and enquired with his eyes if I was okay. I nodded.

"That's not what I meant." Maya recrossed her ankles and dug her toes back into the sand. "I think the whole 'united' part of the prophecy means you have to be in league with a selachii."

Many choice words tumbled through my mind. None of them repeatable. "We don't know if the prophecy refers to me."

"Yes, we do. You're the only mermaid who walks the land."

"Fine." I gripped the spindly armrests of my beach chair. "I accept that part. But Wade is not the only selachii who can walk. I'll find another if I have to be united."

"Do you think you can? From what your brother has told you, it doesn't seem as if the selachii want much to do with the merfolk, or the other way around."

"Maya." I pushed her name out through gritted teeth. "I don't have the pearl, and I don't see how I'm supposed to get it back. There's no point in discussing it. And besides, Dylan says only one species can use the pearl. Your book must be wrong."

"I don't think so—"

"It *must* be. Dylan and Nerida *told* me." I jabbed my finger in the air, emphasizing my point.

"*They* could be wrong." She let the thought dangle

between us. "Personally, I'd take the words written in a book over the accuracy—or should I say *inaccuracy*—of a spoken story that's been handed down through generations, any day. You've played Broken Telephone. Does it ever come out the same as when it started?"

I shook my head, then averted my gaze. She was spouting things I didn't want to hear.

"No, it doesn't." I didn't like the tone in her voice. "Trust me. I think 'united' is the key."

"But you're the only one who can read the book. What if you have it wrong?"

"I don't."

"Maya, come on, you can't even tell me what language it is—"

"I'm not wrong, Cordy. I promise."

The horn sounded three times, signally the surfers to enter the water. Maya and I rose and walked to Trent.

"Hey, Cordy." Trent stood and rested a hand on my arm. "You okay? After last night?"

My throat thickened and gurgled, and I managed a small nod. He slung an arm around my shoulder and squeezed me close to him. He smelled of sunblock and sand and summer vacations. Nice things. Comforting things.

"Good luck," Maya said, and punched his arm.

"Thanks guys." He picked up his board, his gaze settling on my face. "We'll try again, another celebration, maybe a barbeque on the beach? Then maybe Dylan can come too."

"Thanks, Trent, that would be great," I said.

He dashed into the water as the commentator spoke into a megaphone.

"Welcome all, to the Californian high school state final..."

The thickening crowd cheered and clapped as Maya and I wound our way to the water's edge. The day was calm with a gentle offshore breeze and waves a steady five to six feet.

"We're excited to see what our first three surfers can do: Ray Jackson, Trent Summers, and Steven Charles in first, second and third place respectively. But anyone of them could take the lead."

My father and Trent's parents gathered beside Maya and me, and we shielded our eyes against the sun as he stood to take his first wave. Trent's parents held a large banner with his name printed in bold black letters. They lifted it high above their heads and whooped and whistled as he charged across his first wave, performing a frontside three-sixty. He came out of it but had more wave to use. He pumped for speed and then did a couple of backside floaters.

"...eight points to Trent Summers, eight to Ray Jackson and three to Steven Charles who wiped out spectacularly..."

"Go Trent!" his mother called into the advancing wind.

My hair whipped around my face. I threw it in a ponytail and tucked it under my Navy cap.

"He is like the king of the ocean." Maya wiggled at my side.

I gave her a sidelong glance to see twin spots of color forming on her cheeks. "You should tell him how you feel."

"Shut up."

I poked her. "You're never going to know if you don't take a risk."

"I'm not a risky kind of person," she retorted. "I like facts and figures. Absolutes."

"There are no absolutes in life."

She ignored me.

"Don't you want to feel his lips on yours? His hands—"

She shoved me and I almost fell in the sand. "We can't all live in a romance novel."

"Yes, we can."

Her eyes turned wistful and a little sad, so I decided that was enough pressure for one day. Hopefully they would find their way to each other eventually. Maybe with a nudge or two. I smothered my wicked grin.

Trent dashed back into the water to catch another wave. The conditions were perfect; the sun shining with promise and the wind whipping the waves a little taller. The dense crowd spilled into the shallows and lined the road behind us. Children with ice-cream smeared faces climbed the beach wall for a better look.

"*...a beautiful aerial from Trent Summers, earning him ten points and putting him way out in front...*"

Maya jumped up and down, pumping my arm along with her. Trent's father stuck his fingers in his lips and wolf whistled. Trent turned and waved before he dashed back into the water for his third wave.

My father sipped a can of Pepsi. "He's really good at this."

"He is," I said, managing a smile for the first time that day.

The next wave was perfect. It curled toward Trent, and he dug his arms into the water, keeping abreast. When he was in position, he popped onto his board, feet perfect, hips twisting to keep his balance. He threw his arms wide as he maneuvered along the crest.

Something flashed behind him. A smudge of something gray. It was only ten feet behind him and closing the distance, fast. I frowned at the indistinct shape.

"...Trent Summers is on fire today..."

Trent leaped into the air, his board seemingly stuck to his feet. He curled over and grabbed the edge of his board behind his front leg with his front hand—a classic skate-boarding maneuver—a melon grab.

That little flash of white dogged his every move, advancing, now maybe only six feet away. I took a sideways step and squeezed against my father. A heavy frown cut across his forehead. Had he noticed something seemed off too?

Trent landed his aerial and flew along on top of the wave. The gray thing remained on his tail. Trailing his every move. Every time Trent turned, it turned. A flashing gray triangle. A fin. The dorsal fin of a great white shark. Advancing. Now only three feet away.

"Trent!" I screamed, but by voice was snatched by the wind. From nearby, I heard a faint shout, one word that chilled my blood.

Shark.

My father stepped forward, squinting to see better. A couple of lifeguards dashed into the shallows, signaling to their counterparts on jet skis further out to be on alert.

"What's the matter, Cordy?" Maya asked. "What's going on out there?"

Trent gained some distance, performed another frontside three-sixty and shot up the lip.

"...another ten points for Trent Summers. He is owning this competition and—"

"Shark!" someone yelled, their voice carrying over the crowd.

"Oh no," I groaned.

My hands went to my mouth as the shark leaped out of the water, aiming its gaping jaw at Trent. Its black eyes rolled up, preparing to feed.

Maya's mouth fell open. My father cupped his hands over his mouth. Trent's parents gaped, unmoving. Their banner fell to the sand. The rest of the crowd on the beach spotted the awful image. A collective gasp weaved through the horde of people. The commentator fell silent. A small child screamed as Trent was plucked off his board by the jaws of a twenty-foot great white shark. Zale. It had to be Zale.

The loudspeakers crackled, and the child continued to scream. The horrific shrieking carried on the wind and swept around me until I could hear little else. Trent managed one last look toward the shore, toward Maya and me where he locked eyes with us, before the blood appeared and the shark yanked him under the surface.

Disbelief rained on my shoulders. It was five years ago all over again. Rooted to the spot, I could only choke on my own saliva. It was happening again. All of it. Numbness threatened to creep into my core, but I shook it off and sought anger instead.

"No," Maya whimpered, desperation lacing her voice. *"No!"*

She stumbled toward the water, clutching her stomach,

her face as white as the bubbling foam. She fell to her hands and knees, clawing at the water and sand. A wave swelled forward and washed into her chest, soaking her hair and clothes.

"No!" I dashed toward the water and Maya. Charging into the ocean, I grabbed Maya and pushed her back in the direction of my father. "It's not safe for you."

Do something, Cordy, she begged with her eyes.

"I'll get him." An uncontrollable rage built inside me. "I'll save him."

I faced the shallows. My eyes on the spot Trent had disappeared. Three jet skis charged over the continuous waves, their riders searching the murky water. The screams of the ambulance pierced the air as it charged across the beach and wove a path through the crowd. It stopped, sirens wailing, emergency responders waiting. But there was no Trent. He was nowhere to be seen.

I dove under the breaking waves and propelled myself out to sea. The shark appeared as a big, dark shadow a little way off. It held Trent's bloodied body in its mouth. I flipped my tail and directed myself toward it. At full speed, I charged through the churning water after the merciless creature, single-minded about my cause, when something yanked my wrist, and I was turned a hundred and eighty degrees.

"No, Cordy," Dylan said, his tone urgent in my mind.

"We have to save him," I said, struggling against him. "You can turn him into a merman. Please."

But Dylan merely held my wrists and treaded water.

I couldn't move, couldn't swim after Trent. "Dylan! Please! He was your best friend. Do something. *Please.*"

"It's too late. He's already been taken. He'll be turned into a selachii. If we interfere now, we will incite a war. A war we can't win. Selachii are stronger than us." His hazel eyes glimmered with pain.

"I can't let him die like this." My tail flipped, but he held steadily onto my arm. And then Nerida was there, and Tammy and the other merfolk, their eyes anxious and haunted.

"There's nothing we can do. I'm sorry, Cordy. I love him too. But he's not dead. He will live a life under the water," Dylan said.

A sob escaped my throat. "But not with us."

"No, not with us."

I struggled against him. I wanted to rail and fight and hit and punch and kill. But it was useless. Dylan was my brother, and the merfolk were my friends.

"I can't let him go like this." I made one last half-hearted attempt to follow the shark. But I could no longer see it, and I had no idea where it had taken Trent.

I retreated to the middle of the group of merfolk. Flipper nuzzled his nose into my chest. I held onto his fin, and he and Dylan led me back to shore. In the shadowy waters of the pier, he hugged me once more before he returned to the ocean.

Emerging from the water on my legs, I picked Maya out of the crowd. The ambulance was parked by the lifeguard station, its blue light revolving and siren blaring. Coastguards on jet skis continued to crisscross the water. They wouldn't find anything. Trent's mother wept on her knees, as his father rubbed her back and muttered indecipherable things. I couldn't find my father. Maya ran toward me.

I could barely meet her hopeful gaze. "I was too late. I'm sorry. He'll be a selachii now."

She stumbled and fell. I helped her to her feet, and she clutched at my hand. "At least he's alive."

"That's something."

"Maybe his parents will take comfort from that." She turned toward the devastated couple.

"No, Maya," I said. "We can't tell them he exists as half human and half shark. We don't know what the selachii have planned for him. It's better he's dead."

She nodded, and then the tears ran down her cheeks. "I love him," she said. "I really, really love him."

"We'll find him again. And we'll make Zale pay. We'll find the pearl and give Trent back his legs, united," I spat through clenched teeth. I looked at my legs. "Did anyone see my tail?"

Maya shook her head. "No, too busy looking for Trent."

I sighed with relief and led her along the beach, back toward Trent's parents.

"Cordy! Thank God!" Dad grabbed me and squeezed me tight. "I've been running up and down the beach looking for you." He pushed me away until I was at arm's length and peered into my eyes suspiciously. "What the hell did you think you were going to do? Go head-to-head with a great white shark? Seriously, Cordelia, of all the asininely stupid things to do. You could have been killed."

"I..." But what would I have done if I'd caught up with Trent and Zale? My father was right, I didn't stand a chance against a shark, particularly that murderous shark. "I don't know. I couldn't let it happen again."

"I know." Dad brought me close to his chest again. "I know." He stared out to sea, over the top of my head at the lifeguards in their futile search. "Something strange is going on."

Maya and I exchanged a look. It wasn't strange when you understood what was going on, scary—yes, but not strange. But I couldn't tell my father. I couldn't tell him what was really going on because then he would ban me from going in the water, and I would never find the pearl or see Dylan again.

CHAPTER NINETEEN

Trent's body was never found. Of course not. Maya and I had known it wouldn't be. To everyone else it appeared he'd been lost to the ocean. A week later, he was officially declared dead.

Dad, Maya, and I arrived at the strip of beach where plastic chairs had been set up for his memorial. A smiling photo of Trent atop his surfboard had been enlarged to almost life size and erected at the front of the seats. Trent's parents sat at the front, his mother crying quietly, his father staring at the steel-gray ocean. An overcast sky shielded us from the sun, and a grief-stricken wind caused small eddies of sand to whisk across our feet.

When the seats filled and students of Point Loma High spilled onto the beach, Trent's father walked to the podium with a wireless microphone. As he switched it on the loud-speakers crackled. His gaze skimmed across the top of the quiet congregation. He cleared his throat and looked at his feet.

"Trent was my son." His voice shook, and he paused, coughed, looked in danger of passing out.

Maya rose and went to his side. He nodded at her, and she turned to face the crowd of mourners with him.

"Trent was my son," his father tried a second time as he held onto Maya. "We loved him dearly." He indicated his wife and then put his arm around Maya to include her in the sentiment. "Although his death was a tragic accident and everything is being done to find the shark responsible, I take a small comfort from the fact he died doing what he loved and that his death was quick. To see a child suffer..." Another long pause. "He was my son, and we love him, and we will miss him every day." He returned the mic to the podium and took his seat.

As the emotions churned through me, I promised myself I'd break the god-forsaken curse and return Trent to the land. I didn't care that only one species could wield the pearl's power; I would find a way to make it work for both the merfolk *and* the selachii, or so help me God, I would take down the High Council myself. And maybe Wade too.

He hadn't bothered to approach me in the days since Trent's attack. At the very least, he should have offered a heartfelt apology on behalf of his selachii leader, but none had been forthcoming. Instead, he'd spent the week staring at me from afar, with black eyes and a downturned mouth. But he hadn't spoken a word. Even Babette had left him alone.

A reverend stood at the front of the crowd, the breeze ruffling his long black gown. "Lovely words, Mr. Summers. We are here today to remember Trent Summers, his life, and his achievements. The high school surfing board have informed me he won the competition by ten points." He pressed a medal into Trent's mother's hands.

"Mr. and Mrs. Summers have decided to donate his prize money. The money that would have gone toward building Trent's surfing career will be used to educate surfers and other ocean users about the dangers in the water, and to make areas safer for surfers." He paused to allow an applause of support to ripple through the crowd. "Now is the time when I'd like to invite you up here to say a few words. If there is a story or anecdote or joke about Trent, then please, now is the time to remember him how he always was, full of vibrancy and the thrill of life."

Maya took the mic. She fingered a delicate, silver chain at her neck. "The world will be a darker place without Trent walking around here. I miss him, every hour of every day. Every second. I never got to tell him that I love him." She looked over the crowd and cast a quick glance at the rolling waves. Her lips curved into a sad smile. "I know if he was here, he'd be cracking a joke and making us laugh. I'm sorry to say I'm just not funny. Not like him. But I will see him again. I'm sure of it, and I will hold on to that."

She passed the mic to my father who reminisced about two-liter bottles of Pepsi and spilled bowls of popcorn ground into the carpet. The crowd laughed, the uneasiness of death shifting and making room for love and memory. We were now free to remember Trent with a smile on his face, a swagger in his step, and the ubiquitous sarcastic comment hanging on his lips.

One by one students filed to the podium, recounting a story here and there, about the first time he surfed, his first wipeout, his acting career, and the Disney movies he performed in. The crowd laughed and cried at the same time, relishing the person he had been.

At the end of the memorial the reverend led us in a hymn. During the last verse I felt someone watching me and glanced over my shoulder. Wade stood at the back wearing the same suit he'd worn the night of my birthday. His eyes found mine and a profound sadness hung between us. He strode away from the mourners, toward the beach and under the pier. He slipped his jacket from his shoulders and threw it to the sandy floor as he disappeared into the shadows.

My father walked Maya and I back to his car. He held onto my arm as he gazed one final time at the ocean. "Maybe they'll find each other out there," he said, his voice thick with emotion. "Dylan and Trent and your mother."

It was the third time I was tempted to tell him the truth, all of it. I looked from my legs to my father's face and followed his gaze to the wintry water. His heart would break all over again for the life Dylan had lost and for the life he was now chained to. And I had a hunch the relationship between the selachii and merfolk was about to become far worse than tenuous. I couldn't put my father in the middle of it. I couldn't have him running into the ocean to Dylan's defense. Zale was dangerous, merciless, and not particularly choosey about his victims. Or perhaps he chose with perfect clarity and cold-hearted calculation.

I couldn't lose my one remaining family member to the ocean, to the selachii, and a life of being tortured by the ashrays. I held my tongue and fought against the urge to unburden myself to the one person who always seemed immortal and who now, suddenly didn't.

Back at home, my father removed three bottles of ice-cold Budweiser from the fridge and set them on the counter for us. Maya gulped at hers and laughed when the foam trickled down her chin. I made popcorn, ate a handful, and then threw some at my father. It fell to the floor and he ground it into the carpet under his feet.

Later in the evening, Maya pleaded exhaustion, retreated to my bedroom, and snuggled into my double bed, leaving a spot for me beside her. I changed into a pair of sweatpants and a T-shirt and sat with my father in the living room. We didn't speak, but instead watched a football game on mute and listened to the ticking of the kitchen clock. The doorbell rang a little after ten o'clock.

My father raised an eyebrow at me and rose to answer the door. "Not a good idea," I heard him say. "She doesn't want to see you."

The hair on the back of my neck prickled and I clutched the armrests of my chair. An unwanted curl of heat settled in my stomach. *Damn him.*

"Please let me talk to her." I turned to see Wade plant a foot inside the door as my father tried to close it.

My father frowned, squared his shoulders. Now they were the same height.

"Please, if I can just talk to her, she'll see I've done nothing wrong. Please, Dr. Blue. I love your daughter. I'd never do anything to hurt her."

My stupid, betraying heart lurched at his words.

"It's a little late for that, isn't it?" Dad asked.

"I really hope not. Please give me the opportunity to prove that to her."

My breath caught in my throat, and blood rushed in my ears. My father took a small step backward, equally speechless. He turned to me, leaving the door hanging open, and looked at me blankly.

"I'll talk to him," I said, getting to my feet. "It's okay, Dad. We'll go for a walk."

Grabbing my denim jacket, I shrugged into it as I stepped out the door. Wade walked a few steps behind me, out of the drive and onto Del Monte. I took a left, toward the ocean.

"Well?" I swiveled toward him.

I'd forgotten how handsome he was. Even after all this time, I couldn't help but get lost in the depths of his blue eyes, like diving into the ocean. His lengthening sandy-brown hair fell effortlessly across his forehead, and the yearning to run my hands through it was almost too strong to resist. The salacious curve of his lips, a jawline that could cut glass, and those entirely edible dimples that begged for my lips. No. I hadn't forgotten, I'd just tried to ignore it.

I was momentarily taken off guard when our gazes locked and I saw the depth of his love sitting there. Waiting for me.

"What is it you think you can say that could possibly make up for what you've done?" I fought hard for control over my emotions. I wanted to lean away from him, but instead I found myself taking a step closer.

"I didn't take the pearl, Cordelia Blue, but I know who did."

We stared at each other. If Wade hadn't taken it, then I wasn't sure I wanted to know who did. I was afraid the knowledge might undo me. But equally, if I was going to get it back, I needed to know who was responsible for its theft. I stood there, gnawing on a hangnail, working up the courage to ask.

"Well?" I asked.

But I didn't get an answer, not right away, because four of his cousins appeared from the shadows. They circled him, slapping him on the back and offering disingenuous smiles. We were still standing on the road outside my house. How the hell did they know where I lived?

"Well done, Wade. I knew you had it in you." Jordan offered a hand, his ugly scar catching the light of the street-lamp. Wade ignored Jordan's extended hand and glared at him.

"We'll get your mother back yet," said another.

"The pearl is ours," said a third, with a furtive glance in my direction.

They left us, racing down the middle of the street, whooping and jostling.

"You said you didn't take the pearl." Anger laced my words and clamped my heart. "They seemed to think you're responsible."

"They're trying to stir up trouble. They don't like the idea of a selachii being with a mermaid." Wade sighed and shoved his hands in his pockets.

"Well, they don't need to worry, because we're not together." But I was angrier with myself, because when I looked at him, I was in danger of losing myself forever. Still, in spite of everything, I was completely in love with him and furious with myself for it.

"Cordelia?" He nudged my arm and pointed toward the beach. "Are you going to give me the opportunity to explain?"

Nerves shot through my stomach. In that moment, I could stay mad at Wade, I could blame him for everything. I could break the curse for the merfolk and get my family back. But looking at Wade's earnest expression, I suspected there was a hell of a lot more to know about the ocean shifter world. And I couldn't refuse even the smallest of his requests. It was impossible. I loved him.

"Yes," I said.

We stepped over the low beach wall, kicked off our shoes, and sank our feet into the sand. The November night was cool and cloudless, and the full moon bathed us in its mystical light, the man in it seeming to wink conspiratorially.

"It wasn't me who took the pearl, it was someone else, someone close to you," Wade said.

There were only two other people I had told of the existence of the pearl. My two best friends. The thought that one of them might have...the hurt stabbed deeply. The world, and my position in it, turned again. But deep down I suspected I knew which of the two had betrayed me.

Tentatively, Wade reached a hand toward me and tucked one of my curls behind my ear. That one light touch completely undid me.

"Your hair, it's beautiful. The way it dances underwater... like a fireball sent straight from the sun to brand my heart with your name."

I guarded myself against the romance of his words and focused on the more salient points. Not once, in any of my searches for Dylan or the other merfolk, had I ever caught sight of Wade. "You've been watching me?"

"Of course. I needed to make sure you were safe."

"Safe?" I asked. "I thought selachii didn't attack merfolk."

He pulled a face. "I've learned a lot this last week. And that's why I haven't approached you until now. I wanted to make sure I had all the facts. But you're right, there are selachii who aren't opposed to hurting merfolk. *You* especially."

Zale must know of the prophecies. I was a threat to him and his devious intentions. "The pearl?"

"Normally I don't like to grass on another guy, especially one I like and respect, but he agreed I could tell you and try and make things right between us."

I braced myself for the revelation that wasn't a surprise.

"It was Trent."

I sighed, the hollow of my stomach filling with...pity, disappointment, sadness...but strangely, I wasn't angry anymore. It was hard to hold a grudge against someone who'd effectively been killed and then turned into a shark.

"What happened?" I asked.

"Caol got to him."

"Caol?"

"Caol is Zale's second in command...his best friend...his... I don't really know what. Apparently, he's been using my mother as a guard against the ashrays. She never said a word. Until I asked. She was trying to protect me, to make sure I didn't involve myself in a ...coo...afraid that Zale would kill me if I went against him. And Caol is the reason her wounds are so extensive." Wade kicked at the sand. "The first time Trent was accosted was during that first surf competition, the one where he wiped out in the tube. But the merfolk were there too, and they prevented Caol from reaching him."

I remembered when I'd first shown Trent my tail. He'd said he'd seen something in the water—a pretty fish. It must have been one of the merfolk.

"Caol finally got to him when he was on his own one afternoon. He took him hostage and asked him to find the pearl on land. Except, he didn't ask, he threatened."

"With what?"

"I'm not sure exactly, but it was enough to make Trent obey. Once Zale knew you had the pearl, it was easy from there."

"But how did Zale know? I didn't have the pearl at that competition. That was the day I found out I was a mermaid. How does Zale know this?"

Wade sighed. "You were right about him. He did kill your mother. Obviously, he knew Dylan became a merman, and he knew of your existence. He's been biding his time, waiting for you to come into the water and experience your first transition."

"So if I'd stayed out of the water, none of this would have happened."

"But you'd never know about Dylan."

A beat of silence passed between us as we watched the waves break on the beach.

"Zale discovered who your friends were," Wade said. "He suspected, when the pearl was stolen, the merfolk might try to hide it on land. As you're the only mermaid who can walk, he put it together and targeted Trent to watch you."

"You didn't tell him I had it?"

"Of course not." He touched my hand. A pressure lighter than air, but it still ignited a small fire. "I didn't tell anyone."

"Does he know we're together? Were?"

"He does. He did. But Zale would never have risked putting a pureblood in the middle of it. God, I feel awful. Poor Trent." He shook his head sadly.

Evidence of Trent's guilt flashed through my head. The diamond earrings for my birthday, the bouts of short-temperedness, suggesting Wade might be innocent of his own crime. He'd tried to warn me about the selachii. He'd asked me to be careful in the water because he knew they were after me.

"That's why my room was trashed," I said. "Because Trent didn't know exactly where it was."

"Yep." Wade swept a foot against the sand in a slow circle. Moonlit waves rolled onto the beach, whispering at us. "He was supposed to vandalize the whole house. But he couldn't bring himself to."

"Jesus. How could he?" Where was he now? What was he thinking?

"Betraying you was obviously preferable to what he was threatened with. I'm going to see him later, and I'll find out."

"Why did Zale turn him into a selachii? He did what he was asked. Why did Zale have to take him?"

"For exactly that reason." He lowered himself to the wall. "He did what he was asked. Zale has more use for him in the water now."

"Eesh." I pictured Trent beneath the surface, confused, threatened, and without a friend. "We have to help him. We have to find the pearl and help him. And Dylan."

"I thought you might say that." A long breath vibrated out of his lips. "And I agree. I will help you find the pearl again. Because it turns out Zale is building an army to take on the High Council. And I will have no part in that."

"He wants the Power of the Sea?"

Wade nodded.

"What would happen," I asked, sitting on the wall next to him, "if he was successful?"

"Hmm." Gazing at the pier, his eyes flashed black. Lights ran the length of the concrete structure, punching small holes of hope into the darkness. "A future that doesn't bear contemplating. If he got his legs back and was able to wield the Power of the Sea... Jesus...it'd be like the reincarnation of the Greek gods with Thor's hammer and Zeus's lightning and Poseidon's sea monsters rolled into one. Not to mention Vortex." He paused as he let the seriousness of his words settle around us.

"Vortex? The creator of Atlantis?"

"That's right."

"Why doesn't he step in?"

"Perhaps that is where Vortex is more like God—he believes in free will."

"But what is Zale planning?"

"Ultimately, I think he might be after Atlantis."

"Atlantis? I thought it was lost forever?" The coldness of the wall and the sand leached into my bones and my teeth started chattering.

"It is. It was." Wade plucked a pebble from the sand and threw it along the beach. "But with the Power of the Sea, there might be a chance. And once he's acquired the magical properties of Atlantis, he'll be too powerful to beat."

"We can't let that happen," I murmured.

"No, we can't. And Trent is going to help us."

I looked at the dark water, the waves crashing to shore with growing violence, and wondered if Zale and Caol were out there, hunting for prey, close enough to hear our whispered conversation.

"Is he okay? Trent?"

"He is." Wade poured a little pile of sand from one hand to the other. "For now. But because of his relationship with you, I know his list of duties is far from over."

"Shit." Tension tightened my jaw. "I need to do something."

"No, you're not safe out there." He dropped the sand and faced me. "That attack on your father in his lab? That was meant as a warning. The truce between the selachii and the merfolk is over."

"What am I supposed to do? I need to make sure Trent's okay. I need to find the pearl and give him back his legs."

Wade brushed his fingers against my cheek. "I'll look out for him, Cordelia. I'll make sure he's safe."

I stared at him. "I don't want you to get hurt, either."

"I'll be careful. As I'm from the original line of selachii, I have influence with Zale, and he has no idea I know the truth about him. I'll get the pearl back for you."

"You would do that for me?"

"Of course."

"Why?"

"I think we make a good team."

Is that all we were now? A team to take down a murderous selachii?

Wade blew out a breath. "I owe you an apology. I had no idea what Zale was up to. I was totally clueless, and he took advantage of me." Wade straddled the wall and traced a circle in the sandy concrete. "I thought he wanted to free the selachii, and because I was so worried about my mother, I didn't stop to question whether he might have an ulterior motive."

The what-ifs rolled through my mind, but there was no point dwelling on them. Something in my chest shifted, softened, and tension leaked out of my body.

"But part of me is angry with you too," Wade said.

My cheeks flushed.

"You didn't trust me."

"You're right. I didn't. I don't know what to say." My gaze shifted to my feet. I'd hurled around so many unfair accusations, all because...I didn't even know why. I had lashed out at Wade, because of what he was, and that wasn't fair. It was unforgivable. "I'm sorry. I didn't know who to trust."

He lifted my chin so I was looking at him once more. "You can trust *me*. It breaks my heart a little that you didn't."

I nodded as a tear trickled down my cheek. "Can you ever forgive me?"

He scanned my face, searched my eyes, an excruciating moment that lasted far longer than I was comfortable with. Then a flash of amusement glimmered in his pupils. "I already had."

A tentative smile slipped onto my lips, but I still didn't know what that meant. I wanted him. Not just as a teammate, but as a soul mate. Like Romeo and Juliet. No, not like them. I refused to let our relationship become a tragedy.

"So, what now?" I whispered.

Wade laced his fingers through mine, making my hopes soar and warmth flash over my skin. "I told you I would never lie to you, Cordelia Blue. I really want to know that you'll trust me."

"I do. I will. Absolutely." I couldn't get the words out fast enough. "Forever."

Wade's brows lifted. "Forever? That's a long time."

I shook my head. "It's not long enough."

He smiled, all his warmth and love going into that smile, and finally I could breathe again.

"Are we...is it...are we okay?"

Wade tilted his head, his gaze dropping to my lips before he locked his eyes on me once more. "Of course we're okay. I think we understand each other now."

"That's not what I meant."

"What did you mean?"

"Are you going to make me say it?"

"Say what?" Amusement flashed through his eyes and I could tell he was teasing me.

But I wouldn't be deterred. "I love you and I want to be with you. *Forever.*"

Wade made a pantomime of looking at his watch. "I don't know about forever, but I'll take the next ten years or so."

I gaped at him, then shoved his chest as he burst out laughing.

"Oh, come on," he laughed. "I had to make you sweat a little."

I arched an eyebrow at him. "I don't think you've actually answered my question. Not properly."

Wade's fingers went to the back of my neck, the heel of his hands cupping each cheek, and he brought my face toward his. He dipped his head, his lips hovering only millimeters from mine, and still he held my gaze. His warm breath swept over my mouth and I parted my lips, waiting for him.

As his lips met mine, the world melted away, leaving the two of us suspended in time. His touch started gentle, a light pressure of his lips, a gentle caress of his thumb as he traced my jaw.

The pressure of his kiss intensified, quickly became possessive, and I matched his hunger with an equal ferocity. His fingers threaded through my hair, pulling me closer, and I ran my hands along his muscular thighs, desperate to touch every inch of him.

He trailed a hand along the sensitive part of my neck, drawing circles with his delicate touch. Soon his lips followed, curving up to nibble on my ear, then along my jaw and back to my mouth.

"Wade," I moaned on an exhale.

The heat of his breath mingled with mine, a heady mix of desire and need. His tongue traced the curve of my lips, teasing and tasting, setting my skin ablaze with delicious sensation. With each tender caress, a shiver danced down my spine, igniting every nerve ending with a fiery longing.

"Does that answered your question?" he whispered.

I replied with another kiss, taking his mouth hostage, dipping my tongue into it, exploring with a ravenous hunger.

Somehow Wade shifted us off the wall and eased us onto the sand. I closed my eyes, surrendering to his touch, unable to deny the pull he had over me. With the waves crashing in my ears and the sand forming a soft pillow beneath my head, his hands swept over my body, under my T-shirt, cupping my breasts, gently at first and then with a building desire. Heat uncurled in my stomach, spread lower, taking me prisoner, until I had to squeeze my legs together to stop from crying out. To be touched by him was an experience incomparable to any other. I couldn't bring myself to make him stop. With my heart pounding in my chest, I raked my fingers through his hair, roamed his body under his T-shirt. I caressed his back, dipped my hand under the waistband of his jeans, touching his ashray wound lightly, hoping my love would be enough to heal him of his affliction. He flinched once, and I moved my hands away, pulling him against me.

Wade was my soul mate. It was a fact without question, and perhaps we'd been together in all our lives and would be forever more. I could never be without him again.

His hand drifted from my breast, sketched a path the length of my stomach, hovered at the waistband of my sweatpants. And then lower, tracing the seam between my legs. I gasped and arched against him.

His thumb found the most sensitive part of me, pressed a gentle pressure, circled lightly until a groan ripped out of my throat and I bit down on the lobe of his ear. His fingers hovered at the waistband of my sweatpants for a second or two, then he dipped his hand inside, past my underwear, and slid his fingers over my silken center.

He found that sensitive spot again, pushed gently until I called out his name to the moon and stars. And then his motions became more forceful, evoking a riot of sensations that spread from my center to the rest of my body. I couldn't move. And yet I couldn't stay still. I lifted my hips and ground myself against his hand, needing more.

There was a tightening in my stomach, a heat swarming across my skin, a building pressure between my legs I could no longer hold on to.

His touch was electric, sending shivers down my spine as his fingers slipped inside me with a slow, deliberate grace. His thumb traced languid, mesmerizing circles over my swollen bud, each motion igniting a spark that spread warmth throughout my entire being. I couldn't help but arch my back, my hips lifting instinctively to meet his hand, a silent plea for more. I ground against him, the need growing more desperate, until the pressure reached a dizzying peak. Then, with a blinding rush, pleasure burst through me, shattering and reshaping me in waves of ecstasy only he could evoke.

I collapsed back onto the sand with a breathy moan as Wade claimed my lips once more.

Just as I was about to slip my hands past the waistband of his jeans, twin streams of light highlighted the beach only a few feet from where we lay.

"Shit," Wade said. "Beach patrol are here."

He yanked me to my feet and we scrambled over the beach wall, grabbing our shoes, and ran halfway along the boardwalk, the lights bobbing after us, a couple of half hearted shouts telling us the beach was closed.

We didn't stop running or laughing until we'd made it halfway to my house. Then Wade pulled me into my arms and kissed me again.

"I don't know how you did what you did back there, but I want you to do it every night," I said.

Wade grinned. "We have the rest of our lives to do that every night."

"Forever," I said, and I meant it.

We stared at each other. Our relationship had altered. There was a depth to our love that hadn't been there before. A bottomless well of emotion that I would guard with my life. A love so deep I wanted to climb inside him. The fierceness of it stole my breath.

"Are you okay, Cordelia Blue?"

I managed a nod, and then, because there were no more lies between us, "I'm kind of scared by how much I love you."

He took my hand and laced his fingers through it. "You have given me your heart, and I will protect it with my life."

If he hadn't been holding me, I probably would have collapsed.

"Oh, and that reminds me, I have something for you." Wade removed something from his pocket. "I meant to give this to you on your birthday." He handed me a rectangular jewelry box. "But things went in a different direction, didn't they?"

A flash of guilt moved through me, but I shook it aside. I opened the present to find a silver charm bracelet. Two charms dangled from the bracelet—one a mermaid and one a shark. "This is the most perfect gift anyone has ever given me."

"You and me against the world, Cordelia Blue." He fingered the dangling charms as he attached the bracelet to my wrist.

"You and me," I whispered, as his eyes flashed black.

Nothing would ever come between us again.

CHAPTER TWENTY

The anniversary of my mother's and Dylan's attack began with a gray filled sky and a heavy feeling at the back of my throat.

I woke next to Maya. Muted light filtered through a crack in the curtain. It had been five years since I'd lost them both. *Five years.*

"How are you feeling?" Maya asked, stretching her arms above her head.

"Better than I thought." I rolled toward her and pulled the duvet over my shoulder. "Wade was here last night."

"Oh?"

"He didn't take the pearl."

"Seriously?" She sat up. "Who did?"

"Trent," I said.

"Oh no." She rubbed her eyes.

"He was under duress, but he's going to help get it back."

"When can we see him?"

"After we visit the cemetery. Wade says we can find him by the rock pools."

"You're back together? With Wade?"

I grinned. "Yes, we're back together."

"I'm so happy for you, Cordy." She hugged me. "At least love gets to work out for one of us."

"We'll get Trent his legs back. Just you wait. I'll figure it out. And then you and Trent can ride off into the sunset and live happily ever after."

"I hope so. I miss him so much already."

An hour later, after I'd showered and dressed in somber colors for a second day, my father planted breakfast before Maya and me—fried eggs and toast. Maya pushed her glasses up her nose. She'd taken to wearing them most of the time now, rather than hunting for her hidden contact lenses. The three of us sat at the breakfast bar in silence. It seemed we were all unsure what to say, how to mark the day, which words would do it justice. Instead we said nothing and ate our eggs.

Dad flicked on the TV in an attempt at normality. The news channel burst onto the screen and a reporter spoke breathlessly into the camera.

"...it's the fifth attack in three months. This behavior is unprecedented..."

The beach appeared behind her. It could have been anywhere along the Californian coast.

"...another great white attack, plucking three victims from their catamaran, killing them..."

"What the hell is going on?" Dad exploded off his stool and marched toward the TV.

Maya glanced at me and jutted her chin at my father.

No. I shook my head. "It's too dangerous for him," I whispered. "When we break the curse. When we take Zale down. Then we can tell him."

Dad returned to the breakfast bar and put a hand on my shoulder. "Cordy, I know you asked me not to go diving. And now I understand. Something strange is going on out there. But I'm asking the same of you. No going in the ocean, okay?"

"Okay, Dad," I lied.

His grip tightened. "Promise me."

"I promise." I crossed my fingers behind my back, hoping the childish gesture would help ease the guilt of my lie.

There was a knock at the door. My father opened the door to Wade, in his suit again, backlit against a pale, gray day.

"Let's go," Dad said.

The four of us piled into my father's car, and he drove to Fort Rosecrans Cemetery, a stone's throw from his lab. Wade held my hand, and Maya tucked her arm through my father's. We picked our way among neat rows of headstones. The clifftop pathways offered views of both ocean and city.

As my father had worked for the Navy all his life, he'd been able to organize headstones for my mother and brother to be erected on the beautiful site. My father visited their graves, not only on the anniversary of their death, but during his lunch breaks or after work sometimes. He'd once explained to me that to have a view of the ocean, a view of his life's work before him as he talked to his lost family, gave him a peace he could find nowhere else.

My heart swelled with pride as we walked through the

rows of marble headstones. My family could be remembered here amongst generals and admirals and other military heroes. Although my mother and Dylan had not fought in a war, they were heroes too, for they'd died in the ocean, bravely, and during the most terror-filled of battles.

Their headstones rested beneath a windswept Cypress tree. Its branches stretched toward the water as if it longed to leave the clifftop.

"I miss you both," Dad said, as he laid a bouquet of roses at my mother's grave. He'd brought a bottle of beer for my brother, as he did every year. "Here you go. Enjoy."

A dense fog curled in from the sea, obscuring our view of the ocean and city. The whispering fog muffled the caw of the graveyard crows and augmented the sound of my pulse in my ears.

We held hands and stared at the beautiful headstones. On previous visits, grief had been my dominant emotion. Now, there were so many more. I clung to hope and pushed it to the surface, willing success for our plan to take back the pearl. The regret that I felt didn't just concern the attack, but of all the secrets my mother had never imparted. I wondered if, or when, she'd planned to tell me of my merfolk heritage.

Later, at home, after my father had fallen asleep on the couch with the TV remote in his hand, I covered him with a blanket and left him a note saying I was going out with Wade and Maya and would be back later. I stuck the note to the fridge next to a picture of the two of us at Shade's the previous weekend.

"Let's go to the beach," I said.

Wade, Maya, and I walked the four blocks to the beach,

but instead of turning right toward the pier, we stepped over the guard rail and turned left onto the rocks. We kicked off our shoes and Wade rolled his trousers to his knees. A foaming surf sprayed us as we picked out a route along the shallow cliff.

"Here," Wade said.

He sat on a flat rock and dangled his legs into the lurching waves. Maya and I sat next to him and waited. It wasn't long before a blond, bobbing head appeared in the middle of the white foam.

"Hey," Trent called, as he gripped a rock and anchored himself there. His shark tail was a dark shadow beneath the water.

Maya's eyes filled with tears, and she stretched a hand toward him. He grabbed it and laced his human fingers through hers.

"What kind of shark are you?" I asked.

"A bull shark," Trent said.

"The type of shark one becomes is a reflection of the personality of the one who turns you, unless you're born into it," Wade said. "Zale's victims will always be the more aggressive species."

"Are you okay?" I asked.

Trent nodded, then grimaced. "I took the pearl, Cordy. I'm sorry."

"I know. It's okay."

He kept his gaze on the rocks. "It's not okay. It's unforgivable."

Maya leaned toward him and pressed her lips against his cheek.

"I'm going to help you get it back," he said.

"We're going to find a way for everyone to get their legs back," I said.

"And punish Zale," Wade added, his black eyes narrowing.

"Are they treating you okay?" Maya asked. "The other selachii?"

Trent nodded. "Yeah. They're not so bad. It's the freaking ashrays that are the problem." Wade rolled his eyes in agreement. "One almost got me last night."

"Where is the pearl?" I asked.

"It's in the selachii den," Trent said. "Under Caol's protection."

"If we can work together, then we can get to it," Wade said.

Trent braced himself against a wave. "Of course."

"We might need some of the merfolk too." Wade glanced at me.

As if on cue, Dylan's dark head popped above the surface of the water, followed by a grinning face.

"Are we having a party?" He flicked his green tail above the water, daring the few who walked along the distant beach to look his way. "Maya, you got hot! You've got that whole sexy-school-girl-slash-geeky-glasses-thing down." He splashed her with his tail, then his gaze fell to her hand where it held Trent's. "Oh...when did that happen?"

"It hasn't," she said, snatching her hand away. "It's good to see you."

Trent turned toward his former best friend. The two of them stared at each other.

With a tentative smile, Dylan broke the silence. "It's good to see you again, buddy."

"You too."

And then they did that guy hugging, back slapping thing with a few dozen 'dudes' and 'sweets' thrown in for good measure.

"Trent's going to help us get the pearl back," I said to my brother.

"Good, because for a minute there I thought I was going to have to poke you with my exceptionally manly merman spear," Dylan said, amusement in his tone.

"We're going to need your help," Wade said. "And maybe some of the other merfolk."

"What's the plan?" Dylan asked.

"We're going to raid the selachii den tomorrow, during the day, when most of them will be out making other selachii," Wade said. "Hopefully we won't have to fight too hard to take it. And hopefully Zale and Caol won't be there."

"*Hopefully?* That's it?" Dylan raised both eyebrows. "That's the whole plan?"

"We have the element of surprise, Trent and I," Wade said. "They aren't expecting it. Certainly not from me. My selachii lineage is the oldest in existence, the most loyal." His eyes clouded. He was turning his back on his own people.

"They'll exile you," Dylan said. "If you're lucky."

Wade shrugged. "So I don't go in the water for a while."

"You can't do that." I nudged him. "What about your mother?"

And what about the pull both merfolk and selachii experienced, that tug toward the ocean which was a physical thing and impossible to deny? It would be like a human trying to deny himself air.

"I'll find another way to help her," he said. "If you get to the High Council, maybe you can plead for her on my behalf."

"Of course." I threw my arms around him. He was doing this for me. And Dylan. Denying his own mother's freedom, which now seemed so close, in the hope that I could somehow magically return legs to the merfolk *and* the selachii. *Oh, Wade. You have too much faith in me.*

Maya seemed to read my thoughts, for she reached for my hand and said, "You're going to break the curse, Cordy, and give everyone back their legs. And we're going to help you, *united.*"

"I hope so," I muttered. I hadn't yet met Zale, and I shuddered at the thought.

"Tomorrow, we'll meet back here in the morning, and then we'll get the pearl," Wade said, getting to his feet. "It was good to see you, Dylan."

"You too, now that you're back on our side," Dylan replied.

"I was never off it. That was a misunderstanding Cordelia and I had."

"It wasn't Wade's fault. I took the pearl, Dylan," Trent said. "I'm sorry. I'm going to help get it back."

Dylan narrowed his eyes at Trent.

"He means it," Wade said. "The only reason he took it is because Zale and Caol threatened him with Cordelia's life."

I gasped. Dylan turned a shade whiter than the cresting foam. Maya squeezed my hand again.

"Why? Why does he hate me so much?"

"Because you're the only mermaid who has legs," Dylan said. "You are the key to breaking the curse and his undoing. He knows that, and he's scared of you. It's better for him if you're dead."

"But we're not going to let that happen," Wade said.

"Trent, thank you." I bent toward him. "I was angry at the theft of the pearl. But now, I guess you saved my life."

He took my hand and held onto it as he bobbed about in the gentle waves. "And I'd do it again."

"Now you're a selachii, because of me," I said.

"No," Trent said. "Don't blame yourself. I had it coming."

"That's true," Wade said. "Surfers are the most at risk of Zale's selachii attacks. Not only are they the easiest to get at, but they're strong and vital and young, all the ingredients for a perfect army."

"He would have gotten me sooner or later," Trent added. "I'm too stubborn to heed safety. I would never have stopped surfing, no matter how many great whites I came face-to-face with."

A swift wind tunneled in from the ocean, flapping my dress and spraying seafoam over all of us.

"Until tomorrow," Wade said.

"Okay." Dylan slapped Trent on the back and shook his hand. He smiled at me and then dove under the water. Trent turned to follow.

Maya shouted his name, but the wind snatched it from her mouth. "Trent!" She tried again, getting to her feet, her throat straining with the effort to catch his attention. But it was too late, he was under the water and out of earshot.

"We'll see him tomorrow," I said. "You can talk to him then."

"Yeah, maybe." She crossed her arms. "While the rest of you dive into the ocean and leave me sitting here, in the freezing cold, wondering if you're dead or alive."

"You can't come with us, Maya," Wade said.

"I know." She cocked a shoulder defensively. "I just wish I could. And I'm worried. I'm allowed to worry."

The deserted beach reflected the anxiety in my heart. Desolate. Desperate. Dangerous.

But no, I had Wade, and my best friends. We could do this.

It was another misty November day, but the sun burning behind the clouds promised a brighter afternoon and perhaps a successful return from our mission. Although the beach was deserted, the three of us walked toward the concealment of the pier. Wade and I shed our clothes and approached the water.

"Please be careful." Maya wrapped her arms around her waist.

She wore a thick, down jacket, her hair in a ponytail tied against the wind. After dumping her backpack on the sand at her feet, she removed lunch and dinner and drinks to last a couple of days, and a first aid kit. The large red cross on the side of the box filled me with dread. Taking up most of the room in the bulging backpack was *The Mermaid Chronicles*.

I hugged her. "We will."

"Please bring Trent back." She wound a finger into the silver chain at her neck.

"We'll do our best," Wade said.

He made no promises. And I wondered then, consciously, for the first time, whether we would all make it out alive.

Maya nodded curtly, pulled her jacket tighter, and retreated along the beach. She slumped against one of the pier's pillars and slipped to the ground. Settling in, she heaved out the mermaid book and held it in her lap, fingers drumming lightly against the cover. She opened the book and stuck her finger in a page. "Next summer, we're going to the Coney Island Mermaid Parade. All of us. On legs."

"I'd love that," I said, as I edged toward the water.

"Look out for Aquaria, the hound, and the seawolves," she called after us.

"Whoever they are," Wade muttered.

"Maya. Stop. We'll be back," I called.

Wade took my hand and, together, we splashed into the water. We dove under the surface. His vertical gray tail swished as he propelled himself deeper. My glimmering red tail trailed behind me, glowing with purpose. We reached the rock pools where Dylan and Trent joined us. A few of the other merfolk and the dolphins hovered further away.

"I wasn't entirely sure you were going to turn up," Dylan said to Trent, prodding him gently with a slim, but dangerously sharp spear.

"I said I was sorry. I meant it." Trent's underwater voice had a gruff edge.

"Okay then," Dylan said. "Let's get this thing done."

Together we swam, merfolk and selachii, equally matched for speed, into the dark ocean toward the selachii den. Wade led us into darker waters where I flinched at every shadow.

"We're here." He turned to face me, pointing into the murky deep. "The entrance is below us, through an old shipwreck. Trent and I will go in first and get the lay of the land. Follow us, but not too closely."

The sunken vessel appeared to be a tall ship of the old world, one I imagined swashbuckling pirates might have commandeered to escape with their loot. The sails and ropes had long since disintegrated, but the wooden framework remained, giving a home to fish swimming in and out of a massive hole in the hull. Other unintentional doorways, created from the erosion of time, gave access to the shadowy interior. Algae covered the wooden framework, and an abundance of sea anemones, starfish, and barnacles gave the impression the ship was covered in jewels.

We reached the entrance and Wade indicated Dylan and I should hide at its edges. The other merfolk treaded water nearby. Wade glanced over his shoulder to look at me, his expression tense, and then he entered the selachii den.

"Wade, how's the newbie coming along?" I recognized Jordan's voice.

"That's what I'd like to talk about. To Zale, or Caol. I'm not happy Trent was targeted. He's a friend. I didn't want this for him." Wade spoke in an icy tone I'd never heard before.

"It's a little late for complaints, isn't it?"

A long silence ensued. Bubbles from my gill slits rose to the surface. Fish swam in small shoals beneath us, and seaweed drifted in clumps overhead. Dylan gripped his spear.

"I still want to talk to them," Wade said.

"They're out hunting." Jordan emphasized the last word.

"I see," Wade said. "When will they be back?"

I peered around the edge of the rotting wood. Wade and Trent treaded water and faced Jordan, who was out of my view. There were a couple of smaller sharks swimming around, and I wondered if they were selachii. Wade made a small gesture with his finger, toward Trent, urging him to move toward the far side of what looked like the main dining area of the ship. I spotted the pearl resting in a glass case on a pillar, and my heart skipped a beat.

Trent edged his way toward the pearl, and I held my metaphorical breath.

"He'll do nicely for the army. I wouldn't worry too much, Wade," Jordan said. "One might think you're not fully supportive of Zale and his mission to regain our legs."

"There's more than one way to do that." Wade's eyes turned completely black.

"Really? Why don't you enlighten us?" Jordan popped into view. His tail swished, and his eyes were black. Tattoos covered his torso and arms. They were mostly pictures of sharks and sea snakes, but in the middle of his back was the enormous head of Medusa and her snake-hair wriggled when Jordan moved.

"Well, well, well, what do we have here?" The voice filled

my head. Thick and gruff, it resonated deeper than the echoes in La Jolla's sea caves.

I turned, slowly, as something like scurrying rodents raced down my spine. Dylan and I locked gazes as a dark shadow blocked out the sun. Dylan extended his spear, ready to defend himself. But as he completed the turn before me, his eyes went wide, and I wondered if the spear would be any use.

"You're easy to spot, Cordelia, with your red hair and tail. We could see you from miles away," Zale said.

Although he was a great white shark, it wasn't his long tail I noticed first. The sheer size of his body caught me off guard. The sun streamed through the water from above, highlighting the curvature of his impressive muscles. He rivaled any professional body builder. Or wrestler. Or assassin. With his arms crossed, his biceps bulged alarmingly. The whites of his eyes flashed at me, emitting a danger I shrank away from.

He smiled, revealing rows of pointed white teeth. They reflected the light, which only emphasized their violent power. He swept his tongue across his bottom teeth, drawing blood from the sharpened points, and then he licked his lips and drew the blood into his mouth.

"There's nothing quite like the taste of blood," he said, and smiled wider.

"I don't think you'll be needing that." A second selachii swam from behind Zale. He plucked the spear from Dylan's hands and snapped it in two.

"Caol," Dylan whispered.

Caol reminded me of every street corner's worst nightmare, at midnight, when misguided youths wearing heavy gold chains and jeans around their asses swaggered across roads, arrogantly ignorant of honking cars or swirling police lights. And in their pockets would not be a pack of illicit cigarettes or a small bottle of whiskey stolen from the corner shop, but a gun. A big, black glistening man-gun with a caliber large enough to punch your heart right out of your body. Caol was one of those. His beady eyes flashed between Dylan and me and toward the entrance to the den.

"What are you doing here, Cordelia?" Zale asked, his bulging arms an impossible barrier.

"Wade..." I couldn't think of a reasonable explanation.

"Yes. I know about your relationship with Wade. I must say, it's caused quite a stir in our little selachii community." Zale's voice dripped with measured cordiality.

"There's a truce...between the merfolk and the selachii—"

"Is there?" he asked.

"Perhaps you don't see it that way," Dylan said, his nostrils flaring, and his chin jutting defiantly. "Considering you killed our mother, a mermaid."

"Ah! Yes. I'd almost forgotten about Samantha Blue. She was quite something." Zale smiled fondly.

"How dare you!" I screamed.

"Now, now, Cordelia. Let's not be getting all emotional." He chuckled. A deep, throaty ugly sound. "I gave her every opportunity to join the side of the selachii. She was a feisty one."

"She could never have been a selachii," I said, attempting to bottle my rage. "She was already a mermaid."

"It's not entirely impossible to switch sides, complicated,

but not impossible. It was such a shame, considering your mother held the last remaining keys to Atlantis..."

She *what?*

Zale took in the surprise on our faces. "But you didn't know that. Mommy dearest didn't share her secrets with you. Oh, the irony!" He laughed from the depths of his belly and then cut it off abruptly, levelling his menacing gaze at us once again. "We could have rediscovered Atlantis together, been free of the ashrays, but your mother chose not to help us. There was only one remaining course left open to her—death. And with her death, the last remaining chance of finding Atlantis died with her. But you're not here to talk about your mother, are you?"

An altercation erupted behind us. A ricochet of shouts emerged from the ship, and the current strengthened around me.

"You're the reason she was afraid of the water," I realized aloud. "The reason she was nervous every time we went sailing."

"I did give her numerous chances," Zale said.

"You ignored the truce, and you killed her." Dylan jabbed a finger at him.

"And I can forget about it again." Zale's voice boomed toward us, scaring small fish. "If you're here to take the pearl. Are you here for the pearl, Cordelia? Dylan?" He looked between my brother and me. Uncrossing his arms, he rested his hands on his hips, or where they would be if they weren't covered by his shark skin.

Dylan and I exchanged a look. There was nothing we could do. Dylan glanced toward his broken spear, but I didn't think it would have been much help against the formidable selachii to begin with. This was the moment when it was going to go down. Zale and Caol waited. Several sharks swam above their heads, their toothy mouths glittering with need.

"Now, Trent," Wade shouted from within the den.

"Why don't we go in and see what the fuss is about?" Zale suggested.

Zale, Caol, Dylan, and I entered through the hole of the ship as Trent smashed the glass box holding the pearl and wrapped his fingers around it. Jordan and another selachii were on him immediately. Trent managed an underhand throw toward Wade. The pearl sped through the water, defying the ocean's currents, straight into Wade's waiting palm.

"Wade? What the hell is going on?" Zale's commanding voice stole through the water and pounded through our heads.

Wade squared his chest at his selachii leaders. "I'm giving the pearl back to the merfolk."

"No, you're not." Caol streaked toward him, eyes flashing and jaws snapping.

"I don't think you're thinking this through," Zale growled. "Are you not worried about the safety of your mother? Those ashray wounds...without the proper treatment...I don't like to think about her chances."

Bubbles erupted out of Wade's gill slits. "She'll understand."

Wade and Zale faced each other, Wade's eyes flashing black and Zale's flashing white. The moment hung in the air, the presentiment of danger and violence and death. And then the proverbial hit the fan, and the whole world turned red with blood.

Caol darted to Trent where he was being held by Jordan and another selachii, and stabbed him with Dylan's broken half spear, the splintered, damaged half. Trent's eyes rolled into the back of his head and blood oozed from the wound under his ribs, the spear protruding.

Before I could help my friend, Zale lunged at me. As he pounced, his body turned a dull gray and his eyes rolled black. His jaw elongated and revealed two more lines of jagged teeth. He turned full shark and snapped at me, intent on only one thing—to kill me.

"No!" Dylan shouted, pushing me out of the way.

Zale's jaws clamped down. But they didn't miss entirely. Dylan screamed, and my blood curdled. It was the scream of five years ago and it brought it all back. Zale had closed his mouth on Dylan's shoulder. I swam toward the struggling pair and dug my thumb into the sponginess of Zale's eye. Blood spurted from the socket, and his agonized wail ricocheted inside my head. But he released Dylan, who swam toward the exit hole, clutching his shoulder and leaving a trail of blood.

I turned as Caol veered toward me, also having turned full shark. His teeth chomped around my tail. The pain of a thousand sharp teeth sliced into me. Caol thrashed and bit and sliced and chewed through my tail like I was no more than a rag toy in a dog's mouth.

"No!" Wade shouted.

He, too, turned shark, the pearl dropping to the sandy floor below. Although he was smaller, he was faster, and he swam straight into Caol's flank, bit down, and held on for the ride. Caol released his grip on my tail, and I scrambled away, leaving a second trail of thick, red blood. But it only enraged Zale and Caol more and they thrashed in the water, drunk on the scent of it, twisting and turning and lunging.

Their teeth missed their marks and gave us the briefest of respites. The water turned hazy with blood. Zale and Caol retreated somewhat to assess their own ugly wounds. We didn't waste the opportunity.

Wade returned to his half human form, retrieved the pearl from the sand and threw it in my direction. The magical jewel arced through the water, impervious to its resistance. I grabbed it and hurled it through the entrance hole, to Dylan. Wade turned toward the selachii holding Trent. He removed the spear from Trent's side, causing him to scream in a new agony, and stabbed it through the eye of a selachii. Then Wade turned on his cousin. Jordan received Wade's message, released Trent's other arm, and swam away. Wade pushed Trent in my direction, and I grabbed his hand and pulled him out of the hole.

"You've just signed your death warrant." Zale's voice infiltrated my head. But his words weren't directed at me, they were shot at Wade. And it wasn't a threat, it was a promise.

I hovered at the entrance, waiting for Wade to join us. Through the hole, Zale and Wade hovered face-to-face, sizing each other up. This would be the fight of Wade's life. Everything depended on it. I couldn't leave him, not to the mercy of Zale and Caol. Wade looked at me, and with a silent pleading in his eyes, urged me to go.

"We have to go, Cordy," Dylan said. "We'll be dead if we stay."

I gripped onto the ragged wood of the hole. "I can't leave him."

"You have to." He grabbed my hand and pulled me away from the ship, toward the surface and the circling sharks overhead.

Another fight took place above our heads. The sharks and the merfolk, swimming around each other, the merfolk scampering out the way of teeth and the sharks dodging spears.

I swam with the pearl in one hand and the other dragging a limp Trent through the water. My tail and Dylan's shoulder leaked blood, seeming to signpost the way of our escape. The merfolk kept the other sharks busy as we swam for our freedom, our lives, and our legs.

Dylan and I limped through the water, him powering his tail and me swimming mostly with my arms. The wound in my tail throbbed with every tiny movement. We held Trent between us, who murmured as consciousness floated back to him. When we reached Ocean Beach, I scrambled out of the water on jelly legs punctured with teeth marks. I threw the pearl toward Maya, and she buried it in a pocket.

Maya wrapped me in a towel. "What happened?"

The afternoon had grown colder, and the sun struggled to burn through the clouds.

"I'm okay." I gasped for breath. "It's Trent and Dylan." I pointed at the water where Dylan clutched at the sand and pushed Trent onto the beach.

Maya ran to them and dragged them a little way to shore. She opened her first aid kit and kneeled at Trent's side.

"You're going to be okay. You're going to be okay. You're going to be okay."

Repeating the mantra several times, she inspected his wound. When she was satisfied he was no longer leaking blood onto the sand, she piled gauze onto the area and wound a bandage thickly around his waist. With his head cradled in her lap, she made him sip water from a bottle.

Trent sat up slowly, one hand prodding his bandaged wound. He winced when he fingered a sensitive area. Leaning on his opposite elbow, he shifted away from the pain. Maya shoved some painkillers in his mouth and then turned to Dylan.

She bandaged his shoulder next and then moved onto my leg. Teeth marks decorated the length of my calf, but they weren't deep, and the bleeding had stopped. She spent the next half hour scurrying between the three of us, checking on our bandages, asking if we needed more pain relief, and feeding us sips of water. Only when we begged her to sit for the millionth time and reassured her again we were fine, did she finally sit. But she kept a frown on her forehead, and her gaze shifted warily between us and the ocean.

"We're okay," Trent said. "We're all okay."

I looked at the water. "We're not all okay." A sob bubbled from my throat.

"Shh." Maya stroked my damp hair and rubbed my back.

"I have to go back. I have to go back for him," I said.

"Not now, Cordy," Dylan said. "Let me talk to the other merfolk. We'll organize a group, a big group with lots of spears. Spears tipped with poisonous coral. Then we'll return for him."

"It'll be too late!" I pounded a fist into the sand.

"They're not going to kill him," Trent said. "Despite what Zale said. Wade's selachii family is royalty. They wouldn't dare."

"I don't think Zale cares about that," I said. "He certainly didn't care about the truce when he killed my mother, and I don't think the threat of Wade's family lineage is enough to stop him." I curled on my side and rested my head in Maya's lap. Tears escaped as I lay there staring at the ocean, watching the waves crest in their eternal motion. Would I ever see the love of my life alive again?

"Maybe Wade got the better of them," Trent said. "Or maybe he had help. He's not the only selachii who's unhappy with current leadership."

I didn't reply. I couldn't. In my mind I was picturing Wade's brave face as he looked toward me, as he urged me to ignore every instinct and leave his side. I had listened for one reason only—the pearl and the power it could wield, that it *would* wield. I'd promised I would give everyone back their legs. I'd promised Wade I would help the merfolk *and* the selachii. Nothing was going to stop me now.

"I would kill for a beer," Dylan said. He lay on his stomach, chin in cupped hands, tail lying flat against the sand. "I haven't had a beer for—"

"You've never had a beer." Trent flicked his shoulder.

Dylan rolled his eyes. "I'm sick of coconut magic."

"Dude, that is strong stuff," Trent said. "Almost took the hair off my balls."

"Next time, guys," Maya said. "I'll bring you both beers next time."

Listening to the conversation of my friends, my eyelids drooped and I drifted off into a semi-conscious state, distanced from emotion. I couldn't allow myself to feel right now. Contemplating the fate that had befallen Wade was too much for me—it would paralyze me, and I wouldn't be able to think, eat, breathe or even be. I couldn't function without him by my side. We were already two sides of the same coin, and I would never be the same if he didn't return from the ocean.

Numbness washed over me, filled my pores, soaked into my soul, and formed a protective barrier around my heart. And there I would remain until I laid eyes upon his beautiful face once again. I fell asleep with those thoughts in my head.

When I opened my eyes, judging by the descending arc of the sun, I'd woken to early evening. "Where are Trent and Dylan?"

"Dylan took Trent back to Mermaid Lagoon," she said. "They'll both be safe there."

"Good." I tugged the towel tighter to ward off the evening chill. "Wade?"

She shook her head. "I haven't seen him yet." She squeezed my shoulder gently.

"What was that prophecy you told me about?" I asked. "The one about loss?"

Maya sighed and then quoted the prophecy to me. Did she now know the entire book by heart? "*The journey to the sunken land will be filled with heartache and loss. The fire mermaid will need to be determined.*"

"I think it's safe to assume I am the fire mermaid. Everyone keeps remarking on my 'flame-red' hair and my 'fiery' tail."

She nodded.

"I've lost my mother. Dylan was taken from me. And Wade..." I couldn't finish the thought. "Although I haven't begun to search for the sunken land."

"Atlantis."

"Yes," I said. "And my mother held the keys to finding it."

Her eyes went wide. "Like the pearl? There's another key?"

"Don't get too excited," I said, scanning the ocean for shapes, for one particular shape. "I have no idea what she did with them. Where she kept them. For all I know she could have had them in her pocket when she died."

That scenario was entirely likely. I remembered when we were sailing, how she would fist her hands into her jacket pockets. I thought it had been an attempt to ward off the anxiety she felt on the water, but perhaps she'd kept the keys with her at all times, in her pocket, and was merely touching them to make sure they were safe. If that was the case, that would mean they were lost underwater. Impossible to find.

"But you do agree." Maya's eyes danced. "The sunken land is Atlantis, and you are destined to find it."

"It would seem so." I shivered. Atlantis. What did it mean? "Whether I want to or not."

"But first we need to concentrate on giving everyone back their legs," she said.

"Any ideas how?"

She hefted *The Mermaid Chronicles* onto her lap from where it had been leaning against one of the pier's pillars. "Not entirely. But I'm sure you need to do it with a selachii. There are many references to a combined power."

Wade. I wanted to discover the secrets of the pearl with Wade. I prayed it wasn't too late.

"Clear as crystal then." I drew circles in the sand and bit back a new wave of tears.

"Let's get you home," she said. "We'll figure it out together."

When I arrived home Maya handed me the pearl, and my father grilled me about cutting class. I'd failed to register, the school had called, my father had been worried, and I'd only recently returned home when night had descended. He'd been about to call the police. I told him I needed some time. Trent's attack. The anniversary of my mother's and Dylan's death. I'd wanted to be alone. His shoulders had sagged, and he'd given me one of his dad hugs.

"I understand," he said. "But you've gotta let me know what you're doing. If anything happened to you..."

I apologized for causing him to worry, said I wasn't hungry for dinner, and excused myself for an early night.

I lay in my bed, not sleeping, listening for the doorbell, hoping every car parking on the street outside was Wade arriving, coming to tell me he was okay. But none of that happened, and I spent the night in a half sleep dreaming of sharp teeth and black eyes and red blood.

CHAPTER TWENTY-TWO

*W*as he dead? Injured? Alive? Imprisoned? My thoughts cycled.

Tuesday morning. Homeroom. No Wade. Perhaps he'd returned from the water late or wounded and merely needed an extra hour's rest before coming to school. I held fast to the tentative hope.

Maya and I walked to class, or rather she walked and I limped on my injured leg, fiddling with the charm bracelet dangling from my wrist. During class, I waited for Wade's head to pop around the doorway, even though he wasn't in sociology.

In the frenzy of everything that happened yesterday, I'd forgotten my vow that I was going to make Zale pay. I laughed bitterly. The teacher frowned. Maya shot me a tender look.

Who was I kidding? Me, a mermaid, was going to make a twenty-foot great white shark with years of experience of killing, yield and beg for mercy? Not likely. No one could defeat Zale, not even Wade.

My heart leaped for Wade's safety, hammering around inside my chest in an irregular pattern like the tiny staccatos of a minnow's tail. The beginnings of another bitter laugh thickened my throat, but rather than risk more frowns from the teacher, I swallowed the internal taunt. I could do no more damage to Zale than the minnow could do to a pit bull. *Oh, Wade.*

I clenched my fist around a pencil and snapped it in two.

My anger simmered under the surface. Zale had killed my mother. He had imprisoned my brother to a life within the ocean. He'd caused my father and me such grief, and now Wade. If he'd done anything to Wade...I vowed again to make him pay, somehow. The memory of digging my thumb into his eye socket gave me a small comfort, the way the squidgy firmness had suddenly given, like a punctured grape. I hadn't hesitated. I'd stuck my thumb right in the corner of his eye and pushed. And I'd do it again. And more. I was capable of far more than I'd ever thought.

I spent the day walking from class to class, in a daze, Maya whispering softly when I needed to follow an instruction. My tentative hope that Wade would emerge safely from the ocean faded faster with every passing hour. When it was time to return home, I felt as though I trailed an entire lake of misery behind me. And that night? I didn't sleep. I lay there again in twisted sheets, touching my charm bracelet and holding fast to the small, silver shark dangling from it.

Wednesday arrived. A repetition of the day before. There was no Wade. Depression hovered. The ocean called to me, but Zale would be there, and he meant to kill me. I didn't intend to give him such an opportunity. That night I dreamed of Zale, rising out of the ocean and taking my mother in his jaws. I screamed, and my father came to me and held me in his arms.

Thursday. Still no Wade. Not even Maya's whisperings could raise me from the depression that crept into my heart. My classes were vague impressions, the teachers on mute. I stared out the window. I stared at the wall. Hope drained out of me. Perhaps I would go to the ocean today. Perhaps I would face Zale, and if I lost, so be it.

But I couldn't do that to my father. He was my one remaining reason to fight. But the exhaustion weighing on me was too heavy to lift. I wanted to lie down and forget, to lose myself in a private inner world where sharks didn't exist and nothing could ever hurt me again.

I dreamed of Dylan, the image of his panicked face, his scream echoing in my mind. And then I dreamed of Wade, his last look before I left him alone to fight. I woke and held the pearl in my hand. I hadn't bothered to hide it in a sock, but instead left it in plain sight in a glass bowl with a collection of other seashells where it blended in. Running my thumb over its smooth surface, I willed it to impart its secrets. Or, at the very least, to make its low thrumming noise, a signal it was doing something.

Friday. I removed the bandage from my leg and found my calf healed. But there was no Wade. That's the day my heart broke, slowly, like sand through an hourglass. My sand, my hope, had passed through the spout and there was no one who could turn the hourglass back over. I no longer felt whole. I would be forever changed. I was beyond repair.

I don't remember being at school. Maya drove me home and settled me on the couch. She and my father whispered in the kitchen.

"We need to do something," Maya said. "She's getting depressed."

"I know," my father said. "I've got an appointment with a counsellor on Monday. She'd been doing so well. I was proud of her when she started swimming again. I thought she'd finally gotten over it, but...maybe not." He sighed.

"It's not just that," she said. "Wade's missing."

"Missing? Are you sure they haven't had another argument?"

"I'm sure," she replied. "It was at the weekend. He was swimming in the ocean. He was attacked by a shark." Maya made up a story to explain Wade's absence, but it wasn't that far from the truth.

"Like Trent?" Dad asked.

"Like Trent." Her voice wobbled. "We've been calling the hospitals...his family haven't found him...we thought he'd gotten away...but there's been no word..."

"Why didn't she say something?" he asked. "Oh, Cordy."

I could feel his eyes drilling into the back of my head. I wanted him to come and hug me, but I was too listless to move or speak.

"I think she was hoping...he would be okay. And now I'm afraid," Maya said. "I'm afraid she might do something...stupid."

"I won't let her," Dad said. "I'll keep an eye on her."

The clock in the kitchen ticked. The doorbell rang. I winced against the sudden intrusion. I knew who it was going to be. Two cops coming to tell me his body had been found and he was dead. The brutal truth wormed into my soul.

"Oh my God!" Maya said, as she opened the door. Something in her voice made me turn around.

A needle of confusion penetrated my depressed brain. There weren't any cops on the doorstep or any member of Wade's family with sad faces and tear-stained cheeks. Would they even have the decency to tell me if something had happened to him? The apparition standing there made no sense, and I couldn't get any clear thoughts to form in my foggy head. Surely this was a dream?

"Cordelia," Wade said, running toward me. He wrapped his arms around me, lifted me off my feet and buried his face in my hair. His tears dampened my shoulder. "Oh, Cordelia."

"Wade?" I prodded his cheek to make sure he was real.

"It's me."

I fell to my knees, and Wade fell with me, and we kneeled there on the carpet, staring into each other's eyes, tears blurring our view of each other. "I thought you were dead." I leaned into him.

"Ouch." He winced.

"What's the matter?"

"I nearly was. Dead." He lifted his shirt to reveal a horrendous wound. A semi-circle of small punctures littered his back and stomach. The impression of Zale's jaws.

"It's good to have you back," Maya said. "We were worried." A sideways glance at me.

"Are you okay?" Dad approached and examined Wade's wound.

"I am now."

"Shark attack?" Dad asked.

He nodded.

Dad gently inspected Wade's stomach. "You were incredibly lucky."

Wade chuckled. "I don't feel so lucky."

"Do you need anything?"

"No, thanks, Dr. Blue. My family took care of me."

"I'm glad you're okay," Dad said.

"Thanks, Dr. Blue. Me too."

Dad retreated to the kitchen and left the three of us to talk.

"How did you get away?" I asked, as we both stood.

"I didn't. Zale went for me and shook me around like I was on some crazy fairground ride. He left me for dead. I was unconscious in the selachii den for two days. Jordan helped. He came to remove my body, realized I was alive and dragged me to safety. My father has recently returned from his latest fishing expedition, and he pulled me from the beach. I've been at home ever since, convalescing. It was touch and go for a while, thought I might have picked up an infection, but we selachii have a way of healing fast, and I was lucky."

"I'll say," Maya said. "And why didn't your father tell us? I've been calling every day."

"Because he's mad at me, and you guys. My father had pinned his hopes on using the pearl to help my mother. He's furious. Now that I'm better, he's kicked me out," he said.

"Your father has kicked you out?" I asked.

"Yeah." Sighing, he pulled me closer. "He's not happy I helped you."

"I'm sorry, Wade," I said. "God, I feel terrible. You did all this for me."

"It's not just for you, Cordelia, it's time to end Zale's reign. He's a dictator and uses violence and fear to control."

"What about your mother?" I asked.

Wade held me against his chest. "I've heard nothing. But I don't think Zale or Caol will kill her. My father is a force unto himself. He is the rightful leader of the selachii—

"I thought it was your mother who was the selachii?"

"She became a selachii when she almost drowned," Wade said. "Dad saved her. And so she's been stuck in the ocean for three years. She looked after the pearl. My cousins? All dad's family. I just didn't know how to tell you at the time, back before you knew what I was."

"So your dad will deal with Zale."

Wade nodded. "I hope. He didn't realize the extent of what was going on. The selachii leader must remain in the ocean at all times and with a family to raise and a fishing business to run, Dad passed the mantel to Zale without knowing who he really was. Now that he's back, he'll be dealing with him."

"This is...complicated," I said, kissing his dimple. "And you can stay here. Dad," I called to him in the kitchen. "Wade's having some problems at home. Can he stay here?"

Dad looked from Wade to me and back again, three times. He took a sip from an open beer bottle, slowly, taking his time to respond. "I guess it would be nice to see the spare room used again. But I'm afraid the only extra sheets we have are bold pink roses."

"He can stay in my room. With me," I said.

Dad nodded, a curt little nod of agreement and I'd never loved him more. "I don't want to hear...anything."

"Dad!"

"Thank you, Dr. Blue," Wade said.

"You're welcome." Dad retreated to the basement room.

Wade laced his fingers through mine and kissed me briefly. "Trent and Dylan?"

"They're fine," Maya said. "I've been to the beach most days. Trent's been accepted by the merfolk. He's safe, and their injuries are healing nicely..."

I vaguely remembered her telling me she had visited them. But such was the haze of my depression that I'd paid little attention.

"...but boy, can your brother drink beer." She laughed.

"He always was the wild one." I smiled and slung an arm around her shoulder. "Have you spoken to Trent? About... you know?" About the fact that she loved him very much and couldn't bear it if anything happened to him.

Maya shook her head. "No. I couldn't deal if he didn't... I'm relieved he's safe."

"You'll never know unless you tell him," Wade said.

"It just doesn't feel like the right time. Maybe later. We'll see."

"Cordy," he said. "The pearl. Is it here?"

"Yes. I'll get it." I ran to my room, scrabbled around in the glass bowl of seashells, and plucked the pearl from the middle of them. Running back to the living room, I showed Wade the pearl.

He gasped and laid a hand over his heart.

No longer white, the pearl turned a deep purple and swirled with striations of color.

"Oh, my goodness." Maya clamped a hand over her mouth and rose to her knees on the couch.

"What's it doing?" I asked, holding it with thumb and forefinger.

"I have no idea." Wade drifted to my side.

As he held out a hand, the pearl emitted its low thrumming sound. I remembered Nerida had made a comment about its noise, that it only performed in a certain situation, but she'd never finished the thought. Had she known a mermaid and selachii needed to use it together? Is that why it started to make a noise when Wade and I were in my room before, back when he first discovered I held the pearl? We'd been so close to the answer.

Wade reached for my free hand as Maya joined us. The pearl turned to lavender and then back to a deep purple. The colors swirled, faster and faster, as though the pearl possessed its own internal whirlwind. Then the whirlwind was surrounding us, lifting our hair and flapping our clothes. Maya stood with us, unaffected by the sudden wind.

"I told you," she said with a proud smile. "United."

Wade and I held hands. The quickening wind plucked my feet from the floor.

"What's happening?" I pointed to an opening appearing in the middle of the silent whirlwind. The entrance to a long tunnel materialized revealing nothing of its exit except for a vibrant, blue light.

"I don't know." A slow smile spread across Wade's face. "But I'm hoping we're on our way to the High Council."

"Maya," I called. "Get my father and go to the beach." Somehow, I knew that's where it was going to end up. And when it was finished, whatever it was, my father needed to be on the beach, by the pier.

A great flash of light blinded me, and then Maya and my living room disappeared.

Wade and I stood together, holding hands. The pearl was gone. I had no idea where we were. A deep, blue light surrounded us and blurred everything else out of existence. Encasing us, it pulsed with solid definition and created a private sanctuary within a perfect sphere.

"Welcome," a commanding voice spoke from the ether. A voice of dignity and distinction, of time immemorial and noble heritage.

Wade and I looked around. A few feet to our side, lit in a paler blue light, a woman sat behind a regal desk in a wooden, high-backed chair. Graying hair was pulled tightly into a bun on top of her head. Her cheekbones were high and authoritative, an old-school rouge applied in thick streaks. Her large blue eyes were wide and watchful, but in their depths, I noted a sparkling of maternal pride, and the crow's feet around them crinkled with affection.

She wore a deep purple velvet jacket with white cuffs that fanned out lacily over her hands. Beneath the jacket was a frilly white blouse buttoned high to her neck and fastened with an antique broach in the figure of a mermaid.

"Welcome." Another voice spoke from the lady's right side.

A second light shone and revealed a man, also seated in a wooden high-backed chair. But his chair was covered in a rich red fabric and piped with sequins. He was shorter, and rounded with a pale balding head, which reflected the seemingly sourceless blue light, and tufts of hair sprouted over his ears. He wore a white shirt covered by a double-breasted black jacket and a black bow tie at his throat. As he looked us over his eyes flashed black.

"Welcome." The third voice came from the lady's left. This one was deep and booming and made me think of Zale.

A light illuminated a new speaker at the table. The man's muscles were equally as big as Zale's, if not bigger. His skin was a warm brown, a deeply sensual tone. His face was broad, his jaw square, and he possessed thick eyebrows that accented his deep brown eyes. His forehead was tall and pronounced and he wore his lustrous, long dark hair in a braid trailing down his back. Shirtless, he'd adorned himself with leather bracelets along the length of his arms. Black markings covered his skin and both ears and both nipples were pierced. He reminded me of an ancient warrior.

"Welcome," said a fourth voice from the warrior's left. Another man. Elderly and gaunt, his skin sagged from his face. His eyes were set a little too far apart and his tongue slithered back and forth between moistened lips. Wispy, gray hair flew about his head in a mad-scientist kind of way, as well as out of his nose and ears.

"The High Council," Wade whispered and squeezed my hand.

CHAPTER TWENTY-THREE

The High Council sat before us, hands resting on the large wooden table, their hard gazes making me squirm. The world was dark beyond them and us, and I couldn't make out where we were or if we were on land or in water. Blue. Up and down and left and right. Blue light shone around us. Under us and in between our tightly clasped hands.

"Welcome," the lady said again. "I am Esmerelda, the merfolk representative. This," she pointed to the rounded man on her right, "is Shane, our selachii delegate." Shane acknowledged our presence with a minute nod. "This is Gal—"

"My name means fire!" The great booming voice interjected, and the man thumped his chest with a fist.

"Yes, thank you Gal," Esmerelda said, with a trace of annoyance. "He is the envoy of the dragon kings..."

"Dragon kings?" I mouthed to Wade.

"...and this is Edward, leader of the eelusionists."

I looked at Wade again. He merely shrugged.

"Together," Esmerelda continued, "we make up the High Council."

"I was beginning to think you weren't real," Wade said.

"Mmmm. As you can see, we are quite real," Shane replied, twiddling his bowtie. "And you have found us."

"Finally," Wade said, not without an element of irritation.

"If we made it easy for you," Edward spoke, raising his pencil-thin eyebrows into high arches, "then we'd have whole lines of people from across the different water species pleading and begging for us to intervene in every little skirmish."

"Skirmish?" I stepped forward. "I'd hardly say the death of my mother, the attack on Dylan, my friends..." I turned and indicated Wade's angry wound, "constituted a mere skirmish."

"No," Esmerelda said. "But then there is the Power of the Sea to protect as well."

Wade did a double take. "It's real?"

"Of course," Gal replied. "But first we need to talk about why you're here."

"The fact that you managed to reach us is a miracle unto itself." Esmerelda clasped her hands together.

Shane tapped the table with one, long finger. "We never thought you'd get your act together, united."

"We were told only one species could use the pearl to reach you," I said.

"Not by us," Esmerelda said. "It's been centuries since Atlantis was lost. Contacting us on Atlantis was easy; we lived there among everyone. But when the island fell, we had to protect the Power of the Sea from falling into the wrong hands, and so came here, to our blue chamber. It was difficult to watch both species blame each other for the loss of the island. And so one pearl was bestowed upon both species to share in the hope that you would unite yourselves once more. Which is what you did." She nodded proudly. "And not just united, but in love. It's taken the strength of your love to transcend centuries of antipathy and bitterness. And I must say, we've been impressed with both of you."

"A test?" Wade dared a step closer. "It was all a test?"

Edward narrowed his intelligent eyes. "We cannot trust you again without knowing you have put your difference behind you. So, yes, the test was necessary."

"I'm not keen on tests." I paused in an attempt to squash the emotion growing in my chest. Anger. I was the mouse who'd been trivially played with by the cat. I didn't want to be angry; I didn't want to ruin the one chance we had to regain our legs. "Especially if it means people have to die." I squashed harder.

"We needed to test the strength of your unity and love, otherwise there won't be a hope for our other causes." Gal pressed his large palms, and his point, onto the table.

"We want our legs back," Wade said, throwing his shoulders back. "Both the selachii and the merfolk. We want our legs back. We *deserve* our legs back."

Edward leaned back in his chair. "Do you?"

Wade looked each one of them in the eye. "Yes."

"Weren't you responsible for losing our homeland?" Esmerelda asked. "We still miss our beloved Atlantis."

Shane, the selachii, glanced at his interlaced fingers, a blush rising on his neck. "Now, now Esmerelda, there's no need to—"

"No," Wade interrupted.

"No?" Esmerelda questioned.

"I wasn't there," Wade said. "It was lost over three thousand years ago. I wasn't there. I had nothing to do with it."

"Ah, I see." Esmerelda toyed with the lace covering her hands.

Wade pointed a finger at Gal. "Wasn't it the dragon kings who stole it?"

"There has been a dragon king on the High Council since the beginning of time," Gal said, rolling the leather bracelets along his arms. "We sit apart from the rest of our species and do not intervene. I was not there when Atlantis was stolen, and I am not responsible."

"As I said," Wade replied. "Neither was I."

A tense silence hung in the air. I squeezed Wade's hand and held my breath.

"And the ashrays." He clenched his jaw. "That was an unnecessarily cruel addition to the punishment—"

"Careful there, young selachii," Edward said, holding up a chiding finger.

"They inflict horrendous wounds," Wade continued, unperturbed, and turned to show them the angry, red gash on his lower back. "My mother..." his voice trembled, "...her wounds are extensive."

Esmerelda frowned. "Yes, I can see how worried you are." She sighed deeply and conferred with her fellow council members. They nodded at her in turn. "We have been watching your progress, the blossoming of your relationship, and it gave us hope a united front would follow." She cleared her throat and touched her mermaid broach. "And we were right to hope, because you found your way to us, and we had decided," she indicated the other three council members, "if you made it here, we would grant you the use of your legs."

A portion of blue wall shimmered and revealed an image of Dylan and Trent splashing in the water at Mermaid Lagoon. I stepped toward the unusual screen, and my heart ached for my brother and my friend. The image was replaced by one of myself on the day I attempted to save Trent, the day I discovered my beautiful red tail. And then Wade in the selachii den with his mother, myself on Mermaid Island on my birthday with Dylan.

Wade pointed at another screen to our left which revealed the early morning Dylan and I were born, in the hospital room, two tiny bundles being handed to my mother. Wade gasped at another screen; an image of him about thirteen, swimming in the ocean. By the look on his face, it must have been the day he discovered his tail.

Our childhoods were laid out from the moments of our births—the scraped knees, the arguments with siblings and parents, the swim meets we both competed in, the medals we won, the many milestones in between—right until this moment.

The events cycled faster and faster and then I locked eyes with the murderous image of a deadly beast—Zale—and the attack on my brother and mother unfolded. My throat thickened. I choked down an indecipherable noise. Wade put his arm around me and hugged me tight. We witnessed the day the ashray chased him and hurt his back. I winced at the agonized wail that came out of Wade's mouth. And then there was the image of Wade, Maya and myself in my living room, the moment we used the pearl.

Esmerelda splayed a hand at the images cycling around us. "It is time for punishment to end."

Wade's hand trembled in mine, and one of his knees buckled. "Thank you."

Esmerelda held up one, bony finger. "There are caveats."

Wade squared his shoulders and faced the four people who were about to change his life.

"First, we will take away the ashrays. You'll no longer have to live in fear of them," Esmerelda said. I smiled at Wade. "Secondly, those selachii and merfolk currently in existence, who are found worthy," she emphasized the last four words, "will have their legs returned. But," she raised a second finger, heavily ringed with a series of blue jewels. "Those humans who are lost to the sea from this day forth and turned to selachii or merfolk, will not have legs. We can't have everyone returning to land merely to turn their best friend into a mermaid."

"Okay." Wade's head bobbed.

Esmerelda continued, "Zale and Caol will be punished for trying to start an uprising."

"I have no problem with that," he said.

"And," Esmerelda said, "you two must consider remaining here, with us, and joining the ranks of the High Council."

"You both showed tremendous courage and strength," Gal said.

"We need new blood on our council, a youthful outlook to help us keep track of the modern world," Esmerelda said.

"I can't." My head spun. "We can't. I need my brother. Wade needs to be reunited with his mother." My voice shook. This could all be taken away with the click of a finger.

Esmerelda sighed. "I figured you'd say that too. In which case, I have a wish—"

"Yes? Anything?" I asked.

Her blue eyes danced. "I want the two of you to find Atlantis."

Ugh. I could no longer deny the truth of Maya's book. Perhaps it was time to accept it. I was the fire mermaid. We were in the process of breaking the curse and returning legs to the merfolk and selachii and now it was our fate to find Atlantis.

"There's no way." Paling, Wade took a step backward and dropped my hand. "The keys are gone."

"There's always a way." Gal struck a fist on the table, denting it.

"Although we do not possess the keys to Atlantis, we know there is more than one set, and they exist somewhere in the human world. We can give you some of the Power of the Sea to help you on your way." Edward clicked his fingers and a stone pillar rose from the swirling floor. Atop the pillar rested a blue orb, about the size of a basketball.

"It's beautiful," I said, walking close to it.

"It is," Esmerelda came to meet me. She poked a finger into the moving sphere, and it disappeared into the depths of the orb. When she removed her finger, it was colored blue. She rolled her thumb across her finger and gathered the blue color into a ball. She placed the blue ball into a small box and handed it to me. "It might come in handy."

"Thank you," I said.

"You are a special girl, Cordelia." Esmerelda placed her hands on top of my shoulders and stared into my eyes. "The prophecies are right about you."

"You know about the prophecies?"

"Of course." Esmerelda laughed. "Who else do you think put the book in your friend's hands? Maya? Is that her name?"

I gaped at her. "You gave Maya the book?"

"Let's just say we nudged her in the right direction. The Power of the Sea holds the prophecies, and the book was our way of making you aware."

"Why?" Wade asked.

"Although we remain physically separate from you, we are not without emotions; hope for Atlantis, affection for the two of you. We thought you two needed a little help to find us," Esmerelda said.

She took my hands in hers. "Many of the prophecies are about you, Cordelia. You are the fire mermaid. I felt it, the moment of your mermaid birth, when you discovered your tail. I felt it deep in the marrow of my bones, and I knew you had arrived. You are one of a kind, with your red tail, and your mermaid lineage is the oldest in existence. It is you, Cordelia, who has the power to find Atlantis. With Wade. Together. United. It's been a long time," she said, wistfully. "But I have every faith in you."

I nodded, several times, my thoughts spinning, my

stomach churning, equal parts excitement and fear threading through my veins.

"In both of you," Shane said, coming to stand by Wade's side like a proud uncle.

"Heed Maya's advice," Esmerelda said. "She has an affinity for the way of the ocean shifters, and she comes from a long line of prophecy interpreters."

"She doesn't know who her parents are," I said.

"No, they were killed in the sea while protecting the merfolk," Esmerelda said. "Maya's place is right alongside us as she has a special ability to understand *The Mermaid Chronicles*. Although her fate is as yet undecided, she is important. Keep her close and protect her."

Perhaps this was why Maya had always loved Disney's Ariel, why she was drawn to the ocean and the lore of merfolk, why she had fallen in love with someone who loved the ocean, the waves, as much as she did.

"We will," Wade said.

"Now," Esmerelda clicked her fingers, "let's see about those legs."

The shimmering and swirling colors of the chamber deepened. Blue light pulsated in rings, ebbing and flowing with an unseen tide. Swirling, faster and faster, until another whirlwind gathered speed within the chamber. I closed my eyes against a flash of brilliant light. When I opened them, Dylan and Trent, Nerida, Tammy and the other merfolk, Wade's cousins and other selachii had joined us—there were hundreds of people within the orb. The four council members stood in a line in front of everyone.

"Welcome." Esmerelda spoke clearly, and her voice

carried above the confusion and whispered conversations. "I am Esmerelda, the ambassador of the merfolk, and this is the chamber of the High Council." Gal, Shane, and Edward gave brief nods of welcome. "We have agreed to give you back your legs. You have young Cordelia and Wade to thank for that. They realized they needed to unite their cause, come together in friendship and love to use the pearl."

Another flash of light, but this time it was a calming blue that trickled through the chamber, and as the light touched each selachii and merfolk, their legs returned and they stood, teetering and trembling.

Some stumbled, others fell, unused to their new legs after many years in the ocean. But everyone smiled, and some cried. A selachii lady with sandy brown hair stretched onto her toes and laughed, long and hard. She walked toward us, toward Wade. As she reached him, she wiped a tear from her eyes and embraced him warmly.

"Thank you, son," she said. "Thank you."

"Glad to have you back, Mom." As Wade hugged her back, the jagged ashray wound and Zale's teeth marks disappeared.

"Cordelia, I've heard so much about you." She pulled me into the family reunion. "Thank you, too."

A tall man, with a thick beard and mustache, approached from behind Wade's mother.

"Dad," Wade said, dropping his gaze to the floor.

"Wade," his father said, staring at his son with black eyes. "I'm grateful for what you've done, you and Cordelia, returning your mother to us." He paused to include me in his unnerving stare. "But this doesn't change anything." His dark eyes narrowed. "It doesn't change what you did."

"Did you not hear what Esmerelda said?" Wade's mother stood between the two of them. "It's because of what he did that all of this is possible. We have our legs back, thanks to these two. They are heroes, Daniel."

His father remained silent. It was clear he didn't agree with his wife's assessment. But then the tense moment passed as Dylan and Trent barreled into me, wolf whistling and whooping and jumping high into the air.

Nerida joined us. "Thank you, Cordelia."

"You knew," I said to her. "You knew the selachii and merfolk needed to be united."

She shook her head. "Not that. I didn't know that. I only came to suspect that recently."

"But the pearl's vibration, you knew what it meant."

"I knew the vibration and the noise meant it was beginning to work. But I didn't know what the conditions needed to be to make it happen. But you did. You figured it out."

"That's not all." Esmerelda's commanding voice silenced our conversation and the revelers in the chamber. "There are those who tried to start a rebellion, an uprising against the High Council in an attempt to steal the Power of the Sea." She gestured toward the beautifully glowing orb atop its pillar in the middle of the chamber. "They will not be given their legs. They will be punished."

"Where are they?" I whispered to Wade. I hadn't seen Zale or Caol.

Wade craned his neck to see above the crowd. "I don't know."

In a private whirlwind of their own, the two mutinous selachii appeared. Zale's eyes widened as he took in his surroundings. He cowered as his gaze swept over the four frowning High Council members. Then he noticed the glowing Power of the Sea, and a smile twitched at the corners of his menacing lips. But as Esmerelda spoke again, a grimace replaced his smile.

"I want you to know we have the power to grant the return of your legs." Esmerelda's voice rose. "We also have the power to take them away again, or to mete out any punishment we see fit."

Gal raised a hand and Zale and Caol's whirlwind accelerated. They spun in circles, faster and faster, until they knocked against each other and cried out. Their screams filled the chamber as the merfolk and selachii looked upon them silently. Zale turned full shark and leaped toward the council with a wide jaw and gnashing teeth. But the whirlwind carried him away. Caol screamed once more, and then they were gone.

"Where did they go?" Wade asked.

"To a place where they can't bother anyone ever again," Gal replied, letting his hands float back to his sides.

"It's selachii hell." Shane smiled a wicked smile. "They will be contained in a whirlpool with a hundred ashrays."

Edward walked a circle around the Power of the Sea. "It's what they deserve."

"Quite," Esmerelda said.

"While I don't want to risk your wrath..." Wade stepped toward the council members. "And as much as those two deserve to be punished, in the spirit of moving forward, away from arcane punishments, perhaps you could take the ashray element of their imprisonment away."

Four pairs of eyes swiveled in Wade's direction. He winced. I tucked my arm in his—united.

"We've done it again." Esmerelda laughed and gripped his shoulder. "Yes, I do see your point. I will concede to take the ashrays away, but they will stay in their whirlpool prison where they can't hurt anyone else."

Wade nodded.

She gave him a sideways glance. "Are you sure you won't consider staying here and becoming a member of the High Council?"

"No thank you."

"Very well," she replied.

Esmerelda addressed the selachii and merfolk behind me. "The rest of you can return to your lives. By all means reunite with your families, but please heed this warning: keep the existence of ocean shifters a secret from humans, from those who do not need to know, otherwise a door will open, one filled with pain and sadness, and it won't be easy to close."

Her words tempered a few of the smiles in the gathering. She inspected the merfolk and selachii for another minute, locking gazes with a few, nodding her head at others, and then the crowd disappeared. They winked out of the giant blue chamber faster than a streak of lightning.

"Where did they go?" Wade asked. We were alone again with the four High Council members.

"Back to the ocean." Esmerelda offered a jubilant smile. "I have something else for the two of you, if you're sure I can't tempt you to stay?"

Man, she was persistent. Wade and I shook our heads.

"Here." She handed us each a large, white pearl. "If you need to contact us again. While we can come to you whenever we wish if we feel we need to intervene, it's not easy for you to come here. You need a pearl. It is the transportation method. Take them." She laid a hand on both of us. "Use them wisely. You don't need to be together to use these. One of you will suffice."

"Thank you," I said, closing my palm around the pearl.

"I expect you'll be wanting to get back," she said to me, a flicker of tenderness moderating the lines on her face. "In time for a special reunion."

Dylan. My father. My heart stuttered in my throat.

"Take care of the Power of the Sea, Cordelia." Esmerelda took one of my hands in both of her own. "Guard the pearls, protect Maya, and search for Atlantis."

Her image faded, her features softening until they dissolved into the air, like a fuzzy hologram. I looked to the other council members. They too dissolved from view.

"How?" I asked before they faded from view completely. "How do I find Atlantis?"

Esmerelda merely shook her dissolving head. But she smiled, and I could hear her voice in my mind. "Trust your instincts. You are the fire mermaid. You are the one."

And then they were gone. Their essence evaporated around us, leaving Wade and me alone. Everything was dark. But we were no longer in the giant blue orb. We were in the ocean. Submerged, in shallow water, beneath the columns of the pier.

"Your hair," Wade said.

Looking over my shoulder, my hair fanned out in a fiery array, long and flowing as if I'd never cut it. I swished my flaming tail in the water, and small fish came to inspect its dazzling sparkle. I really did look like I was on fire.

Wade and I swam to shore. We emerged on legs, the pearls and the box containing the Power of the Sea grasped firmly in tight fists, to find a huge gathering on the beach. Dusk reigned over the horizon, its hues of deep pinks and soft oranges filling the sky. At the deepest part, where the sun dipped beneath the water, a swatch of vibrant red made the sky appear on fire too.

"There you are." Wrapped in a thick wool jacket, Maya rushed toward us. "United. I told you, didn't I?" She jumped about on the beach, kicking sand into the air, a triumphant smile on her lips.

"Yes, you did." I threw my head back and laughed, the weight of my lengthened hair tugging at my scalp.

"You've done it. Together, you did it." She pointed to the gathering of people on the beach, stumbling around like drunks, adjusting to legs once again.

Wade grabbed my hand and kissed the back of it. "We did."

"Where's my father? Dylan?" I whispered, afraid if I spoke any louder, my voice might dissolve this magical dream, and I would be left standing on the beach, alone.

"Here." Dylan smiled an impish smile and wrapped his arms around me. He wore jeans and a hoodie. It was weird.

"Dad?" I asked.

My father emerged from the shadows of the pier in his shorts and sandals and a new Navy baseball cap set backward on his head. He stumbled toward us, as if he too had only recently regained the use of legs, and when he reached Dylan, he clawed at him in disbelief. He fell to his knees and cried.

"Dad," Dylan said. "It's okay. I'm here."

I helped my father to his feet. A swelling of triumph filled me as he and Dylan embraced. They both cried a flood of tears, trying to speak at the same time.

"I've missed you so much," Dad said.

"I love you," Dylan said.

Maya, Wade, and I cried too, and my father widened his arms for a group hug.

The clusters of people on the beach dispersed to begin their new lives. Trent approached us with his joyous parents in tow. He embraced Maya and whispered into her ear. She turned and brushed her lips against his. He plucked her off her feet and twirled her in a circle, his lips finding hers this time.

After a few minutes, when Maya, Trent, Dylan, Wade, my father, and I had walked to my house, my father lined us up on the couch and posed his first question. "Will someone please tell me what the hell is going on?"

We told him. All of it. From the time of Dylan's attack to me discovering my tail, the merfolk and the selachii, the uneasy truce, the magic of the pearl and the existence of the High Council. Dylan and I took turns showing my father our tails in the bath. He wept again, with joy and the incredulity of it all.

"So this is what you've been up to all this time." Dad shook his head. "How did I not know?"

I placed a hand on his cheek. "Sometimes it's harder to believe the things that are right under your nose." I rubbed his stubble. "And, Dad, humans aren't supposed to know. This is a big secret."

"I can see that. Of course, I'll keep the secret." He kissed the top of my head and then handed out sodas.

Dylan swapped his for a beer, popped the cap on the bottle and swigged it down in one.

"I suppose we should drop the whole 'Dr. Blue' thing, if you're planning on staying here, Wade. The name is Chris." My father stuck out his hand.

Wade took the offered hand and found his arm pumped vigorously a few times. "Thanks...Chris. I think."

Dad laughed and took a swig of his own beer.

"It's not over," Maya said.

"What do you mean?" Dad asked.

"Cordy and Wade need to find Atlantis." She rubbed her hands together, like she was warming up.

"Atlantis?" Dad asked, as if he hadn't heard correctly.

"Yep," Maya said. "It was real, *is* real. And Cordy's going to find it."

I groaned. "Time and place, Maya. Maybe we can get used to having Dylan back before we go charging off on the next adventure."

"Do we have to?"

"I need a minute." I hugged her, remembering the council's warning to heed her advice and protect her.

Dylan reached for another beer. My father automatically swatted his hand away, then he laughed and said, "what the hell!" and passed him a second bottle.

Dylan regaled my father with stories of his life in the sea: his passing girlfriends—Tammy and he had broken up—evading the selachii, learning how to spear fish, the mermaid island and coconut magic, Flipper the friendly dolphin, Zale and Caol and their punishment. He talked into the night and my father hung on to his every word, only stopping to order pizza and answer the door when it arrived.

"Everything you do needs to be united," Maya whispered in my ear. "That's the key to all the prophecies, Cordy. I've been studying the book. It's so much bigger. The entire selachii history is in there now. I've figured out how to interpret it. It's all changed—new pages, new prophecies. Selachii and merfolk together. I'm sure you'll find Atlantis. *Together.*"

CHAPTER TWENTY-FOUR

$\mathcal{A}$tlantis.

I couldn't wrap my head around it. The myths and legends that surrounded the ancient island were true. All those books, those movies...were real, or at least offered some semblance of the truth.

When everyone had left or gone to bed, I grabbed Wade's hand and took him to my room. We put our pearls and the box containing the Power of the Sea into the glass bowl and buried them deep within the various seashells.

"Do you think we can find it?" I asked. "Atlantis?"

"I don't care about that right now, Cordy." He placed his hands on my hips and turned me toward him. The desire sparking in his eyes made my breath hitch.

His gaze raked unabashedly over my body, electrifying my skin, curling heat through my stomach.

"It's time," I said, reaching for the zipper of my hoodie.

Wade watched my fingers as I slid it open, inch by inch,

painstakingly slowly, teasing him even though I couldn't bear to wait.

The hoodie fell open, revealing my bikini top beneath. Wade's eyes roamed over my skin, drinking in every inch of me.

"Jesus Christ," he muttered.

"I think you'll find my name is Cordelia Blue," I said.

He laughed and reached for me, held me tight against his chest.

"Wade." I wrapped my arms around his neck. "It's over. It's all over."

And finally, the relief surged through me. The joy of bringing Dylan back from the dead, and Trent too. The vengeance of my mother's death soared though my heart and made my chest feel light and bubbly. But there was something stronger causing my skin to tingle with such intensity it broke out in goosebumps. It was the anticipation of Wade's touch, of his fingers on my skin, gently removing my clothes.

In the semi-dark of my bedroom, I tugged off his shirt, unbuttoned his shorts, and gave him the same once over he'd given me.

"I want you," I whispered. I took my time touching him. Starting with the curve of his arms, then ran my hands over the expanse of his defined chest, the tautness of his abs. All the time his hardness pressed against me.

I moved my hand to circle the length of him. With gentle strokes, I drew my hand up and down the silky hardness of him. He groaned into the shell of my ear and freed my breasts from my bikini. When he dipped his head to take a nipple into his mouth, every nerve ending went into overdrive. Never had I wanted anything more.

"Cordelia..." my name came out in a raspy growl as his hands wandered across my naked skin, touching every part of me, slipping two fingers between my legs. I almost buckled.

His thumb circled the desperate tip of my need, pressing gently, until I moaned his name into his ear.

"I like that I can make you sound like that."

I smiled against his lips. His fingers slid deeper inside me and his thumb stroked my swollen bud. All I could do was cling to his shoulders as I spasmed against him. He kissed every inch of my skin until I could do nothing but give myself over to him.

"I don't just want you," I whispered. "I need you."

Wade chuckled as he kissed me long and hard, then nudged me onto the bed. He pulled away to stare into my eyes, with such passion, with such intensity, I thought I might melt away. His blue eyes sparkled brightly, like the depths of a deep ocean, and then they flashed black, and I smiled at his selachii side.

"I've never done this before," I told him, handing him a condom. "Have you?"

"Once or twice," he replied. "Do we need to talk about it?"

I shook my head. "I don't care about the past."

He smiled and tore open the condom wrapper with his teeth. He handed it to me and I gently rolled it onto him, relishing his quiet murmurs as my fingers brushed against the most sensitive part of him.

"I love you, Cordelia Blue," he said, as his lips brushed against mine.

"I love you too," I replied, and lifted my hips to meet him.

He paused at my entrance, holding my gaze, making my muscles quiver in anticipation. I felt the pulsing need of him and a deep heat coiled low in my stomach.

"What are you waiting for?" I asked.

"I want this moment to last forever," he replied.

"Forever," I echoed.

Finally, he lowered himself into me. I clenched around him, pulling him deeper, until he paused once more.

"This might hurt. But only for a second," he said.

I nodded and dug my fingers into his rear, pulling him deeper. He thrust his hips and the moment of pain burst over me, quickly followed by an ecstasy I'd never felt before.

Our bodies melded into each other perfectly; my head buried into the crook of his neck, nipping at his skin; his stomach pressed flatly against the curve of my own. Our hips met as if they were made for each other, coming together with a desperate urgency. Together, with my legs entwined in his, we found our rhythm.

Heat danced over my skin, bringing with it a riot of new sensations that blew both my mind and my body. Spasms made my limbs jerk and I had no control over my movements, could only lift my hips to match Wade's even strokes, taking him deeper each time.

I wrapped my legs around his waist, clawed at his back, bit at his ears. My breath came in rapid pants as pressure built in the very center of me. A tantalizing pressure I could no longer contain.

Music reached my ears, but I paid it no mind as the physical sensations took my body hostage. A consuming wave of ecstasy shuddered through me. I bit into Wade's shoulder as the orgasm crested, streaking from my center to my fingers and toes, burning through every nerve ending, blazing across every cell of my existence. Nothing had ever felt so deliciously, exquisitely, painfully blissful. As Wade groaned in my ear, his own release mirroring mine, I arched my back and pulled him deeper, unable to keep from crying out.

Wade called my name, twice, and collapsed against me. But then he raised his head and frowned. "What's that noise?"

It sounded like pan flutes. I thought I'd been imagining it, or that every young woman heard the fanciful, elusive notes during her first time. But the sound surrounded us, thick and visible, and it reminded me of ancient people in ancient times standing on green covered mountains in a dense fog, their lips blowing into flutes, creating physical musical notes that would take to the air and fly away like doves.

"I thought it was me," I said.

"No. I can hear music, or something, and it's getting louder." Together we climbed out of my bed.

"We need to get dressed, before it wakes everyone else," I said.

We dressed hurriedly as the music enveloped us. While it remained mystical and beautiful, the growing volume suggested it might be building to some sort of crescendo or explosion, and I had no idea where it would lead.

"It's coming from the kitchen." Wade darted along the darkened hallway.

I followed him. In the kitchen an eerie blue light throbbed through the room in time with the music. Wade opened cupboards and pulled drawers out. It was the set of drawers below the breakfast bar, the third one down. Wade tugged it open. The music stopped and the blue light winked out. The sound of the ticking clock took its place. No one else had woken.

"Whatever it is, it must be in here." Wade rifled through the sticks of chewing gum, the lone die, the loose change, and the envelopes. Clarification settled in my mind. I knew what was making the noise. But I had no idea what it meant.

"Here," I said, moving a couple of envelopes aside. "I think this is it." I pulled my mother's keyring from the drawer, the keyring with the three jewels attached. "Could this be what we're looking for?"

"Cordelia..." Wade's eyes sparkled as he held them to the light. "You have keys...and I know exactly what to do with them."

I gasped. "The keys to Atlantis?"

"I can't say for sure, but we've taken a huge step in the right direction."

Atlantis. It was real, and perhaps not lost forever.

THE END

Read on to see how Cordelia and Wade start their journey to Atlantis...

Thank you so much for making it all the way to the end. I hope you have enjoyed Cordelia's adventure and are excited to discover the rest of her journey (4 more books in the series). If you did, leaving a review is the best possible present for an author!

You can do it here: **https://geni.us/ SecretsoftheDeep**

Cordelia and her friends have been living in my head for several years now and I'm so thankful to be able to share them all with you. Without you, my dream of being a novelist would never have happened, so from the bottom of my heart —Thank You!

Maybe the next time you're at the beach, you'll cast your eyes out at the ocean and wonder where Cordelia is in that moment or maybe what coconut magic actually tastes like!

If you're interested in my other books, you can read the first chapter of all of them on my website at www.marisanoelle.-com, or buy from any bookshop. Please sign up to my mailing list to get the latest news, free stories, novellas, and chapters from all my other books.

And you will receive the first three chapters of ***The Shadow Keepers*** **FREE!!!**

Turn the page for the first chapter of ***Quest for Atlantis...***

ACKNOWLEDGMENTS

Well, folks, they say it takes a village to raise a child, but I'm here to tell you, it takes a whole circus to birth a book! So, grab your popcorn, because I've got some shout-outs and thank-yous that are more entertaining than a juggling act on a unicycle!

First up, my writing group, The Rebel Alliance. You guys are like the Jedi Masters of encouragement, and I couldn't have done this without you. You've had my back for so long that I'm pretty sure you have a permanent imprint of my book cover on it!

And speaking of covers, Fay, you're the Picasso of book design. Seriously, the cover is so gorgeous it's practically doing the cha-cha on its own. Bravo!

Now, let's talk about Team Swag. We navigate the treacherous waters of publishing together, and boy, do we make a splash! When it comes to sharing knowledge, we're like the Avengers of advice-giving. What a fantastic bunch of writers and friends!

Neil, my rock, my Steady Eddie. You stole my heart in a single night and have been guarding it like a precious gem ever since. I love you more than a mermaid loves the ocean (and that's saying something).

To my kids, Riley, Lucas, and Quinn, thanks for being the

wind beneath my writerly wings. You're my plot problem-solving superheroes, and you always rescue me! Just promise me you won't be embarrassed if I show up at your school fairs with a stack of books.

Mom, you're the eagle-eyed proofreader of my dreams, even if we occasionally find a typo or two. Let's just blame it on Dad when that happens, shall we?

To my early supporters, you're the MVPs of my writing journey. Sasha, Michelle, Nikki, Adrian, Darcy, Hetty, Louise, you've given me advice and feedback that's worth its weight in gold doubloons!

Twitter, oh Twitter, (and you will always be Twitter) you've been my trusty sidekick in this adventure. The writing community there has made rejections feel like mosquito bites at a barbecue—annoying but manageable. You all know who you are, and I couldn't have asked for better virtual friends. Thank you!

And then there's Booktok! What a wild and wonderful place I've stumbled into. You've made me buy so many crowns I'm starting to feel like royalty. Thanks for supporting my journey, engaging with me, and even buying my books. You're the crown jewels of my author life!

A big shout-out to my A-level English teacher, Michael Fox, who taught me to first think for myself and second defend my ideas. You're the reason I can write more than a grocery list!

Last but not least, a standing ovation for my readers. You are the true stars of this show, and I wouldn't be here without you. Stick around, because there are more books in my circus tent, and I promise they'll be worth the price of admission.

Oh, and if you fancy learning more about my books and want to be in with the chance to win exclusive giveaways, sign up to my website below!

www.MarisaNoelle.com

Turn the page for the first chapter of *Quest for Atlantis*...

ABOUT THE AUTHOR

Marisa Noelle is the author behind a treasure trove of middle-grade and young adult novels that dance through the realms of science-fiction, fantasy, horror, dystopian, and mental health. From unraveling mysteries to diving deep into the human psyche, she's your go-to wordsmith for adventures that'll tickle your imagination.

Marisa's literary exploits include "The Shadow Keepers," a spine-tingling tale to keep you up all night, and "The Unraveling of Luna Forester," a masterpiece that snagged the prestigious First Place Incipere Award, rocked the WriteBlend Finalist stage, waltzed as a BBYNA Semi-Finalist, and took its place on the Bookshelf Finalist shelf. With dystopian being one of her favorite genres, you can expect fast-paced thrills from the world of "The Unadjusteds Trilogy," a rollercoaster ride featuring "The Unadjusteds," "The Rise of the Altereds," and "The Reckoning," perfect for fans of Divergent, Maze Runner & The Hunger Games. And don't forget to dive into "The Mermaid Chronicles," a series that will plunge you into the depths of "Secrets of the Deep," lead you on a wild "Quest for Atlantis," challenge you to "Fight for Freedom," send shivers down your spine with "Ghost Pirates," and leave you craving "Vendetta." She also writes steamy romance under the pen name Savannah Warner.

When Marisa's not weaving literary spells, she's helping mold the future of MG and YA authors as a mentor for the Write Mentor program.

When not writing, Marisa likes to imagine herself as a mermaid, and can often be found in the local pool...or lake... or ocean. Despite her undeniable bookworm credentials since she was knee-high to a grasshopper, the author gig took Marisa by surprise. You see, she had a secret past as a bit of a science geek during her school days. But hey, science and storytelling make a surprisingly magical concoction! Currently, Marisa calls Woking, UK, her home sweet home, where she resides with her trusty squad, including her husband, three amazing kids, and a furry four-legged friend named Copper.

Marisa loves to hear from her readers. You can find and connect with her at the links below.

Twitter & Instagram: **@MarisaNoelle77**
Tiktok: **@MarisaNoelle12**
Website: www.MarisaNoelle.com

Turn the page for a sneak peek into *Quest for Atlantis*...

THE MERMAID
CHRONICLES
BOOK TWO
QUEST FOR ATLANTIS
MARISA NOELLE

QUEST FOR ATLANTIS

Mermaids are being hunted...

They are no longer safe in the human world....

When one of their closest mermaid friends is imprisoned in a science lab, Cordelia and Wade insist on taking up the quest to find the lost island of Atlantis, a sanctuary for all water species. But the island is guarded by the dragon kings, an ancient and formidable race who are determined to keep it for themselves.

Cordelia and friends must travel to distant pockets of the earth to collect the magical jewels that open the portal to Atlantis. But no one remembers how the jewels work, instructions are non-existent, and tensions are rife as Wade's ex-girlfriend appears on the scene determined to win him back.

Cordelia's heart breaks as she watches the love of her life waver. When Wade is fatally wounded, she fights for her right to be by his side, inciting a rift between the merfolk and selachii once again.

Can Cordelia and Wade repair their fractured relationship before it is time to face the dragon kings, or will the fate of Atlantis be lost to them forever? The race against time has never been more treacherous, and the fate of merfolk hangs in the balance.

CHAPTER ONE

For six months, we had lived with secrets, hiding our true selves from the human world. Dad had forbidden any search for Atlantis until after graduation, but today was the day we finally crossed that threshold. Graduation marked the end of waiting and the beginning of our journey.

"Today we get the keys back," Maya said, as she smoothed down her skirt.

"Yes, we do," I replied, trying to push the swell of excitement away. It's all I'd been able to think about for the last six months. Dylan and I had argued with Dad constantly, but he'd remained steadfast in his decision, and wouldn't even listen to Wade's parents when they'd stormed over demanding the keys. Eventually, Dad had taken the three keyrings that had belonged to my mother and hidden them somewhere. Argument over.

Maya curled her hair around her finger. "And we graduate..."

"We do."

I stood in front of my full-length mirror, dressed in my maroon cap and gown for the graduation ceremony. The sleeves were cuffed in a wide, gold ribbon and I wore a golden sash around my neck.

"So...?" She raised an eyebrow, which looked huge behind her black-framed glasses.

"Maya," I said slowly, coming to sit by her on my bed. "We can't turn you into a mermaid."

She dipped her chin. "It's the only thing I've ever wanted."

"You heard what the High Council said. No turning best friends into merfolk and selachii."

She lurched to her feet. "No, no I did *not* hear what they said. I wasn't there, because I'm not a mermaid. And if I was there, I'm sure they would make an exception for me."

I looked at her pleading expression and sighed. "What about your siblings? You foster parents? Don't you think they'd miss you?"

"Nope." She pushed her glasses up her nose. "Not in the slightest. I'm supposed to go to college at the end of the summer and I don't plan on coming back. I'm eighteen now and officially an adult. They've stopped receiving financial support for me and they could care less where I go."

"I don't think that's true," I said gently.

"This is my life," she snapped, tossing her hair over her shoulder. "Surely it's up to me what I want to do with it? Why can't you see that?"

"Maya." I stood to face her. "It's not an exact science. It's too dangerous. No one wants to take the risk."

"It is still my choice to make."

"Besides the fact that I don't actually know how to do the ritual and we'd have to find someone who did—"

"Dylan." She said, her arms crossed and her face flushed. "He's been shown how to perform the ritual."

"And what if it didn't work? What if you really died? Then how do you think Dylan and I would feel, knowing we were the ones who couldn't save you?"

"I—"

"And then," I continued, "you seem to conveniently be forgetting about the fact that any new merfolk and selachii can't come out of the water. You won't have your legs anymore. You'd be stuck in the ocean at night, on your own, while the rest of us sleep in nice, comfortable, warm beds."

"I don't care!" She threw her hands high.

"You need to be protected," I said, trying a different track.

"I can protect myself."

"That's not what I mean." I slumped into the armchair in the corner.

"You told me my parents had been involved, my real parents, that my family had always been protectors of the merfolk. Holders of *The Mermaid Chronicles*. That I have a role to play. It makes sense for me to be a mermaid, Cordy. You know it."

"The High Council insisted you be protected," I agreed. "But I don't see how I can do that when you're in the water and I'm on land. It's not like you can keep the book in water, anyway."

She gaped at me, started to speak, then clamped her mouth shut as she sank down on my bed again, facing me.

"I'm sorry," I replied, getting to my feet and approaching her. "I think you need to be on land. Where you're needed. And where you're safe."

"What about what *I* want?"

"Let's find Atlantis. Then we'll see."

She sighed and looked out the window at the ocean beyond. "I am *not* happy."

"I know," I said, arranging her mortar board atop her head and fanning out her blonde curls around her shoulders. "But I think it's the way it has to be, for now."

"I still want to come with you," she said.

"I wouldn't leave you behind," I replied. "We'll need you and your book. My father wants to come too. So, when we find out what it is we have to do, or where we have to go, if there is any way for you two to come with us, with your human legs, then I'll make it happen."

She gave me a curt nod. "I guess that will have to do."

I hugged her. "The last six months haven't been all bad, you know. Being valedictorian is nothing to sniff at."

She smiled. "It was my dream. For a long time. Then going to Harvard. But so much has changed. There's so much more to the world than we thought. There's so much out there to discover...I can't just sit back with my nose in a book."

"Unless it's *The Mermaid Chronicles*," I laughed.

She gave me a curtsey. "Naturally."

"Knock, knock." Dad popped his head around my door. "Look at the two of you. So grown up. Young adults embracing the world." He shook his head and wiped a tear from his eye. "Your mother would be so proud, Cordy."

"Thanks, Dad," I said and gave him a quick hug.

"Okay, enough of your old man crying embarrassingly. It's picture time. Wade and Trent are here."

"Give us one more minute," Maya said.

Dad left and Maya walked to the full-length mirror for one final look. She swept her brush through her hair once more and passed a shimmery lip balm over her lips.

"How is it without Wade being here?" she asked.

"Hard," I replied. "I miss him."

Wade had been living in my house for the last six months. His father had remained steadfast in his disapproval of Wade's relationship with me, a mermaid, and it was only recently, after months of us trying to wear him down that he had finally relented to allowing Wade back into the family home, although we still had a very steep, uphill path to climb before he was ready to accept me as his son's girlfriend.

Wade had only been gone a week, and I really missed the curve of his body wrapped around mine each night. He'd taken my virginity, as well as my heart. And my soul. And without the warmth of him pressed against me...I could no longer sleep.

"But he needs to try and make things right with his father," I sighed. "Family is important."

"He'll come around," Maya said, squeezing my shoulder.

"I hope so."

I doubted it.

There was something about Daniel Waters that was cold and unforgiving. His eyes did that flashy black selachii thing constantly and he spent much of his time in the water. With Zale's exile, it had fallen to him, the rightful leader of the selachii, to restore order among his people, even though he didn't want it. He was a fisherman, he wanted to spend his days at sea, and now he had to split his time between managing his shipping empire and keeping calm over his people. He was stressed and tense and not very warm or fuzzy around the edges.

He was about to leave on a three-month fishing journey and his son dating a mermaid was a complication he didn't need or couldn't be bothered with. But Wade had refused to toe the line and Daniel Waters had come to grudgingly accept his son's rebellious attitude. But I wasn't holding my breath for a scented invitation to the house. I was pretty sure that would never happen.

I mulled these thoughts over as we drove to our graduation ceremony at Point Loma High. Wade, Trent, Maya, and I accepted our diplomas while Dylan watched with my father, both dressed smartly in suits, and cheered and whistled. Dylan hadn't bothered going back to school, and much to my father's annoyance, had done nothing to further his education. Instead, he'd gotten a job at a garden center, then spent his evenings drinking beer. Too much beer.

The crowd applauded as Maya stood on stage in front of the podium, a huge smile on her face.

"We all know life is about challenges," she began her valedictory speech. "That's nothing new. You only have to turn on the news to see how people are suffering. You only need to look at the homeless person on the street corner. You only need to see failed college applications, foodbank receipts, or the dark shadows under someone's eyes to know life isn't always smooth sailing..."

I squeezed Wade's hand. We'd been through so much, but I knew we hadn't yet scratched the surface of everything that waited for us.

Feeling eyes on me, I glanced over my shoulder to see Wade's father frowning at my back. I kept my face neutral and turned back around. Daniel Waters was just going to have to go screw himself. I squeezed Wade's hand harder and didn't let go.

"...choosing how to cope with it is what matters," Maya continued, pushing her glasses up her nose. "Learning to ask for help. Taking the hard step. Showing support to someone you don't like. Being brave will make you grow and help you to face future challenges..."

"She sounds like a fortune cookie," Dylan chuckled.

"Oi." Trent smacked his shoulder. "That's my girlfriend you're talking about there."

Dylan raised his hands in mock surrender. "Next thing you know she'll be saying *with great power comes great responsibility.*"

"...you don't have to be free of fear to be brave. Being brave is being afraid, and doing it anyway," Maya addressed the crowd, her gaze skimming the tops of our heads. "With great power comes great responsibility..."

Dylan burst out laughing, earning a few scornful looks. "Called it."

"Okay, okay," Trent said. "So I made her watch all the *Spiderman* movies. I guess it had an effect."

"The sentiment remains the same," I said, patting Trent's shoulder. "With great power *does* come great responsibility." I looked at Wade. Reaching the High Council six months ago hadn't been easy. I had a feeling finding Atlantis was going to be ten times harder.

"...on the brink of adulthood, our whole lives ahead of us, to accept the unexpected and embrace the difficult. Together. United. Only then will we triumph!" Maya tore her hat off and threw it in the air.

The audience stood and offered her a thunderous applause.

"She's talking about us," Wade said in my ear. "United."

"She is," I replied, blinking back the heat of tears.

After the ceremony, we gathered on the front lawn, flipped our tassels over and threw our mortar caps in the air. My father took pictures. Wade's father approached and shook hands with his son and Trent, his selachii subjects. He ignored Dylan and Maya, and I felt lucky to receive a curt nod of acknowledgement.

"I can't make the party," Daniel said to his son. "We're leaving in an hour."

"I understand," Wade replied. "It's work. How long will you be gone?"

"Most of the summer," Daniel replied. "Then I'd like to take you out. Now that you've graduated, it's time you became part of the family business."

"Yes, sir," Wade replied. "After we find Atlantis—"

Daniel scoffed. "The island has been lost for centuries. You'll never find it."

"Still, I'd like to try." Wade looked at me. "*We'd* like to try."

Daniel didn't spare me a glance but shook his head at his

son. "If you haven't found it by the time I'm back, I'll expect you on the boat."

Wade dipped his chin. "Yes, sir."

Daniel Waters walked away and I breathed a sigh of relief.

"Don't mind him." Wade's sister took his arm. Marina was back from college and often softened the vibes between Wade and his father. "He's a grouch by nature. He'll come around. Especially when you find Atlantis."

"*If* we find Atlantis," I warned.

"We will," she said.

"We?" Wade asked.

"Yes, I'm coming with you. This is a summer adventure right? Well, I've got the next three months to do nothing but help you."

"Thanks, Marina," Wade said.

"Okay." My father slapped his hands together for attention. "Everyone back to my house for the party."

Trent and his parents, Maya, Wade with his sister and mother, and Dylan and I followed my father back to our house on Del Monte. There we could talk freely and openly about who we were and what we were about to do. But before my father would consider relinquishing the keys to Atlantis into our grasp, I knew he wanted a proper celebration.

On the deck in the backyard, he had laid out a meal for an army; shrimp with Marie Rose sauce, crab and lobster bites, spring rolls with plum sauce and mini hamburgers and hot dogs. There was a couscous salad and a green salad and another salad with a number of beans I couldn't name. There were mimosas for everyone, and my father held his glass high as he raised a toast.

"Congratulations to you all," Dad began. "I know these last few months have been hard on you. Not only have you had to pretend to concentrate on your studies and ignore the fact that I hid the keys, but also, you've had a very big secret to keep. You have had to keep part of yourselves from the world. Perhaps the most important part. It's been challenging. There have been rumors in the press, but at least here, you are in a safe place, and you can share who you really are with everyone here."

"Hear, hear," Trent's father exclaimed.

"I couldn't have said it better, Chris," Wade's mother added.

As I went to Wade and slipped my arm around his waist, I noticed his shark tooth necklace dangling at his throat. It glinted in a ray of sun, seeming to emphasize my father's words. I pressed a kiss to his cheek and he wrapped both arms around me. I felt his cell phone vibrate in his pocket. Pulling away, he removed his phone and read a message on the screen. His brows knitted.

"We need to go inside," he said to the small gathering. "The news channel."

Inside, my father flicked on the TV with the remote. The screen came to life and a pretty, blonde reporter stared into the camera. A picture over her left shoulder showed a shot of sand and ocean, and the big bold letters after 'breaking news' read **_Mermaids? Are they real?_**

"_...well, that's the questions on everyone's lips..._" the camera panned to another female reporter standing on the beach. A beach I recognized. La Jolla. *"...it seems as if here, behind me, a mermaid—and I can't believe I'm actually using the word—was seen diving into the water and flicking a beautiful blue tail...and now we go to our eyewitnesses..."*

The eyewitnesses were a couple in their twenties who had been taking a stroll along the beach early in the morning. They had seen a young woman walk down the beach and into the water. Moments later a shimmering blue tail appeared and she disappeared beneath the waves. There was a video. It had been caught on camera.

"This is not good." Marina frowned.

"They need to be more careful," Dylan said.

"As do you all." Dad grimaced. "Very careful. We can't afford this kind of exposure."

"Especially as we're all about to take off in search of Atlantis," Wade's mother added.

"The journey to the sunken land will be filled with heartache and loss. The fire mermaid must be determined," Maya quoted solemnly.

"I must say," I considered aloud. "I never thought the prophecy might be about exposure to the world. But that would cause heartache."

"See?" Trent looked at Maya. "Now is not the time to contemplate becoming a mermaid. It's even more dangerous." Obviously, I wasn't the only one Maya had kept on at during the last six months. I looked at Dylan and noted the guilty expression creeping across his face. Had Maya been wearing him down too?

"Cordelia Blue, it's going to be okay. We'll be careful." Wade circled his arm around my waist and brought me close. He planted a kiss on my lips and his eyes flashed black.

"You've gotta stop doing that," I said. "Or you'll be the next specimen in a net."

"We need to go to Corona Del Mar, now," he said. "I'm certain that's where the keys are to be used, then we'll know what to do."

"Will you be back tonight?" Wade's mother asked. "Stephanie and her mother are arriving this evening."

"I don't know," Wade replied. "We might be late. Maybe I should stay here tonight?"

"No, don't do that." His mother flapped around him. "Come home, no matter how late. It's so good to have you at home again. And Stephanie and her mother would love to see you."

The party was cut short, everyone's appetites muted, and now Wade and I had a mission to complete. Trent's parents and Wade's mother and sister left. Wade and I prepared ourselves for Corona Del Mar. My father handed me my mother's key rings and a flash of blue light sparkled through the room. Everyone gasped.

"What's it doing?" Maya asked.

"I don't know," I replied, rubbing a thumb over the three small jewels. "But they know it's time too."

Wade and I made our way to my jeep. We would drive to Corona Del Mar, up the coast a couple hours, and not risk exposing ourselves until necessary.

"Wade," I said, as I climbed into the jeep. "Who is Stephanie?"

He fastened his seatbelt, taking care over the latching of

the buckle. "My sister's best friend from when we were living in San Fran. They go to college together now."

"And why is she getting involved?"

Wade sighed, looked out the window. "She's a selachii. Was attacked in the water one day. Marina feels guilty. She wouldn't be a selachii if it weren't for my family. But it was my fault, really."

I put a hand on his arm and his gaze dropped to the contact. "Why is it your fault?"

"We were together when it happened."

"Together?"

"Yeah, I was only a few feet from her, Marina was closer to shore and...it happened so fast." He raked a hand through his hair.

"It's not your fault."

He lifted a shoulder. Wouldn't meet my eyes. "And yet I still feel guilty." He looked at me then, his eyes searching mine. "She wants to help find Atlantis, and I can't really say no."

A thread of unease wound through my limbs. The group to find Atlantis was growing larger with every passing day, and now a stranger was going to walk into the middle of it and demand...I don't know what, call it a woman's intuition... but I didn't like it one little bit. I didn't know who Stephanie was, but I sure as hell didn't want her anywhere near Wade.

To carry on reading, click here:
https://geni.us/QuestForAtlantis

9 781916 893245